T0208373

An Isle of Fancy

Where Good Trumps Evil

a novel by

Rocky Wilson

iUniverse, Inc.
New York   Bloomington

An Isle of Fancy
Where Good Trumps Evil

iUniverse books may be ordered through booksellers or by contacting:

iUniverse
1663 Liberty Drive
Bloomington, IN 47403
www.iuniverse.com
1-800-Authors (1-800-288-4677)

Because of the dynamic nature of the Internet, any Web addresses or links contained in this book may have changed since publication and may no longer be valid. The views expressed in this work are solely those of the author and do not necessarily reflect the views of the publisher, and the publisher hereby disclaims any responsibility for them.

ISBN: 978-1-4502-1419-3 (sc)
ISBN: 978-1-4502-1424-7 (dj)
ISBN: 978-1-4502-1421-6 (ebk)

Printed in the United States of America

iUniverse rev. date: 4/23/2010

Another novel written by Rocky Wilson and published by iUniverse is Reviewers Choice Award 2010 acclaimed SHARENE Death: A Prerequisite for Life

DEDICATION

This novel is dedicated to the wonderful people of the island nation of Malta, located in the heart of the Mediterranean Sea.

Although the first draft of An Isle of Fancy was written on that island years ago, other than the fact both fictional Dalilennon and real-life Malta are places where good trumps evil, the author absolutely draws no parallels or comparisons between the two. Dalilennon and all characters on it are figments of the author's imagination, while Malta is a real, living place with residents who feel and hurt and love like other people around the globe.

ACKNOWLEDGMENTS

There really are few acknowledgments that go along with the writing of An Isle of Fancy, it being primarily a solo venture generated by and through the author's imagination.

Still, the generous support and encouragement given this project by friends and fellow believers Guy and Irene Siverson have been priceless. Whenever the author required prayer or technical assistance to keep this novel headed where it needed to go, Guy and Irene always were available and more than willing to help.

Possibly some peripheral credit should be given to the individual who, in 1981, rented a flat to the author at 43 Parallel Street, Sliema, Malta, where the author's rental included a balcony view of the Mediterranean Sea. For it was from that site, in hand-written journals, that the novel's first draft was written and completed during a six-week period of time.

Too, some accolades might be directed toward the long-forgotten stimulus that caused the author, at a much later date during his seven-year stay on the island of Oahu, Hawaii, to perform a complete rewrite of the original manuscript, using what's today an obsolete word processor.

At the conclusion of the current publisher's 23-page critique of An Isle of Fancy, the publisher described this novel as "the most unusual book ever." Up until An Isle of Fancy's date of publication, no one other than representatives from that publishing company and the author had read the text. Still, the author always took the publisher's summation of this work of humorous allegorical fiction to be a giant compliment, and willingly, without reservations or fear, offers An Isle of Fancy to the reading public.

Rocky Wilson

As always, however, the author acknowledges that anything good in this novel is of God, and anything less than that of his own choosing.

Contents

A black Fiat ascended final turns to Herr McCoffee's estate, only the driver inside. That driver bent and shut off a jabbering car radio, muscled the oversized steering wheel into a stiff right turn, then eased the foreign rig into full view of Herr McCoffee's picturesque holdings at the top of a hill.

Trees, ones tenderly nurtured for centuries in the dry climate of Eglicata, sprung with purpose from the unnaturally green front lawn that encompassed McCoffee's large hacienda at the center of his property. Chalk-like yellow dust ringed the lawn's lush mondo grass like nondescript borders to bright, bold paintings.

The nose-grabbing dust billowing behind the arriving vehicle briefly engulfed the Fiat when Max, its driver, braked to a halt some fifty meters from the estate's wrought iron main gate.

He shut the key.

The vehicle, in need of a carburetor adjustment, coughed once (loudly, Max thought,) then shuttered to silence. It had been good transportation, but its days were numbered.

Max surveyed the scenery around him through dark Italian sunglasses.

He paused in thought. What he knew in his head was enough to topple champion foosball players from glory to ignominy in an instant, or cause Jesus to cry.

Politicians from distant lands, especially industrious Darius, would have bartered litchi fruit and precious metals to learn secrets locked inside Max's mind; secrets about McCoffee's giant fowlawarfare being groomed and stoked with lambs to conquer the world, and about the ever-shorter list of potential dissidents capable of slowing the powerful Herr's diabolical intentions to squash anyone in his path. If need be, Herr McCoffee would squash those opposed to him like stink beetles beneath gumshoe boots, and Max knew it.

Practicing cerebral avoidance concerning the dire consequences to him, his wife, and his four sons were he inadvertently to speak aloud in his sleep or share classified information during one of his occasional flings with that damned imported drink tequila, (even taxi drivers have their weaknesses,) Max looked to the ocean and smiled.

"I wonder how many soccer tickets I'll get for today's duties?" he asked of himself, all the while counting in his head the expected stack of Eglicatan currency he'd receive for services rendered.

Far to his left, closest the ocean, stood small buildings where servants were housed, and beyond them larger buildings where vehicles belonging to the Herr were protected from the hot sun and occasional rain storms.

Baby one-cycle tractors for tilling the useful soil, a kerrozin for exercising horses, stately automobiles from all over the world to impress visiting dignitaries, and even a golf cart or six were kept behind the bright-colored walls of the taller buildings that dwarfed the adjacent servants' quarters like a Toyota Tundra to a Volkswagen Beetle, or Goliath to David.

The bold, forest-green door upon the largest barn, at least three end-to-end '59 Chryslers in width, made the flat, unpainted servants' quarters closer to Max appear tiny, even inconsequential in comparison. It was through the latter where some of Max's countrymen now peeked out.

Herr McCoffee's mansion itself was stately, even more so here in this pastel setting near the sea with nothing of comparable grandeur in sight. Admittedly, placing it next to any of Eglicata's huge churches or public gathering facilities would have tainted the structure's visual and cubic wonder, but, by design, no towering churches or other non-McCoffee facilities were within view. Hence, there was no competition for praises one might want to voice about what Herr McCoffee had built.

Max waited and lit a cigarette. It was a dry, unfiltered smoke he'd rolled from tobacco imported from Turkey.

Waiting in front of McCoffee's main gate was anything but uncomfortable for the taxi driver-chauffeur. He was both patient and dexterous. Two minutes with tools, and the highly visible TAXI sign on top of the Fiat could be demoted to the trunk next to the spare tire and lug wrench. When his duties for Herr McCoffee were completed, Max would reverse the process and again serve the public as a taxi driver.

When that switch came, however, his pockets again would be lined with more tax money than other taxi drivers could earn in a week. Max could drive visiting dignitaries to tennis courts, soccer matches, and even lewd bars where handsome tips to promote forgetfulness were commonplace.

Max's immediate family, including his sons ages fourteen through twenty-one, was proud of his stature among Eglicatan taxi drivers. They knew little regarding the nature of their father and husband's calls into service from the powerful Herr, even less of what actually transpired while he was away, yet always felt puffed with pride whenever the telephone rang and Max hastily gathered tools to break down the red-lit TAXI sign.

Other taxi drivers took note, too, speaking quietly and urgently on their radios to ensure Max wasn't slowed by traffic.

Max, now puffing on his second hand-rolled cigarette, used a bare hand to wipe yellow, dusty chalk from the Fiat's chrome bumpers and front grill. He'd even spray the chrome with mist from an aerosol can and wipe surfaces clean with the blue kerchief he carried in his back pocket if time permitted.

A mere face among millions, Max had been fortunate enough to come under Herr McCoffee's favorable eyes when, years earlier at fate's decree, he had driven in broad daylight upon a major altercation only two kilometers from where he now stood in dust under the bright sun.

Born of poor, proud parents, Max instinctively had bailed from his auto (an even older Fiat,) and joined ranks with what at the time had been the losing cause. Max had suffered a black eye and nearly battled himself to exhaustion before the adversaries, equally worn, had limped away. Time revealed that Max's hastily chosen allies in that mini-war were private dance instructors returning to their homes after teaching members of the Herr's internationally acclaimed chess team how to relax from the rigors of their stressful, governmental vocation.

Hence, it was only appropriate that Max become the Herr's number one chauffeur.

He retained the position by keeping his mouth shut.

A pulsing, desert-like wind surged gnarled tree limbs and ruffled Max's straight black hair. Like most days on Eglicata, the day was warm, and Max wiped perspiration from his forehead.

Max's blue kerchief was laden with dust and the Fiat's front grill shiny when the wrought iron gate opened and two of Herr McCoffee's more prominent advisors stepped into full view under the bright sun.

Ms. Sylvia Smitharomance and Manual McGetitdone blinked rapidly, almost in unison, as they walked abreast toward Max and the waiting black vehicle.

Ms. Smitharomance was a stately beauty with an aura of toughness about her she couldn't have hidden had she wanted; much like an orange-colored rose semi-hidden among thorns or a Greek goddess with tattoos hidden out of sight beneath billowing white robes.

McGetitdone, with arms like Popeye after consuming seven cans of spinach, had a disagreeable demeanor that no one addressed in his presence. With narrow, black eyes, McGetitdone's face was marred by a deep scar that changed colors depending on his mental state, much like a chameleon. A purplish red meant to stay away from him at all costs. A pink hue indicated Manual was in heat.

Max smiled and pocketed his dark glasses for a time.

"Hello, Max," said Ms. Sylvia in an alluring tone. "We'd like you to take us to the home of Mr. McView by the sea. The fact he doesn't know we're coming will make it pleasant for all of us."

Max opened a door on the rear left side of the vehicle, near a small dent made when his youngest son inadvertently had backed into a tree at age eleven after washing the taxi in moonlight, then ushered Ms. Sylvia and Mr. McGetitdone inside. He fought to suppress a mischievous grin as he scooted under the oversized steering wheel, adjusted the inside mirror, and drove away.

He'd driven for this pair before.

The Fiat left tracks in the dusty road, tracks destined to survive even beyond the time when chalk-like, swirling dirt molecules would settle back to earth.

McCoffee's two political advisors in the back seat were quieter than Max was used to. This made him uneasy, placed waves of queasiness in his gut about what soon could transpire. He glanced into the rear-view mirror in front of his right shoulder, and saw Smitharomance and McGetitdone sporting distant looks, as if each was engrossed in thoughts continents away.

Max, as per his instructions, was driving the advisors to the home of a retired lawyer who'd long been a critic of the McCoffee regime. The nature of such an unusual visit troubled Max, but only to a point. He knew his role was not to think, but to do.

"It's a beautiful day, eh?" he offered to an ominously quiet duo behind him.

Birds flew out of the Fiat's path, and donkey masters thoughtfully stepped out of the way as the black automobile passed over the dusty road.

In his thoughts, Max, again practicing avoidance in regards to the immediate future, fully expected to put the TAXI sign back in place that day. Sightseers and lovers would want rides.

Being a taxi driver as well as a chauffeur, Max took mental note that an additional twenty-four kilometers had registered on the Fiat's odometer when he stopped the vehicle by a small dwelling near the sea.

Ms. Smitharomance kissed McGetitdone on the lips and rubbed the bulky man's chest with an open palm, while Max watched through the mirror. She said in a clear voice, "Do what you need to do, Manual, but don't kill him."

"And you," she said to Max, "stay here and keep the engine running."

Then she and Manual McGetitdone walked to the dwelling's front door, knocked, and were allowed inside.

Max knew signs weren't good, especially for Mr. McView, but neither had or wanted any antidotes to the situation. The long-range safety of his family, and, of course, good seats at the next national soccer match, were more important to Max than the life of this old lawyer who stubbornly refused to bow to Herr McCoffee's power and authority.

In the many years he'd worked as the Herr's primary driver, Max had witnessed many unusual events.

Ms. Smitharomance, for example, had made love in the Fiat's back seat to no less than three different men on trips even shorter than this one. In addition, delegates from other countries had requested one-way trips to lewd parts of Eglicata's capital city. And, on one occasion, an indignant ambassador from another land had bad-mouthed Herr

McCoffee in every breath from government headquarters almost to the airport, then been removed from the vehicle and never seen again.

And certainly this visit to the aging lawyer had a bad smell to it as well. Max knew enough about the man now inside the small cottage with Manual McGetitdone and Ms. Smitharomance to be confident the old man would say nothing to please McCoffee's henchmen, or rather henchman and henchwoman. The retired lawyer, very intelligent and very white of hair, had been an outspoken opponent to Herr McCoffee's rise to power years before, and hadn't wavered in that opposition to the present day. Most such antagonists to McCoffee's regime had been put to rest quietly, but McView's highly visual popularity had kept the Herr at an angry distance.

Max, while waiting in the driver's seat of the black Fiat, pondered about the personality traits of the diplomats he was waiting for.

The man, a strong brute, had ridden Herr McCoffee's coattails to prominence, and done nothing since then to compromise that position. Manual McGetitdone wasn't a man to be crossed.

The lady with him, Ms. Sylvia, was highly intelligent and highly valuable to Herr McCoffee's administration. She'd risen to political eminence like cream to the top of newly drawn milk. It was written in the stars, possibly her fate. Even her promiscuity, a personal priority, had done nothing to slow her rise to power. Maybe it had helped. Herr McCoffee, intelligent as well, quietly was leery of her fast-rising political clout, and consciously elected to do whatever was necessary to keep her happy and allied with his government.

Max, still waiting, tossed a third well-puffed cigarette out the Fiat's window and watched as its glowing tip lost its heat in the Eglicatan dirt.

The afternoon sun lazily lingered on the countryside and seashore around him, and Max became drowsy. Oh, to be at home where he could argue with his sons. They'd soon marry and move away. Unfortunately, he thought; things always change.

Max, yawning, fingered the crucifix chained to his neck and experienced a moment of peace. He'd turn in his handwritten bill for this excursion to the Herr's main business office in the morning and be recompensed shortly thereafter in sound Eglicatan paper money and soccer tickets. And that paper money would be good for buying potatoes, milk, and pasta; tickets to a cock fight or Shakespearean drama for he and a chosen son; buying a new metal strip for his TAXI sign; or maybe even, God forbid, that red dress the Mrs. had been coveting for months.

The soft pooch of feet on dust rattled Max's eardrums, rallying him from a state of daydreaming back to one of reality. He stepped out of the Fiat--unaware that his right boot stepped on and buried three sedentary cigarette butts in the process--held the door to the back seat open for Ms. Smitharomance and Manual McGetitdone and, with no verbal instruction or interchange of any kind, drove the pair back to Herr McCoffee's estate.

Max, through his rear-view mirror, saw McGetitdone holding his right hand with his left, then watched as Ms. Smitharomance bent over and caressed McGetitdone's injured hand with her tongue.

Not wanting to hear anything that could further implicate him in this nefarious deed, Max was unable to block from his hearing one decipherable statement from behind him as the trip progressed to McCoffee's mansion on the hill.

"Rightjet is dangerous."

The name vaguely was familiar to Max, but not enough to tie it to anyone he knew. Besides, with a good paycheck and soccer tickets on the morrow, what did he care about some stranger named Rightjet?

Inside the Palace

After advisors Smitharomance and McGetitdone were dispatched to interrogate McView at his seaside cottage, Herr McCoffee turned to watch the door close behind them, then paused in thought. Another step was being taken to realize his plan for world supremacy; world supremacy for Herr McCoffee, not for Eglicata.

He glanced over his left shoulder to his own five-foot-high portrait, pompously placed above the finely carved acacia wood table near where he stood. The scowling personage in the portrait, with penetrating eyes, peered over McCoffee whenever Eglicata's finest minds gathered to meet at his decree. Members of McCoffee's cabinet, such as fisheries experts, the nation's economic brain trust, defense specialists, and national chess players not only were conditioned, but programmed to see a second Herr McCoffee, one larger-than-life, peering down at them during every minute of every meeting.

A few feet stage-right of the Herr's virtual throne under the portrait was a closed door that led to the ruler's private study. That door afforded the international leader an opportunity to remove himself from the outside world, gave him license to cry for more personal wealth, pray for more power to achieve his carefully detailed goals or, most commonly, lust after the black widow of his cabinet who wouldn't consent to marriage ... or even any more sex.

Long ago, practically at the eve of his vault into power and fame, Herr McCoffee had stolen at night to her quarters, made passionate love mindless of the lady's own marriage intent, and proposed a marriage union of their own.

She'd laughed.

"Do you think you could satisfy me and millions of Eglicatans as well?" she'd cajoled mincingly. McCoffee, in disbelief, had groped for more physical pleasure that night, only to have the woman titter his intent away.

"But I love you," he'd gasped well into the night, and she'd laughed seductively from the back of her throat. She knew the powers he had to conquer the world were useless in her bed.

"I will be on your cabinet and very valuable to you," she'd concluded near daylight the following morning as she'd buttoned up his silk Hawaiian shirt. "We must always treat each other respectfully with the best interests of Eglicata in our hearts." She'd offered the final statement with a smile, a gentle slap on his weary butt, and nudged him toward the door.

True to her word, Ms. Sylvia Smitharomance was in Herr McCoffee's cabinet when next they'd met--in the same room McCoffee now occupied. And their compact, at her insistence, never had been violated. She was, indeed, a "very valuable asset" to a young government.

But that compact had been made nine years earlier when McCoffee's Eglicata had been tottering on stilts, threatening at any moment to stumble and crash into oblivion with another ruler or two scrambling to replace McCoffee's government with one of their own. Ms. Sylvia Smitharomance had been as valuable an ally in the early days as now.

But not, much to Herr McCoffee's chagrin, sexually.

A man of wisdom himself, the Herr repeatedly had denied personal desires to try and augment their professional relationship. He ached inside when McGetitdone, Norbert Nodahead, and other key advisors looked at her lustfully. He ached even more when he'd see her look back at them, smile seductively, and wink.

Much had changed in those nine years. A fledgling government--blessed with vast resources, agreeable people, and a unifying leader--practically had bolted into the world's consciousness. Almost any school child anywhere now could approach a world map with a push pin and tag Eglicata's location with confidence.

But, as the world and the Eglicatanese people had begun to think of Eglicata as a progressive nation, Herr McCoffee, behind symbolic waves and smiles, began harboring that vile ambition that felled both Alexander and Hitler ... total conquest.

And he was close.

Still alone, Herr McCoffee ventured through the arched doorway stage-right of his throne and into his private study. His eyes raced to the photo and charts along the nonwindowed interior wall to the right of that inner door.

"The leaders of Darius would love to see this," he articulated for only his ears to hear.

"My beautiful fowlawarfare," he said soothingly, like a televised game-show host talking to children, "you will take me to paradise."

McCoffee's eyes, filled with adoration, focused on the wall-sized photograph of a bigger, much bigger than life bird.

"Sweet fowlawarfare," he said, "you must stay alive until Darius is mine. You must be the one that carries out my plan, the attack that will end all wars."

The photo on the wall depicted a gigantic cassowary, or ostrich-looking creature with serviceable wings, rippling sinewy muscles, and a leathery coat of armor that, theoretically, could withstand and accurately, like a boomerang, slingshot back at sources any firepower generated from conventional or unconventional weapons.

"I don't know precisely why your mate chose to die," said the Herr with a level of compassion in his voice normally reserved for emotional, public speeches made during halftimes of soccer matches when scheduled women's mud-wrestling matches, replete with giant-screen televisions equally spaced around the national stadium, were cancelled because of low-hanging fog. It was the same type of compassion McCoffee sometimes voiced when unexpected lulls arose during thrilling chess competitions.

"But I do know, as do you, that you are the end of a line of nine years of selective inbreeding. You are the ultimate weapon for peace, and you soon must fly to conquer Darius."

Still, Herr McCoffee wasn't pleased with his minisoliloquy.

"Why did she die?" he demanded of the giant flying bird's photo, the house-sized flying bird held in place, as depicted on his wall, by sizeable anchor chains. "Why did she die?"

A knock was heard on the door to his study.

"Come in," barked Eglicata's most powerful figure, now in a grumpy mood.

A short White man walked into the study briskly, bowed to his ruler, then waited for permission to proceed.

"Mr. McDove, I think," said McCoffee with instant interest. "I believe you've been working on the death of the fowlawarfare's mate. Speak up."

"By our calculations," began Mr. McDove, "the Mrs. Fowlawarfare died of indigestion. She simply was unable to digest her food intake as quickly as it was consumed. We feel the fowlawarfare himself may be endangered by the same ailment. He, too, eats a lot of sheep."

"I know he eats a lot of sheep, McDove, and I know he's vulnerable to the same illness that struck the Mrs. Fowlawarfare."

Herr McCoffee spoke these words in the repetitive singsong dialect of a patient, understanding, yet cunning politician. Then his voice changed inflection like Nathan addressing David after David's anger was kindled about a rich man having the audacity to take a poor man's only lamb instead of one from his own humongous flock, (although the analogy ends there.)

McCoffee's voice went cold. "What I need to know is what the antidote is."

"We thought you'd want to know that," quietly responded the short White scientist who was confident in his position and in no way unnerved by being in the presence of such a renowned world leader.

"And?"

"And we found one called disadvantageous. It works by breaking down mutton fiber … "

"I don't care HOW it works," exploded the highest of diplomats suffering under a world filled with strain and stress. "I want to know where to get it!"

"Our computers currently are working at full speed to find that out," said McDove. "Apparently, disadvantageous used to be plentiful, in fact a noxious weed in many places on the planet. But man, for decades, has deemed the plant worthless and made a concerted effort to make it extinct."

"Does it still exist?" asked the ruler, now a bit more composed.

"We think so, Your Excellency. The computers at this very moment are trying to pinpoint a location where it still grows."

"Very well," said Herr McCoffee. "Inform me immediately when you have additional news to share."

After opening the door and preparing to leave, McDove hesitated in the arched entrance to the study, turned, and spoke boldly. "I'd like to say it does me great honor to work with the Eglicatan government in this quest for world peace."

A cold stare from Herr McCoffee sent him packing.

Slightly less than two hours later, Ms. Smitharomance and Mr. McGetitdone knocked on the Herr's study door, seeking admittance. Herr McCoffee recognized McGetitdone's staccato pecks on the door, grunted assent to their entrance, then busied himself with pen-upon-paper activities upon his roller-top oak desk to accentuate his personal importance.

The near silence after the two entered the study was deafening. Only sounds from a muted pendulum clock on the wall by the door and pen scratches were audible.

McGetitdone felt uncomfortable in a reverent sort of way, and Ms. Sylvia plopped down in a stuffed maroon chair.

The ruler of Eglicata, aware he was being watched, hurried his pace to finish mundane, yet consequential tasks.

"I heard news of Viola," said the Herr while looking up from white mounds of paper.

McGetitdone immediately glanced to the wall photo of Viola's mate before Herr McCoffee could continue.

"Apparently, she died of indigestion … "

"Small wonder," quipped Ms. Sylvia Smitharomance.

Herr McCoffee no longer thought to reprimand Ms. Sylvia in small groups. She nearly was his master.

"Vic could be endangered as well unless we locate the proper antidote quickly," said the Herr. "Apparently, there's a plant named disadvantageous that will break down mutton fiber at a fast rate. The problem is locating a source of the plant and getting it to Vic in time. We can't do anything until a source of disadvantageous is found."

Sylvia Smitharomance leisurely gazed around the study, noting the bright streams of sunlight peeking through latch-string blinds above and behind McCoffee. The broken rays of light striped his own desk like a studious zebra. Ms. Sylvia held no reverence for their leader, a point Herr McCoffee painfully was aware of. And the witch hunt she and Manual had just returned from had done nothing to alter her view. The old man, as she'd expected, had told them nothing about Roger K. Rightjet.

For nearly nine years, the Herr relentlessly had pursued and eliminated those who'd contested his rise to power, and the list was getting short.

But Rightjet was a special problem. An influential young lawyer who'd worked with the previous government, Rightjet had fled Eglicata for distant lands. On two occasions, McCoffee's agents nearly had tracked the lawyer down, only to have him flee again to another land. It had been seven years since Rightjet had last been seen, but sources said the old lawyer knew his whereabouts.

"He told us nothing," Ms. Sylvia said to the ruler still writing on papers at the oak desk. "We beat up the old bastard and he told us nothing. He asked us to thank you for the honor of your visit."

"The old man's still alive, Your Excellency, and he knows where Roger K. Rightjet is hiding," interjected McGetitdone loyally.

"Hiding, huh!" snorted the well-toned lady with youthful, shapely features ranging from fluid calves to soft-curved buttocks to her lightly painted, alluring face. "He'd probably call it living by now."

"Enemies of the state of Eglicata must be sought out and destroyed," barked Manual McGetitdone, much like a Marine drill instructor in an introductory speech to new recruits.

Another knock on the door, and Norbert Nodahead, a third close advisor to the Herr, was granted admittance into the study dwarfed by the presence of a wall-size photograph of a giant bird. Like the other two, Nodahead had been with the McCoffee administration from its inception. He, Ms. Sylvia, and Manual McGetitdone (all present and accounted for in the Herr's study as we speak,) were the only original cabinet members still around. The most recent to leave, one Poncho McTea, had dipped from prominence a few years back.

No one looked to the most recent arrival in the room for news. He was more of a 'yes' man, capable of achieving uncanny goals by listening, offering subtle direction, and, with multiple nods of affirmation, efficiently doing the Herr's bidding. Pudgy in stature, Norbert sported a thin, black mustache that adorned a pale, ill-looking face. Norbert was worthy of distrust and scrutiny from his fellow cabinet members, especially the newer ones whose grasp toward power, as of yet, largely was unsubstantiated. Like an unscrupulous, lithe, buoyant swimmer in a pool, Norbert Nodahead had no misgivings about pushing off the skull caps of others to attain a better vantage for him. He felt those unable to defend themselves shouldn't even be in the pool--period.

It thrilled Norbert whenever his small, plump, unassuming body no longer was a liability.

Norbert only had begun to nod over the latest fowlawarfare news when another knock was heard through the stout teak door. McDove next was ushered into the study so recently bodied only by him and the nation's leader, Herr McCoffee.

He'd done his packing.

"We've found it, Your Excellency," stated McDove with pride. "The disadvantageous plant only grows on the distant isle of Dalilennon. It grows rampantly there like a noxious weed. You also must know," continued the peace-loving, White scientist/botanist, "that the weed's chemistry for digestive purposes is very sensitive. To obtain a useable crop to treat the fowlawarfare, it must be planted on a given day, harvested fourteen- and-a-half days later, and transported in wet gunny sacks."

McCoffee was perking with enthusiasm.

"Thank you, Mr. McDove," he said. "Your efforts for peace won't go unrewarded."

McDove exited, closing the big door behind him, and the nation's leader laughed loudly, mercilessly.

"Do you know who's on Dalilennon at this very moment waiting to aid our mission?"

Too hyped to slow the news and maximize the power he held over all, Herr McCoffee proceeded speaking with dashes of overt animation.

" … none other than my wonderful cousin and former cabinet member, Poncho McTea. From prominence to banishment, and maybe now back to prominence. So wise and forward-thinking of your Herr to ship Mr. McTea to the very island we'd need to deal with at a key future date."

"Does he even remember your name?" asked Ms. Sylvia Smitharomance pointedly, as if holding a pitchfork or an electric prod to derail McCoffee's vain display of pride.

"We do communicate on occasions, mostly on our birthdays and Halloween, and the last I knew Poncho was dying to get back into Eglicatanese politics. Maybe now," concluded the Herr with mock divinity ebbing through his words like a stone-cold cobra or a rock-hewn machete, "maybe now Cousin Poncho will get another chance to do what needs to be done.

"Tonight, I'll text him instructions to plant a crop of disadvantageous."

Blokehead's Gambit

The overhead fan slowly moved the wave-like, shimmering heat on a harsh Dalilennonian afternoon, leisurely sweeping in a clockwise direction at a tortoise's pace too slow to stop fine dust from gathering on the fan's blades. The switch to trigger a faster speed on the fan, one that actually gave some relief from the heat, was outlawed during working hours because it rifled papers off desks of the girls who worked there.

Three women regularly worked at the G.C. Corp.'s main office, many less than the bold, occasionally illuminated outdoor sign would indicate. Two other women would join the three every-other Tuesday when the exporting firm's products for shipment were prepped, boxed, and loaded on the isle's most seaworthy vessel, the SlipSparrow, then shipped to distant ports.

Of the five women who worked there, Ms. Nancy Droosha was the only one who knew what a distant port looked like. She'd debarked from the SlipSparrow four years earlier. What had begun as a lark, a dare, had evolved into a comfortable, leisurely life without fanfare on a complacent, lovely island a quarter of the world away from what had been her home.

Swatting at a large black fly that had no reverence for her position at G.C. Corp. or her beauty, Ms. Nancy Droosha reminisced about her past home in Darius. A fight with her family and her lover had driven Ms. Droosha angrily from the nest, and prompted her daring, defiant plunge into the sea to spite those whom she loved. Fortunately, the SlipSparrow, Dalilennon's most seaworthy vessel, had been heading home following a trading mission to Darius, and those aboard ship had rescued the drowning maiden. Deck hands on the SlipSparrow had netted Ms. Droosha from the ocean's cool waters and, drenching wet, she'd waved meekly, resignedly to her native land as the tidy vessel had sailed onward toward what for her was a new world.

She laughed now about the argument she'd had with the vessel's captain who, once determining her health was intact, had insisted passage be paid in cash. Her Darian money, not plentiful and wet, had been unacceptable. Ms. Nancy finally had resolved the matter by signing her name to an agreement, typed on the spot by the captain's secretary, stating that she would pay her passage once she reached Dalilennon and found work.

"Where's Dalilennon?" she'd asked after signing her name.

But times had been good, and Ms. Nancy found a job working for the G. C. Corp. immediately following her arrival in Dalilennon, or would that be "on" Dalilennon, it being a small island and all? Apparently, the skills of Darisian women were highly coveted, and the ship's captain had paved the way for Ms. Nancy by radioing ahead to his brother-in-law, who'd been given the odd name of G.C. at birth and was looking for some good help for his exporting business.

Nine months elapsed before Ms. Nancy Droosha was free from debt. She no longer owed the SlipSparrow's captain for her extended sea voyage of albatrosses, storms, and near tilts. The original price of passage had been reduced when the athletic, 5'7" Ms. Droosha had proven her mettle by working above deck throughout the voyage amid crushing seas and sail-snapping winds.

Now dressed in white to protect her from the heat, Nancy looked at the two women working at nearby desks, young women whose futures soon would include husbands and babies.

What else was there to do on Dalilennon?

Ms. Nancy Droosha had peaked, been promoted as high as she could go, hardly one year after beginning her career at G.C. Maybe it was time for her to think seriously about going home to Darius. That very thought had angered her during her first three years on Dalilennon, but now the glamour of being the most coveted, most beautiful foreign woman on the island had worn thin. Especially with no males she'd met who'd generated any hormonal interest within her.

"Adronica," she said in her caring, yet authoritative voice. "Have the bees from the Southside been prepared for shipping? And I don't mean

Grattzi Farms' packing, either. We're responsible for each container's safe passage and must do all of the packing ourselves."

The lazy-eyed woman responded in fast Dalilennonianese that Ms. Nancy had learned to understand. "It's late in the day and it only takes two hours to prepare the bees. So-o let's do it in the morning and go home early to our families today," said Adronica.

"You know better," responded Ms. Nancy Droosha. "Go do it now, you and Xandra, and I'll come help you in a few minutes."

Ms. Nancy's eyes sparkled as she looked at the beautiful, olive-skinned Xandra who'd heard every word. "Maybe the three of us still can go home early. Now move along, and I'll join you shortly."

The two girls left through a side door and Nancy Droosha suddenly was alone beneath the tired, sweeping overhead fan.

"She knows we need tomorrow to crate the birds."

Nancy began working on her paperwork, quantities of which hadn't changed between Darius and Dalilennon. Easy work, mundane work, and now, after nearly four years at G.C. Corp., boring work. Her pen, without conscious thought to its repetitive strokes of motion, swept through the heap of papers, and her mind wandered toward memorable smiles.

Priest Precious. What a special human being. The wiry man in his late 50's who'd sought her out after a communal mass, listened without interruption to her awkward tale of anger, spite, and eventual leap into the sea, then had opened his home to her for frequent visits with tea, sometimes wine, and always hard-crusted bread.

Priest Precious was legend on the isle of fancy. Boasting a sparsely toothed grin, he'd once told Ms. Nancy of leading a children's benefit parade on a tricycle--in his priest's frock. He'd also admitted plunging into the sea himself, once again clothed in his frock, in an attempt to swim to the mainland for medical supplies. He'd been hauled aboard a vessel, exhausted, some 1,211 kilometers short of his goal. He also admitted, under pressure from sweet Ms. Droosha who'd heard the story from another source, once challenging the Dalilennonian government to a boxing match. His ploy had been to alter governmental intentions to remodel an aging church into a gymnasium. The gym had usurped the church only after the precious priest had been felled, minus two teeth, by a ringer on a one-day visa from a cold, northern country whom good King Nocturnal had imported for that very purpose.

'What a man, what a priest, what a friend,' mulled the twenty-nine-year-old beauty while absently sorting and filing shipping forms on a lazy Dalilennonian afternoon.

Then there were Jean Paul and Mary, mischievous orphan twins who'd always tried to figure ways to …

"Who owns that ratso donkey?"

Nancy looked up and recognized the man speaking to her through the doorway as the handsome, ordinarily discreet, well-tanned foreigner she'd seen many times attending masses performed by Priest Precious. In his current state of obvious anger, however, the man wasn't handsome or discreet.

"Sir, do I need to remind you that you are addressing a lady?" retorted the world-traveled secretary now torn between dismay and laughter.

The man's eyes, incensed, were riveted on hers. "Burros, donkeys, jackasses, it's all the same to me. All I know is that ratso donkey bit me on the butt! It's a public nuisance, and I'll have no part of it."

By now, Ms. Droosha again was in control of the situation and informed the handsome stranger who wasn't looking particularly handsome, while looking him straight in the eye, that the donkey he was speaking of was named Blokehead and was the property of Miss Prissy Hampshire.

"And if you can get any satisfaction out of Miss Prissy," Nancy added with a wry smile, "you're a better man than I am."

Roger K. Rightjet suddenly felt foolish; his block of icy anger melted instantaneously by a pretty smile. He didn't know how to leave and retain any semblance of dignity, but knew it was time for him to go.

Her beauty fanned his embarrassment.

"Thank you," he mustered lamely, and exited from the same street-side doorway from where he'd appeared. A patch of denim was missing from a rear pocket of his pants.

Ms. Nancy Droosha then flashed her biggest smile of the waning day and said, for anyone who had ears to hear, "And now for the bees."

The Nose Pickers

To most people, the art of nose picking is something that should be practiced behind closed doors.

Young women often lock doors behind them, or, better yet, practice the art of picking their noses on the toilet (loo,) where chances of discovery, at best, are minimal.

More brazen than their female counterparts, young men, especially at the door of a long-sought date, often dive in recklessly to get that last mound standing between themselves and an evening of comfort, peace, and pleasure. Even on such occasions, however, the young cavalier often is most conscious to take note of the comings and goings of others; letting a quick whirl and a shoe tie, a placid gaze toward the heavens above, or a hasty march to the men's room provide him with cover whenever necessary.

Even so, these actions rarely provide our cavalier the relief he's seeking, for there's always the lingering doubt that the job only might have been half done.

All in all, the art of nose picking is, as it should be, a private affair. No well-groomed young man likes to see the girl of his dreams picking her nose over dinner, and no young lady appreciates a beau who takes a quick dig before a good-night kiss.

But, just as good Copernicus said, "No, the earth's round," and swift Revere said, "Two if by sea," so has history been blessed with folks anxious to buck the odds and prove their way is best.

Just such a brave leader was Dalilennon's second in command, Mrs. King Nocturnal, who'd been known to espouse the bounties of nose picking by the hour.

"An excellent massager of the nose's interior," she'd say gravely while reaching within. Or ...

" ... it stimulates the nasal membranes, allowing one to better appreciate the flowers of spring ... " Or ...

" ... since breath is life's essence, why slow it with clots?" etc., etc., etc.

The good Mrs. King was so adamant in her support of nose picking that no one could remember, at least in the previous ten years, speaking to her for any thirty-minute span without the Mrs. King's finger inserted into a nostril and her definitive arguments on the subject of nose picking articulated with grace and dignity.

Two close friends of the Mrs. King, Ms. Patty Pickly and Ms. Frannie Finger, had cemented their respective roles in the Mrs. King's entourage years earlier by forming a snobbish club to support the art of nose picking; a club that, even if it didn't meet officially other than on every-other holiday--circulated flyers and practiced daily. The two women often were seen gaily picking away while mimicking their royal leader near the Mrs. King's brass throne.

Let it be known that Mrs. King Nocturnal hadn't always been a strong supporter of the art of nose picking. In fact, when she'd first married the good King some twenty-six or twenty-seven years earlier, she'd been both a lady of queenly etiquette and, to coin an often misused phrase, a fox.

But time gradually had eroded her visible grandeur. Life in the upper stratum of society proved hard on what had been a twenty-two-year-old bride of humble origins.

When she'd tried to organize ladies on the island to throw a benefit church bizarre, the kindly good King had explained such was not her role. "Separation of church and state," he'd said. When the young Mrs. King had asked her many friends to attend a kingly ball, the good King had said, "No. Commoners and state only are allowed to mingle on select occasions." When she'd tried to organize an island-wide art contest for children and adults, the good King, with a knowing smile, gently had thwarted those efforts as well. "I'm the only one qualified to judge such an event," he'd stated lovingly to his pretty bride, "and I have many more important things to do."

That rebuke had hurt the most.

And while the good King had sauntered away to ponder his next meal or cabinet meeting, the good Mrs. King had retired to cry in royal frustration. Such was the plight of a genteel woman who could have anything she desired: almost.

The repeated denial of her wishes, over time, drained the strength of the good Mrs. King's spirit, who turned her attentions to self-loathing and an oversupply of cream tarts. Her self-esteem plummeted and her weight skyrocketed.

Ten years before the start of our story, a story that began, if you remember, with Max's black Fiat making a cloud of dust while approaching Herr McCoffee's Eglicatan mansion about nine years after McCoffee had assumed power in Eglicata, Mrs. King Nocturnal devised a plan that wouldn't be denied; a plan she would launch within the confines of the Dalilennonian palace that would establish her rights as the Mrs. King of the isle of fancy.

Good King Nocturnal ignored her challenge initially, finding it too commonplace to combat. But when nose picking became the norm in his chambers, he regretted that oversight. Still, being a man of virtue most of the time, good King Nocturnal did nothing to stop his wife's chosen habit. Instead, he endured.

For good King Nocturnal, overall, was a good king who cared for his people, his family, and his God. He was a fourth-generation king on Dalilennon who took his role of sovereignty seriously. Not as serious, perhaps, as had his predecessors who'd risen to every challenge to make life on the island, for the most part, free from want and troubles of any significance.

For today, the isle of fancy routinely glistened without challenges in tropical sunlight well removed from the rest of mankind. Dalilennonians occasionally left the isle to visit other countries and a few foreigners moved in, but, all in all, the ongoing climate of warmth and more warmth translated into uncontested peace and contentment for all of the good King's constituents who, like O.J. playing football for man y years, only knew a path of tranquility.

Whereas former King Nocturnals diligently had worked to solve water and engineering issues, the current king, spouse of the tart-eating Mrs. King, had few problems of merit to combat. Cabinet meetings were held regularly, but often were mundane, dull, and yes, even boring.

The hottest cabinet meeting in memory had come within recent times after Priest Precious had challenged the state to a boxing match. King Nocturnal had huddled for hours with top advisors Malcolm Straight and Poncho McTea (the two never agreed,) to solve the perplexing dilemma.

Mr. Straight's proposed solution was to form a committee to study the pros and cons of the church/gymnasium controversy that had sparked the spunky priest's challenge. McTea thought the priest's bone of contention totally was uncalled for because the priest's goal was diametrically opposed to his personal wish of replacing the old church with a gymnasium. McTea told good King Nocturnal, in unequivocal terms, that suggesting such a boxing match not only was an act of wanton disrespect to the good King's administration, but bordered on treason.

"Back down from this overt act of aggression and we'll open the gates to civil disobedience, to a trampling on the hallowed flag of Dalilennon," he'd said. If a boxing match was to be held, McTea demanded that a true boxing champion, one who couldn't lose to the "puny" priest, be commissioned to put the disruptive rabble-rouser, aka church leader, in his place.

The argument between the two top advisors had waged long before good King Nocturnal's patient ears and eyes. Then, as quickly as Priest Darrell Precious's tart challenge had opened the controversy, a decision was reached.

Good King Nocturnal, aware it was past his dinner time, suddenly rocked to his feet and admonished the two advisors for their inability to compromise. Sternly, he stated that the correct choice of action was blatantly obvious, then exited in a huff, leaving the two top advisors to determine the matter's outcome.

After the door of the conference room they were meeting in closed behind the good King, Poncho chuckled, mimicked good King Nocturnal's, " … the choice is blatantly obvious …, " then informed Malcolm Straight in no uncertain terms that a boxer from a cold, northern country would be hired to do the job.

Livid with anger because of known personal limitations, Straight packed his satchel and walked away.

And that's how Priest Darrell Precious, looking for a right and getting a left, lost two teeth. It also was the pivotal behind-doors de facto political decision that felled an aging church, leaving in its wake a renovated gymnasium with a golden, rarely used boxing ring; a floor shuffleboard court; a badminton net; a Jack LaLanne treadmill; and a fancy marble desk with chairs on two sides that could have been used for international chess competitions if anyone on Dalilennon had known of and mentally been prepared for such a strenuous sport.

A Tetherball Pole Subdues Julian K.

The second longest-staying non-native on Dalilennon, next to Poncho McTea, was the agreeable-looking gristmiller who'd arrived seven years earlier after being chased off an island or two since leaving his homeland in the dead of night. He'd landed as a sorrowful lawyer and taken the first job opportunity his multi-punched visa would allow; a slower-paced, more physical job than that of being a lawyer. And, in the early days after his arrival on the isle of fancy, that job routinely had left him caked in white.

Gristmilling on Dalilennon was a tedious vocation long before Roger K. Rightjet selected it as his new career. Multitudinous sacks of grain were unlabeled daily, slit with long knives, and dumped into grist vats where patently slow wooden paddles crushed the kernels of wheat along vat walls, forming the soft, cake-like powder that covered the clothes of gristmillers.

At a later time, much later in homes and café kitchens, a dash of yeast and some water would be added, and that white powder would be transformed into hand-crafted pocket breads or the fat-loafed bread types preferred by most Dalilennonian women.

But, for now, the white powder was dumped from the vat onto a rubber conveyer belt (old Dalilennon was old, but not archaic,) where six natives patiently plucked dark husks of wheat, crushed insect bodies, and other impurities from the powder as it passed by. Once beyond the reach of this crew of impurity pickers, the ground wheat, still on the same black belt, was routed to another room where a clumsy two-armed work of science dumped flour into several sizes of double-papered flour bags. The bags manually were sewn shut for buyers of what had been wheat, and now was flour.

A small battalion of bag-toters next hauled the sacks to warehouses.

Most of Dalilennon's wheat output came to the efficient gristmill on wobbly, wooden-wheeled carts drawn by donkeys.

Once gristed, bagged, and sold to small grocers, the flour moved to store shelves and, eventually, into the homes of many Dalilennonian wheat growers. Meaning wheat growers who sold their crops to the mill, and there were many, often were first in line to buy flour produced in that same mill. And why not? They'd earned precious money selling wheat to the mill, so it only was right and proper that they return the favor, and in so doing provide food for their families.

Roger K. began his gristing career as a bag-toter carrying product from the bagging room to warehouse shelves. It was a dusty "no brainer" with ample workload, and Roger K. excelled. Virtually in no time at all, he was promoted to sack duster (i.e. dusting sacks in the warehouse to tune them for store shelves,) and, once again, he excelled at the task.

It was only a few months into his new career before Roger K. Rightjet noticed a subtle shift in the treatment he received from his fellow gristers. Instead of awe at his foreign birth or patronage for his ambitious work pace, fellow workers began viewing Rightjet with genuine respect. Many natives, however, took bets on the side whether the healthy, active foreigner soon would jump ranks to a newer, more ambitious career, or instead simply lose his gusto for life and succumb to the everyday mundaneness of being an average gristmill worker on the isle of fancy.

None knew Roger K. well. They knew he laughed and smiled broadly. They knew he was intelligent and punctual, but they had no way of knowing the inner hurt that drove his daily energies, kept him rapidly moving in an attempt to squelch memories of his past.

Rose thorns continue to fester until they're extracted permanently, you know.

Roger K. frittered away little time in pubs and pool halls, electing instead to pocket his moderate income and, as the years progressed, purchase a small, whitewashed adobe home.

The purchase of the structure he would call home should have been a nightmare, Rightjet being a foreigner and all, but fate OK'd his intent. The day Roger K.'s wanna-be purchase papers had crossed the desk of good King Nocturnal was unusually hectic at the palace. The pilot light on the Good King's royal stove had flickered into nothingness because of a lack of propane, and the hungry king had deferred all political decisions to his advisors while he pined for food; during an elapsed time of about 22 minutes and :03.1 seconds.

During his absence, Poncho McTea, in defiance of Malcolm Straight's wishes to the contrary, had rubber-stamped approval of Roger K.'s housing application without noticing Rightjet's honest Eglicatan disclaimer on the document's upper right-hand corner (or was it the lower left-hand corner?).

Elated at the quick approval of his submission for home ownership, let alone governmental approval of any kind, Roger K. Rightjet assured his gristing bosses he wasn't quitting to accept a higher-paying job, and moved into his new house.

The mortgaged living quarters was moderate with running water, hard-baked adobe walls, and springy, dwarf-needle trees in a front yard where tree limbs tossed freely, fluidly, on recurrent ocean breezes.

Yet, it was a garden space to the rear of the dwelling that nurtured the unlikely hero's wounds. It nurtured him far better than any doctor could; better than most any nurse.

Roger K. tapped the dirt with solid iron implements; bought seed from the island's sole seed outlet; planted and nurtured vegetables, fruit, and flowers; and, through the ensuing years, with time, patience, and prayer, flushed personal poisons out of his system. He learned that submerged rose thorns, no matter how severe their initial pain might be, surface and relinquish their sting over a course of years. Poignant memories remain, but the physical pain of abused love subsides when daily counterbalanced by the colorful, ongoing, life-sharing bounties of Nature.

Even if scars remain as visible reminders, the pain can go away, or at least lose its grip on those who hurt.

The man of few words and foreign blood paved a path that touched many in an isolated, beautiful, yet tired nation. Roger K. gained numerous friends and admirers he never met simply by being his friendly, yet almost reclusive self.

The biggest irritant to him during the course of his seven years on Dalilennon had been periodic, well-intended jabs at his chosen gristmilling profession.

"You're too gifted to work here," they'd say after gaining his confidence. "Why don't you work in the banks? … the schools? … in the government? … in shipping? Why don't you work where the money is greater and the toil less demanding?"

Invariably, Roger K. would respond in a rote pattern of answers, employing as many as it might take to pacify his well-meaning, but intrusive interrogators.

"I want to learn your country's culture from the bottom up," he might respond. Or, "Someday, the art of gristing will be forgotten and I'll know an unknown trade." Or, "I've had money before and found it didn't satisfy."

His most common response, however, always was offered with a smile and a twinkling eye. "A man's gotta do what a man's gotta do," he'd say.

And so, Roger K. Rightjet, a disillusioned man of twenty-five when he arrived on the isle of fancy--not dissimilar to Nebuchadnezzar grazing in fields to learn life-saving lessons God wanted him to learn--gradually eased forward to become a contented vegetable-fruit-flower gardener age thirty-two who earned a living wage working in a gristmill.

Little did he know that his life of contentment and leisure soon would be usurped by the past he so wanted to forget.

But even that's a big leap ahead in our story.

On a given, seemingly inconsequential evening long after Priest Precious's tooth letting and well into the tenure of Mrs. King Nocturnal's nose-picking charade for equality, in fact about the time Herr McCoffee (thousands of kilometers away,) gathered his closest advisors to first unveil a most fowlawarfarish plot, did Roger K. Rightjet sit rocking in his adobe-walled home—alone, and at peace.

He'd experienced a minor twinge of nostalgia minutes earlier when something in his garden, as often happened, had triggered thoughts of his past: Roger K.'s once flourishing law career snuffed into obscurity by Eglicata's unstable political climate like pansies in a drought; his personal, thwarted love affair with a beautiful, sensuous lady who'd betrayed Roger K.'s trust; the ensuing years of self-doubt and quandary when life's merits only existed for him on a Scrabble board or the 22nd and 23rd verses of the next-to-last chapter of the ninth book of the New Testament which he, being a methodical reader, only encountered every 1,189 days.

He now recalled, while rocking on his porch in the warm Dalilennonian evening, racing to his love's private abode for a final plea for her to join him on his flight from their homeland. And, once again, he remembered seeing the official limousine, with its chauffeur standing outside the driver's door, and he, Roger K. Rightjet, watching as the light in her bedroom went dark, confirming what he'd suspected and didn't want to know.

"Never again. Never again," he muttered protectively through tight lips nine years after the fact. "Never again will anyone do that to me."

And during the past nine years, seven of them on Dalilennon, no one had come close. In fact, his amiable lifestyle at and around work belied the fact that only one person other than himself ever had been granted admittance to Roger K.'s Dalilennonianese home. And even the beginnings of that relationship, or friendship, had been anything but cordial.

It had happened like this.

Roger K. Rightjet, as he now was, had been rocking in the low, back balcony of his split-level "flat" at twilight, the time of day when he invariably debated on the proper moment to retire for the evening. Visibility was dimmed acutely by the coming night and small fruit trees he'd planted in his yard looked to be mere outlines of wispy, dark blues. The secluded stone walls surrounding his property, which efficiently removed Roger K.'s world from any other, were mere shadows in the night.

Then, (reverting at this point to present-tense narrative to share this exciting piece of prose,) without warning, Roger K. heard an unexpected sound that spelled intrusion, and a willowish, twilit form audibly dropped from the surrounding stone wall like an apple from a high tree or a catfish breaking water in a slough vainly attempting to corral a low-flying butterfly or gnat.

Unseen, Roger K. crept to a closet near an open doorway and secured a portable aluminum section of his tetherball pole.

Then, he stalked the intruder.

Step by wary step did Roger K. Rightjet, in near silence, slip down the slight stairway leading to his patio. Inch by inch, without making a sound, he slid open the bamboo-trimmed glass door between his house and the patio and, in the quiet of the night, walked straight ahead and approached a fruit-yielding pear tree (Roger K.'s personal pride and joy,) where what looked to be an alien life form was munching on a newly picked green pear: "grazing" so to speak.

"What are you doing here?" demanded the property owner authoritatively, and the startled intruder dashed for the wall, almost scaling it with cat quickness before Rightjet grabbed the dark-robed invader by one foot and forcefully yanked him back to earth.

"Can these bones live?" gasped the garbled transient who broke free once more and, again, tried to scale the wall. 'Thump' hard on the skull with the tetherball-pole section, and the frocked outsider fell silent at Rightjet's feet.

Roger K. dragged the invader to his patio, lit a lantern for light, and surveyed his prey.

"E-e-ehc," was Rightjet's vocalized first impression of what he saw. "Who, or what the deuce do we have here?"

At Roger K.'s feet, comatose, lay an unusual sight. He assumed the creature was human, but would have sought a second opinion were one to be had. He, for scraggly facial hair did hint of that gender, was atypically contrived, but probably human. The twirl at only one end of an embattled mustache that groveled for space with pockmarks and pimples; the long, curved eyelashes that would have been a redeeming feature in the eyes of any mother; the mud-stained priest's frock covering tattered khaki pants and a greasy white dress shirt; and the bright red high-topped tennis shoes with Mickey Mouse shoelaces all hinted, sort of, that the creature was human.

"You are Julian Knotsofoolista," stated Roger K. Rightjet evenly as the taser-like stun began to wear off his captive.

"And you swing a mean tetherball section," came a surprisingly clear reply as Mr. Knotsofoolista gingerly rubbed the back of his head. "Nobody plays tetherball anymore."

"I'm told you're the crazy man of Dalilennon; that you're everywhere and nowhere, with all the answers to questions no one wants to ask. Is that so?"

By now, Julian Knotsofoolista had risen to one knee. He continued to rub his head. "Nobody uses a tetherball section as a weapon," groaned J.K.

"I did, and it worked fine," said Roger K. "Well, are you crazy?"

"Sure, sure," said Julian Knotsofoolista with no attempt at guile. "Just give me a minute to get my head straight. Being crazy ain't easy, you know."

"Where do you live?"

Roger K. was experiencing empathy for this funny little creature, the inexplicable bond that unites the lonely with the lonely.

"Got a fancy cave," quipped the newcomer. "Don't worry. I feel some craziness coming on now." He groaned a little for his head, maybe for show, and stood up. "Am I captive?"

"I've more questions to ask you," stated Roger K. Rightjet, not unkindly.

"Listen, bucko," retorted Julian Knotsofoolista, speaking in a surprisingly up-tempo voice. "Things are tough in this world. I got hunger, you don't got hunger. You got fruit, I don't got fruit." His voice now was melting into a sing-song lilt. "So why can't I eat some of your fruit?"

"You did," said Roger K. evenly. "And since you weren't invited to do so, I'd be a fool to invite you back."

"Why put a yoke upon the neck of disciples?" asked the crazy man in his inimitable 'crazy' voice.

"Are you a disciple?" asked Roger Rightjet.

"Then shall the lambs feed after their manner."

Roger tried another, more genteel tact. He began slowly, grasping for the right words as he went. "Are you a being who deserves special treatment? Is it right for you to invade my yard for fruit? I'm asking this in a religious sense."

"No. You have a valid point. I should grow fruit in my own cave and not bother someone like you."

"Hear your own words," laughed Roger K. Rightjet. Then he pointed Julian Knotsofoolista toward the gate that separated Roger's personal space from the outside world. "Come back any time when I'm here, announce yourself, and you shall be fed."

"Grattzi," said the crusader as he marched calmly, proudly, through the gate with frock rustling and maroon high-top tennis shoes mincing through the dirt. The whites of Mickey Mouse's laces flashed their appreciation as the unusual visitor disappeared from view.

And that was how Roger K. Rightjet met the elusive Julian Knotsofoolista, a man whose comings and goings were legend on the proverbial isle of fancy. And every bizarre encounter (could there be another kind?) any Dalilennonian had with Knotsofoolista was documented in fact, gossip, and folklore. The seemingly strange antics of Priest Precious with his boxing and swimming escapades were almost commonplace, maybe boring when paired next to fanciful tales regarding Julian Knotsofoolista.

Family members living abroad, and there were a few at distant ports seeking excitement and/or riches, attentively scanned letters from home or copies of the island's linotype-generated monthly newspaper in search of new J.K. adventures. They not only understood and accepted such stories as gospel, but readily shared them with nonbelievers from other lands who appreciated the humor in Julian's stories, laughed heartily, yet couldn't comprehend the profound truths being told.

And the documented stories, those appearing in the occasionally accurate monthly newspaper, were every bit as juicy as the gossipy-lettered ones.

For instance, there was the recorded account of Julian K.'s unanticipated "raid" of a sizeable gambling session at the home of high-ranking Dalilennonian diplomat Poncho McTea. Knotsofoolista reportedly entered through an open front door, leaped upon the green gaming table around which Poncho and friends were seated, and loudly enunciated a Bible verse.

" … for the evil man has no future; the lamp of the evil man will be put out," he'd proclaimed.

Then, amongst a covey of startled diplomats, Knotsofoolista reportedly had abandoned the gaming table, regained the doorway, flicked off the light switch in Poncho McTea's illicit gaming parlor, yelled "Proverbs 24:20" as if he were Paul Revere holding an unlit lantern, and zipped away, supposedly to safety.

Yet, on that occasion, Julian Knotsofoolista had left a trail that Poncho McTea, an irate, powerful Poncho McTea who'd been holding a full house of jacks and twos at the time of the intrusion, could follow. Only one person on the isle of fancy would pull such a daring stunt, and McTea sent blue-clad officers to the caves to find him.

Not an easy assignment, but on the seventh day leery police officers discovered the suspect-culprit sitting in a trance-like pose in a recessed Dalilennionian cave lit by a flickering, pulsing, dancing torch set in a high wooden stand placed near Knotsofoolista himself. The officers approached the frocked figure cautiously, and found him quietly humming an eerie tune. Julian, quite obviously, was in another world. After consultation with crack Officer Oliver Ogilvie, who was heading the investigation, Dalilennonian policemen wound their arms to form a human chair and carried the entranced sort-of representation of the human species to jail.

Police records say the frocked crusader stayed in his humming trance for four days, no food and no water, before "all hell" broke loose. During the additional four days that followed Knotsofoolista's hellish awakening, amply fed and watered, the would-be priest dented the eardrums of the island's police department with screeches and howls of anguish. Two officers stayed home with headaches and crack Officer Oliver Ogilvie spent as much time as possible working on outside assignments.

By the evening of the eighth day after Julian's arrest, every dignitary who'd been at Poncho McTea's gaming party at the time of Knofsofoolista's raid simply wanted to put an end to the affair. Being discovered gambling at Poncho McTea's residence was bad enough without every officer on the Dalilennonian police force, save crack Officer Ogilvie, pleading for the return of the "crazy man" to the streets or caves where he belonged.

Those dignitaries pressured Poncho until, against his better judgment, he relented, and dropped all formal charges against Julian Knotsofoolista.

Poncho McTea dearly wanted to nail Knotsofoolista to the proverbial rood, but backed off when he realized the political 'perks,' the Dalilennonian political 'perks,' that dropping those charges would provide him with. After all, Poncho McTea was first and foremost

Eglicatanese, not Dalilennonianese, and had a better handle on how better to achieve power than did his unsophisticated peers.

Knotsofoolista had raised a different set of hackles at a recent Easter service when Priest Precious blissfully had been engrossed in the presentation of a hard-hitting sermon of sacrifice and resurrection. It had been an evening service with waning rays of sunshine slicing through a stained-glass representation of Christ suffering on the cross. Attentive parishioners had looked through Priest Precious's lofty words to Nature's enhancement of the multi-colored, painstakingly placed pieces of glass above the priest when, if possible amongst such a politely attentive throng, a hush swooped over the proceedings like a passing cirrus cloud.

The precious priest had felt the emotional quietness, inwardly been charged by it, and resolved to throw even more love, more conviction, and more faith into his fervent, heartfelt oratory.

Then a snicker, a titter had usurped the congregation's silence; then a second one. Priest Precious had continued delivering his sermon, yet experienced sharp pangs of disappointment and personal failure. He saw the eyes of his parishioners tilted high above him and resisted the urge to turn around and look as well. Would God seem humorous to these children of faith?

Another large titter had followed, bordering on outright laughter, and Priest Precious had turned to see what each member of his congregation already was looking at: Julian Knotsofoolista climbing on the outside of the stained glass (in frock, of course,) holding to a rope obviously dangled from the church's steeple. Knotsofoolista was centered perfectly between the stained-glass cross and the down-turned sun, casting a shadow on the base of the church's east wall.

Once he knew he had the priest's attention, Knotsofoolista had yelled for everyone to hear, "For the Lord sees not as man sees; man looks on the outward appearance but the Lord looks on the heart," then had remained unspeaking, unmoving, dangling, waiting for the priest's reaction.

And it had come quickly.

Without a spoken word, Priest Precious, in the eyes of his entire Easter evening congregation, motioned for Julian Knotsofoolista to retrieve his rope and go home. Which he did, well aware of the precious priest's authority to make such a binding, poignant request, by whatever means he deemed prudent.

Unlike the gambling party, no official complaints ever were filed for that unsettling, but memorable Easter occurrence.

Stories about the garbed marauder ran rampant upon the isle of fancy with no one even attempting to separate truth from fiction.

Roger K. never tried. Too many honest folk had seen and believed too many incredible things about the man.

At the garden Roger, too, had believed.

J.K. was something else! Seeing the black priest's frock with high-topped maroon tenny runners beneath it had been enough to raise his eyebrows several notches, but Mickey Mouse's laced appearance as well had brought the whole experience home on a more personal level.

Roger K. Rightjet respected Julian Knotsofoolista the man even more than he respected Julian Knotsofoolista the legend.

And so, the two men became friends.

Few people knew of Knotsofoolista's nocturnal visits to Roger K. Rightjet's home for fruit, conversation, and occasionally for tea. But word did leak out, and the number "assuming" that a Knotsofoolista-Rightjet relationship existed soon was far greater than those "knowing" of such.

The prissy nose pickers in the Mrs. King's entourage often would discuss the strange suspected relationship between the two men.

"It's sex," would say Ms. Patty Pickly while squeezing a juicy find between her thumb and forefinger.

"I think he teaches him those devilish quotes," would respond Ms. Frannie Finger while knowingly nodding her head.

And the good Mrs. King would remain noncommittal, letting her thoughts move on to the day's next meal or cream tart. Then, remembering her position of prominence, she'd add to those with ears to hear, " ... since breath is life's essence, why slow it with clots?"

Ms. Prissy the Midwife

And so it went in Dalilennon, with Ms. Nancy Droosha systematically accomplishing all tasks at her work station while dreaming of requited romance; the Mrs. King holding court with one finger up her nose and the other cradling a velvety cream tart; Priest Precious (needing new bridgework,) feverishly looking for novel ways to share his pious ideals in defense of church and country; good King Nocturnal heartily trying to raise the kingdom's stature without making decisions; Mr. McTea, foreigner whom he was, becoming more and more influential in the affairs of Dalilennon; Malcolm Straight becoming more and more concerned with the affairs of Mr. McTea; Julian Knotsofoolista in hiding, awaiting the proper moment (be it full moon or Easter,) to again spring forth in the misunderstood causes of revelry intertwined with virtue in its purest form; Ms. Patty Pickly and Ms. Frannie Finger wiggling and waggling their fingers and tongues, only mindful to please the Mrs. King; and the mischievous children Jean Paul and Mary trying to wrangle Blokehead to the rear of Roger K. Rightjet who gardened, worked at the gristmill, and sought the anonymity, not to be found, that had brought him to the isle of fancy seven years earlier.

And then there's Ms. Prissy Hampshire.

Nothing about Ms. Prissy was normal. Honest attempts at documenting the elderly lady's physical appearance on paper run the risk of her reading such excerpts, and Ms. Prissy Hampshire, to be sure, is no common adversary.

Ms. Prissy always had lived at the base of Dalilennon's only mountain in a pastel, adobe two-room dwelling. The simple gate leading to her home provided direct access to a narrow grass-tufted walkway where

Blokehead the donkey, when home, was known to take provender and abide.

Ms. Prissy once had been a sought-after midwife, called to homes throughout the isle at all hours to prep expectant mothers, then help deliver sputtering Dalilennonian infants who'd invariably, upon opening their eyes, see Ms. Prissy's haggard face and cry long and loud. No buttock whacks were required to usher these chosen children into life, to initiate crying and breathing, because any child's first sight of Ms. Prissy's wrinkly, grinning face less than a meter away couldn't help but serve that very purpose.

And it was the culmination of her midwifery career that most unsettled Ms. Hampshire in her later years. A Dalilennonian pioneer, or near pioneer in her chosen vocation, Ms. Prissy Hampshire delivered hundreds of newborns without birth-certificated acknowledgment of her contributions to life, often without sharing so much as her name and, more often than not, without payment.

The lack of acknowledgement and/or remuneration bothered Ms. Prissy not a lick during her working days. She blindly trusted that justice would prevail. But when Ms. Prissy prepped herself for retirement in her early 70's, the capable midwife found herself with no government pension. Previous midwives on the isle, only two on record, had filed for and received pensions without question. Ms. Prissy hadn't.

Apparently, hundreds of faces now populating Dalilennon had forgotten their roots, their midwife, and no one stepped forward to champion Ms. Prissy's cause.

The good King Nocturnal had forgotten, the busy Ms. Pickly and Ms. Finger had forgotten, and even Malcolm Straight had forgotten whose skilled hands had ushered them upon planet earth.

Even so, the good King and Mr. Straight gladly would have approved a pension for Ms. Prissy had Poncho McTea's heart not been set elsewhere.

The foreign advisor to the good King adamantly proclaimed, "Her name doesn't appear anywhere. Not one birth certificate or business receipt for services rendered has Ms. Prissy Hampshire's name on it. She has to be a moocher!"

By the time good King Nocturnal and Malcolm Straight returned from the public library in a futile attempt to discover a definition for the word 'moocher,' Poncho McTea had ruled in their stead, which legally was permissible according to DRS 666.6, which stated that Poncho made the rules when his superiors, or superior, were away on an important fact-finding mission.

"Not one penny to the alleged midwife," he'd proclaimed.

Ms. Prissy took the news in bad temper. She even took Blokehead, Jean Paul, and Mary with her to "storm the castle" in defiance of the decree. Their onslaught, however, had been repulsed by blatantly under worked palace guards, but not before tensions ran high when those same guards heatedly urged the scrappy "old rip" to lodge her protest through the mail.

Blokehead had brayed and stamped about angrily like a miffed Brahma bull tossing a no-name cowboy, but even his dramatic antics failed to get the protestors beyond the initial wave of palace guards.

Then, suddenly, their attempted onslaught was over.

Like a triple-bagled tennis player, Ms. Prissy exited the palace grounds with nothing. She'd neither write to fill a form of protest or ask another for help in doing so. Pride. Ironical, isn't it, that summits of pride thrive beneath the crevices of poverty--often behind stoic, unblinking eyes.

The incident scarred, jaded Ms. Prissy's sensitive heart which chose to bury the injustice beneath an exterior shell of renewed crankiness.

Friends rallied to offer support. The raucous orphan children and Blokehead went to lengths to unveil Ms. Prissy's crooked, yellow teeth in grudging guffaws. Too, an oddball from the caves frequently came to supply humor, fruit, and water-shy vegetables.

And their efforts helped. Righteous adversity loves company, feeds on it for survival. But, still, the hurt was deep.

And that was when Ms. Prissy Hampshire, who'd brought into the world a notable percentage of Dalilennon's current population, never asked for any remuneration or turned any down, and blindly left her future first to fate and later to charity; that was when she made a survivalist decision to bury her injustice and live the remainder of her life as a poor, craggy ex-midwife.

Hence, the future of peaceful Dalilennon was left in the hands of a potpourri of dignitaries, a priest with missing teeth, a penniless ex-midwife, foreigners, children, and a 'ratso' donkey ... a virtual cross-section of God's calling to service.

In the days ahead, Ms. Nancy Droosha, Priest Precious, Mrs. King Nocturnal, good King Nocturnal, Malcolm Straight, Julian Knotsofoolista, Patty Pickly and Frannie Finger, Jean Paul and Mary, Roger K. Rightjet, Ms. Prissy Hampshire, and a handful of others, including crack Officer Oliver Ogilvie, would have their valor tested when Herr McCoffee's devious plan involving the island microcosm--a mere steppingstone on his quest for power, a catalyst to the total conquest he unabashedly yearned for--would unfold like a military burial at sea: with the flag of Dalilennon refusing to accompany the corpse.

Invasion by Night

It was dark, so dark that unseen clouds left no openings for moonlight or celestial auras to peek through. The washing sea recklessly clambered upon unseen rocks, splashing loudly with a mist-hissing drone. The hissing was so rhythmical that surely one could make blind dashes into the surf without dampening a sole were senses tuned to time an initial rush into the dark, receding sea with divine discernment, divine grace.

Julian Knotsofoolista quietly sat watching in the direction of the black sea, the fire in his elevated seashore cave dying to its last embers behind him. He knew the shoreline intimately, had spent numerous hours outlining its features before and after the sun had set on many nights. Tonight, with the moon shaded by clouds, there was little to see.

He lit a filtered cigarette and playfully toyed with the orange light it radiated. He gauged what he could and couldn't see while puffing from the rocky entrance of his chosen dwelling. A soft breeze lightly puffed the dying embers of his campfire, softly accenting the back side of the black frock he wore almost daily, for warmth as well as appearances.

Julian's quick, black eyes sought minor flashes of white generated by waves turbidly rolling ashore. He'd spent many nights watching from this same post, but few this dark. Still, like a winged owl or a raccoon, Julian Knotsofoolista wouldn't be ready for sleep until more nocturnal surveillance was accomplished.

Normally, his was a lonely, tedious job. But someone had to do it.

Then, Julian caught a brief glimpse of light well off shore in the rolling sea, but was unable to focus on it before it dropped from view.

This could be caused by the moon peeking through a cloud, but Julian K. sensed more. He waited, looking toward the light's source for more than a minute.

A similar quick flash of light next was seen to Julian's immediate left, along the coastline, and, not being a fool, he deduced the two flashes were of one and the same intent.

J.K. crushed the butt of his cigarette beneath the sole of his right tenny runner on the rocky exterior of his cave, donned his black, tie-string Zorro hat, and cautiously walked toward the sandy beach next to rocks two-hundred meters below. Navigating the familiar path in maroon high-tops, even in dense darkness, wasn't taxing to Knotsofoolista's keen, developed senses.

An on-shore signaler, with a lantern, came into view about fifty meters away when the caped crusader rounded a rock face. J.K. elected to stay put. The white sands on the shore, even in darkness, could give him away if he tried to get closer.

Julian Knotsofoolista remained at a curious distance, not suspecting the severity of the plot unfolding in darkness before his very eyes.

The distant overhead moon filled a temporary cloud opening with golden light, and Julian K. watched a rowboat, after what he knew had to have been a perilous journey through the bay's surf-pounding rocks, bounce into the shore's backwash. One individual could be seen maneuvering oars, while two others jumped from the boat into the chest-high surf. The skilled rower completed the surf-to-shore sojourn alone.

The two who'd jumped from the rowboat ignored the moon-visible individual holding the lantern on the shore, and merged into a wet, intimate embrace.

Julian tilted Zorro, and scratched his head.

Whereas the return of clouds and the night's darkness dimmed Knotsofoolista's view, so too did the crushing surf override any chance he might have had of overhearing conversations.

The two who'd jumped from the boat and embraced waded ashore, shook hands separately with the individual holding the lantern on the white sand, and followed his lead inland along a northerly island route:

… which is tricky to describe because what's northerly on a small island quickly becomes southerly when one reaches the north shore and has to turn around; meaning land previously described as northerly becomes southerly. Still, this geographical observation, astute as it might be, could hold true on larger bodies of land if one turns around often enough.

Anyway, without hesitation, Julian Knotsofoolista followed the threesome at an angled tack that would keep him off the white sand.

The final figure, now ashore, with the mantled second lantern seemed content to wait unseen in what now was a beached rowboat.

Julian followed the three at a safe, relatively close distance, utilizing his highly trained ability to traverse the stone-strewn path, in red tennis shoes, without making noise. He heard portions of sentences, of statements, but couldn't identify the language being spoken. His curiosity was aroused doubly.

After a walk of some distance, the lamp-led trio of conspirators stopped by a high metal gate apparently placed there to protect a private farm plot. The man with the lantern, whom we know as Poncho McTea, unlocked the gate with a key and ushered admittance to his Eglicatan guests. All three huddled together closely once inside the stone walls surrounding the garden plot, especially the two who'd come by sea, and spoke in whispers, often pointing to one portion of the tilled garden area.

Julian K., standing outside the gate, barely could hear or understand what was being said. He only caught the words "King Nocturnal" and "disadvantageous" spoken in an understandable dialect over the course of a fifteen-minute discussion, the latter term obviously referring to the noxious Dalilennonian weed that continually threatened the island's chosen crops.

Voices got louder, and the three conspirators returned to the gate. Julian recognized McTea, still holding the lantern, but neither of the other two. One of them, he was certain, dressed all in black, was a woman.

Knotsofoolista followed the invaders as they walked back to the rowboat and watched, whenever moonlight would allow, as two of them scrambled aboard, then were rowed into darkness by the skilled boat driver. Just before they dipped from final view, a slice of moonlight saw fit to grace their exit, and Julian saw the two shore invaders silhouetted in yet another embrace.

Poncho McTea, his lantern extinguished as he watched them leave, was followed to his home by a would-be priest who knew not in whom to confide this startling piece of information.

Lacking an answer to this perplexing dilemma, Julian Knotsofoolista returned to his cave and promptly went to sleep.

Love, and Blokehead's Gambit, Part 2

Priest Precious was aglow.

It was the third week of Lent and the church was filling rapidly. He stood in the church's foyer shaking hands with latecomers, mentally rehearsing portions of his upcoming sermon between "good to see you"s and "how's your mother?"s. Everyone seemed to have dressed gaily for the service, reflective of the sun's brilliant presence, both outside the church and peering inside through windows and colorful stained-glass icons of Christ, saints, and hints of a newer, better world.

The good priest took special notice when Ms. Prissy Hampshire selected a seat near the middle of the church, then said a short, silent prayer in hopes of thwarting any interruptions Blokehead the donkey might have planned for the occasion … any possible interruptions Julian Knotsofoolista might be plotting as well.

When Easter did arrive, it would have been two years since Knotsofoolista had upstaged Priest Precious's brilliant sermon, distracting his congregation with J.K.'s bizarre rope-swinging antics.

"You'd think he was Tarzan," mumbled Priest Precious under his breath nearly two years after the fact.

But today was brighter, held more promise for good.

Priest Precious joined in the choir's procession from the back to the front of the church. There, the choir split off and sat in jury-box type seats to the left of the chancel, while the precious priest grabbed a seat in a gold-colored chair to the right of the chancel. He'd rest there during the singing, then reverently stroll to the pulpit. He felt like a new, born-again man as he watched the orphan twins light candles signaling the commencement of the Lenten church service.

As a lay (as in "Biblically untrained,") speaker began announcing upcoming church events, a pretty friend of Priest Precious's was ushered to a seat in the front one-third of the sanctuary. That pretty friend of his, Ms. Nancy Droosha, settled in the seat next to Roger K. Rightjet, and felt warmed by fate's kindly intervention. She flashed a smile at the handsome foreigner and watched as his cheeks glowed red in embarrassment.

"To conquer in love" began Priest Precious once the singing had quieted, gaining the congregation's rapt attention as he christened the sermon's theme while walking to the pulpit.

This time Nancy flushed.

The priest spoke of a white horse from Revelation, the sometimes futuristic book of the Bible where collective fates are unsealed. He read one verse from the sixth chapter of Revelation, citing the white horse's rider as a supreme conqueror.

Roger K. blushed a second time at his own selfish thoughts of wanting to ride into Ms. Nancy Droosha's life; she, so beautiful and so soft, sitting next to him in spirit and in body--and, potentially, in love.

"Love one another in brotherly affection," said the priest. "Outdo one another in showing honor."

'Sounds like the ticket for me,' thought Roger K. introspectively, peeking to view Ms. Nancy's reaction to the sermon.

"Hold fast to love and justice, and wait, … " the priest pronounced to a hungry, attentive congregation.

'I will,' thought Nancy Droosha coyly, but not irreverently, while sneaking a peek of her own at the handsome donkey-hater who'd already displayed a rich, healthy singing voice while joining melodious offerings made by the choir.

" … with love in the spirit of gentleness," piously pronounced the reverent speaker whose words undeniably were pure, a lesson for all.

Roger K. Rightjet envisioned himself as a gardener rather than a gristmiller, even seeing himself as a pureblooded rider on a white horse who wanted to arrive in the life of the woman sitting next to him, whom we know as Ms. Nancy Droosha, and have her covet his newfound wholeness in white. He was moved by the priest's sermon, stirred even more by the pulse-catching beauty sitting next to him: a true fox who seemed unafraid to look into his eyes and soul, then smile.

The precious priest's words, ones of virtue and wholeness, spoke of readying for the upcoming day of judgment, by "cleaning out stables," and doing one's utmost to prepare for that special day by accepting and applying the unabated powers freely available in the unconfined glory of God's unconditional love.

With tears in his eyes, the touched, emotional priest closed his sermon with yet another provocative parcel of candor. "Let all that you do be done in love," he said.

Then they prayed, sang another song or two, and were dismissed to the exits, to the bright Dalilennonian sunshine that washed over kings, scalawags, and church attendees without discrimination.

"It was a wonderful service," said Ms. Nancy as she and Roger K. filed side-by-side out of the tall church.

"It will inspire me forever," concurred the gristmiller, readying to capture the thrill of the moment, the love dancing all around them. "Would you care to dine with me this evening?"

Nancy shaded slightly, catching her breath in an attempt to not appear too anxious, to keep from hugging him and shaking him and exclaiming, 'That's what I've wanted all along!'

"Yes," she responded demurely, "I think that would be nice."

His heart beat excitedly as they crossed the winding street to a dark green patch of mondo grass flanking the ten to fifteen tired, dusty automobiles that had transported faithful Dalilennonians to church this Sunday morning; where they'd heard the mystical words of revelation and love and conquest that had elevated the moods and spirits of this would-be hero, would-be heroine, the owners of those cars, and others.

The warm sun was a salve to Roger K.'s ego, an apparent portent of things to come. He openly laughed from the heart at Ms. Nancy's wit, her color, and her gently penetrating eyes.

But peace and joy can be short-lived.

Neither of them saw the cumbersome intruder until it was too late. One moment they were looking at the sea, crazily talking about white horses and goodness; and the next moment, if you'll pardon the phrase, all hell broke loose.

Lacking edification from the morning's sermon he'd been barred from attending, Blokehead the donkey, with no small amount of coaching from a pair of acolyte-clad orphans, found Roger K. Rightjet's right rear pocket and, in one delicate maneuver, stripped him of it.

Blokehead, braying in pleasure, then lumbered toward the sea with Roger K. Rightjet--lacking the presence of mind to even ask the name of the woman he'd just arranged a date with--chasing after the donkey in dogged, heated pursuit.

Although a trifle miffed, Ms. Nancy Droosha had to chuckle as her white knight raced away yelling at maximum amperage, "Come back here you ratso donkey!!"

"He'll never catch 'em," chimed a craggy ex-midwife who'd sidled up to the side of Ms. Nancy during the unexpected burst of excitement. "He ain't goin' ta catch my sweet donkey."

Dalilennonian Motorcade and a Hot Fan

Roger K. Rightjet spent the next eleven days burrowing into his work and his gardening hobby. He was embarrassed and, even at his best, admittedly no match of wits with the female species.

Did his impromptu chase after a ratso donkey (He'd finally gotten in one kick, he smiled.) embarrass, or even anger the attractive lady from church? Had his total lack of propriety pointed him irretrievably to the lady's doghouse? Would she even speak to him again?

These questions, and the lack of personal inner faith that accompanied them, kept Roger K. from attempting reconciliation. Instead, he buried deeper into his gristing duties, daily fighting off the urge to appear unannounced, with Blokehead nowhere around, at the pretty lady's place of work, aka the main office of the G.C. Corp.

The cyclical nature of the universe again had unveiled itself in Roger K.'s life predicament. He'd come to Dalilennon seven years earlier to, in addition to the fact his life was in peril, bury memories of a discordant love affair. He'd long carried a hurt for a near marriage that only had ended when he'd learned, almost first hand, of his intended's promiscuous bent--for sex, not love. A scar on his heart had healed the wound, a scar so sensitive to potential pain he'd consciously tried to deny anyone access to his inner self.

Roger K. had become a very self-protective man.

Yet, suddenly, the beauty and smile of the lady at church threatened this protective mode.

On this particular Thursday afternoon, Roger K. Rightjet was the only employee left working at the gristmill, sweeping and cleaning up. All of his peers had taken leave to view a previously unknown spectacle in Dalilennon: a motorcade. Dignitaries from the distant land of Eglicata were being given the royal treatment.

Roger K., had he attended the occasion, would have recognized an alluring beauty sitting prom-like and wooing onlookers while smiling and waving from the motorcade's lead car.

Poncho McTea had organized the procession with little notice and even less encouragement from good King Nocturnal.

A total of four cars comprised the colorful motorcade, including the only convertible on the island, a red Lincoln with wide fenders where Ms. Sylvia Smitharomance sat, front stage-left, smiling and waving as if she were Venus or another Roman goddess of exquisite beauty and sensuality.

Sitting high with their butts on top of the backseat of the convertible, their feet where such posteriors normally went, were Manual McGetitdone and Norbert Nodahead. They smiled like hatless cowboys riding horses in a parade, with Manual's medium-length black hair loosely tossing about in the gentle, swirling sea breeze. Norbert's hair likely would have done the same, except his latest order of hair-growing gel hadn't arrived in time for the sudden trip to Dalilennon, and the hair that now sat on his head, sparse at best, would have required a hurricane to be tossed about loosely.

Sylvia blew loving kisses to the people she wished to deceive.

The second car in the procession held the bulky Mrs. King Nocturnal and her court of two: Ms. Patty Pickly and Ms. Frannie Finger. The duties for the three of them during the motorcade, though not officially sanctioned by the good King, included waving from open windows and doing their respective nose things.

The third vehicle, a painful lemon green in color, sported arch rivals Malcolm Straight and Poncho McTea looking out opposing back-seat windows. Straight had threatened to boycott the affair before succumbing to good King Nocturnal's begrudging pleas for a show of unity. Malcolm Straight, with little enthusiasm, waved sparingly through his back-seat window, in sharp contrast to Poncho McTea's overt displays of joyful, arm-pumping exuberance. Poncho waved as if his frantic displays of cheer and spirit might earn him a date with the prom queen two cars ahead of the lemon-green vehicle in which he and Straight were passengers.

Priest Precious and Ms. Nancy Droosha sat in the back seat of the fourth and last vehicle in the parade, the black one.

Nancy had argued at length with governmental authorities that she did not win any lottery to be in the motorcade, in fact had entered no such lottery in the first place. But her arguments fell on deaf ears.

It had been decreed by good King Nocturnal that she'd won the lottery and would ride in the motorcade; so nothing else need be said.

Priest Precious had done his best to calm Ms. Nancy's objections, and now, rarely smiling, she perfunctorily waved from one back-seat window of a dusty, black Mercedes; the precious priest exhibiting a little more vigor with smiles as he waved through the other back-seat window.

Ms. Nancy Droosha's strongest desire at this moment was to extricate herself from this public scene, to return to the quiet confines of her work.

The motorcade slowly wound along a seashore route, along a series of traversing turns. Dogs on flat roofs barked at the multi-colored procession that attracted fewer and fewer onlookers as the motorcade progressed toward the rise above the sea. Many viewers of this previously unknown sight on the isle of fancy straggled back to their work stations, disappointed in what they'd just witnessed. The few that did persevere and continued watching and walking with the motorcade soon were joined by a new wave of spectators at the crest of the hill.

This new wave of spectators, thanks to Mr. McTea, had been paid in advance with quality guitar strings and dental floss (all but three had chosen dental floss,) to appear, at that very moment and place, to cheer on the Eglicatan-based convoy. However, their contrived enthusiasm ebbed, then completely disappeared when the final leg of the motorcade, the last half-mile from the crest of the hill to good King Nocturnal's lofty palace, erupted in confusion.

Witnesses give varying accounts of what actually did undermine the final leg of the McTea-instigated motorcade.

Crack Officer Oliver Ogilvie, away at the time on a windswept walk by the sea with his wife, soon afterward was asked to reconstruct the events of that final half-mile. With his usual aplomb, the good officer researched those events and, as best he was able to recreate them, dictated what he uncovered to the good King in the following manner:

"The first strike came against Mr. McTea in the form of sun-ripened tomatoes. We don't know the precise number of tomatoes thrown because an early 'hit' on his face sent Mr. McTea scrambling for cover on the floorboard in the back-seat of the ugly green car. His cabin mate, or would that be back-seat mate, Malcolm Straight, didn't feel threatened by the barrage, noting that the volumes of tomatoes thrown at the vehicle came from behind a stone, farm wall along Mr. McTea's side of the car.

"The half-dozen policemen patrolling the motorcade rushed to the site of the uprising and prepared to converge on the culprits. An old farmer aided those policemen in their efforts by pointing them to a nearby shack. Armed and ready for any conceivable test of valor they might encounter, my men focused their energies and spent the next forty-five minutes carefully stalking that rundown building.

"They found it to be empty.

"By now, so to say, my men had placed all their eggs in one basket, and had left the motorcade naked of police protection. Returning from the empty shack, determined to quell any additional civil disobedience in its tracks, my men questioned two children with a donkey, but they'd smiled and said they'd done nothing wrong.

"While our patrol was away stalking the shack, the crazy caped crusader from the caves, Julian Knotsofoolista by name, reportedly jumped out from among the crowd and leaped upon the hood of the final car in the parade; the black one with Priest Precious and the fair Ms. Droosha in its back-seat. Knotsofoolista wore his usual garb of black priest frock and red high-topped tennys. He even wore his black Zorro hat.

"The strange one reportedly carried a lighted lantern, swung it wildly, and yelled at the top of his lungs, 'One if by land, two if by sea; a prophet isn't without honor except in his own country.'

"The driver of that fourth vehicle, the black Mercedes, then warned his passengers to 'hang on,' and tried to 'pop the clutch' and tumble the intruder. As he tried to do so, however, the black Mercedes winced, then stalled along the final leg of the parade route, scant hundreds of meters from the motorcade's goal: good King Nocturnal's palace.

"As the hand-picked driver of vehicle number four fought with the stubborn ignition, the caped crusader, much in the same vein as The Lone Ranger or Batman, descended from the car's hood to the pebbled road, and zipped out of sight.

"Earlier, I'd instructed my men not to pursue the bizarre one a second time for fear they'd get lost in the caves.

"I'm told Priest Precious and Ms. Droosha abandoned the vehicle and the motorcade at that point, and walked back to town.

"And there was more harassment to come! According to eye witnesses, an ugly old former midwife named Ms. Prissy Hampshire sprang from the crowd to berate Mr. Malcolm Straight riding in car number three, claiming she held the winning motorcade lottery ticket, not Ms. Nancy Droosha.

"Poncho McTea remained huddled on the floorboard on the other side of the back seat of that same vehicle, hence Straight took the brunt of Ms. Prissy's wooden cane across his hands and arms as he unsuccessfully tried to reason with her through the window. His urgent assurances that he'd form a committee to get to the heart of the matter apparently carried no weight with the former deliverer of Dalilennonian babies who'd finally found a representative of the nation's government to whack, twack, and vent her anger upon.

"The driver of the lemon-green car then accelerated his automobile, drove wildly, and passed the number two vehicle in the procession, hence triggering momentary errant jabs from the studious nose pickers, who quickly regained composure and resumed their nasal activities. Still, the driver of vehicle number three, passing vehicle number one in his haste, remained unable to shake loose Ms. Prissy Hampshire who was standing on the car's running board, hanging by a mirror, and demanding justice for retired midwives.

"And that's how Dalilennon's first official motorcade arrived at King Nocturnal's palace: with three of the four vehicles it started with; most of its original dignitaries present in one state or another; and an angry former midwife wielding a cane.

"Ms. Sylvia Smitharomance, I'm told, arrived without consequence in vehicle number one, (which now would be vehicle number two if calculated on arrival time and not departure time,) still basking in the sunshine and tossing kisses like high school royalty, and Misters McGetitdone and Nodahead continuing to wave and smile from that car's back seat at a crowd that no longer was there. The Mrs. King and her two friends safely arrived right behind them; in car number two or car number three depending if one wants to count front to back, or back to front.

"You know better than I regarding what happened after everyone's arrival," said crack Officer Oliver Ogilvie to King Nocturnal. "Hence, I conclude my report."

The report Ogilvie submitted to the good King and his advisors only was shared after he'd conducted numerous interviews, yet was OK'd with minimal discussion because even more weighty occurrences followed the weighty events immediately following the motorcade. (If that makes any sense!!!?)

After the operable vehicles were driven away and three donkeys were employed to drag the black Mercedes to an auto repair shop, the remaining dignitaries--or at least those not off in pursuit of cream tarts such as the Mrs. King, Ms. Patty Pickly, and Ms. Frannie Finger--and good King Nocturnal, whose whereabouts during the odd motorcade remain a mystery to this day, gathered for a momentous meeting in the chambers of the good King.

Missing for that meeting, and probably not invited in the first place, were Priest Darrell Precious and Ms. Nancy Droosha who nearly were home by now, or, in Ms. Nancy's case, back at work.

Since momentous meetings with international diplomats were heretofore unknown in Dalilennon, at least during the reign (and possibly lifetime,) of the good King, there were no formal rules of conduct to abide by, no Roberts Rules of Order fresh in anyone's mind. And so, good King Nocturnal, being dexterous as well as kind, undertook a semistrange, impromptu approach to the meeting that left Straight and McTea, who never agreed on anything, uniformly scratching their heads in disbelief.

Good King Nocturnal assumed the role of a Cub Scout den mother wanting new parents to feel at ease at a Weblos initiation, and summarily took it upon himself to grab each participant at the meeting, with one exception, by the back of their right arms and guide them to the seat he'd picked for them around a large oak (or was it teak?) conference table. The exception, of course, was Ms. Sylvia, the only female in the entourage, for, to honor her gender and maybe her striking looks, the good King escorted Ms. Smitharomance to her seat promenade-style.

Then, good King Nocturnal took to his throne and waited.

Manual McGetitdone, after chancing a glance at Ms. Sylvia's tan legs visible beneath the mini-skirt she'd donned for the motorcade, broke a lengthy silence after it became clear the good King had no intention of using his authority to speak first.

"I suppose you're wondering what brings us to Dalilennon?"

The good King nodded in assent, and Manual McGetitdone, with help from Ms. Sylvia and Norbert Nodahead, delivered a well-prepared presentation proposing a mutual defense pact between Eglicata and Dalilennon. The benefits for Dalilennon, according to the three Eglicatanese diplomats, would be dazzling. Eglicata would become a major ally responsive to the isle of fancy's every need; be it medical supplies, technology, television sets, or straight-out brotherly armaments for defense.

The room's inhabitants, except the good King, all sat along the King's long, wooden conference table that faced to the north and south, and they gazed toward good King Nocturnal whose throne pointed back at them from the head of the table in the east. From his elevated perch, set at a considerably higher level than even this talk of preservation and munitions was privy to, good King Nocturnal listened, ruled in his mind, and said little.

Good King Nocturnal watched with silent amusement as a child crept into the conference room, unnoticed by the Eglicatans or the king's advisors, and cranked the little-used heating fan in the room to the max. King Nocturnal gravely nodded in assent when young Jean Paul, fresh from a tomato patch, looked toward the king and flashed the biggest of mischievous grins.

Good King Nocturnal always had liked the giant heating fan. He'd installed it during the first year of his reign, twenty-six or twenty-seven years earlier, to combat each year's three- to-five days of cool weather, and it had paid dividends. Granted, today wasn't such a cool day, but a few added degrees of warmth wouldn't bother. The good King had a mischievous streak of his own, and began wondering whom from among his guests or advisors would be first to protest the coming hike in room temperature.

Norbert Nodahead soon began to wilt. His bald head, which wouldn't have been bald if his hair-stimulant gel had arrived before he'd left Eglicata on this lark to help secure a warped type of world peace, began seeping, weeping with sweat, as did his face and neck. He wiped all aside with a white kerchief and continued listening attentively to what was said by all. (Wasn't that his role in life?)

Ms. Sylvia, too, felt the rise in humid heat, as did Manual McGetitdone. Like Norbert, they chose to ignore the inconvenience.

When Poncho McTea began grumbling about "that damned heater," Malcolm Straight took liberty to rise from the table and open a hinged window placed in the wall several steps to the end of the table away from where the good King was seated.

The Eglicatanese diplomats droned on with their devious ploy, not noticing when a rope flashed outside the plane of the open window on their blind sides; not noticing when red tennis shoes, then a black priest's frock with a skinny body inside it clambered down the rope to a listening vantage out of sight just below the sill of the open window.

"And so it is, Your Excellency (a name to the good King's liking that often was repeated that day,) that the mighty nation of Eglicata, fearing for the safety of our friends at sea, wish to join Dalilennon in an unprecedented pact of goodwill, trade, and neighborliness highlighted by this sturdy defense treaty I hold in my hand.

"As neighbors in the good cause of national defense, all we need to do is share our natural resources to protect everyone's common good. If anyone attacks Dalilennon, heaven forbid, the good nation of Eglicata will be there posthaste to do whatever it takes to defend your beautiful island," concluded Herr McCoffee's occasionally articulate strongman, Manual McGetitdone.

"And vice versa," nodded Norbert Nodahead, and in so doing earned immediate, wrathful looks from his Eglicatanese peers. "Excuse me. Excuse me," said the uncomfortably sly little man who wished to be agreeable and grandiose at the same time.

As knuckles on the rope outside the window grew whiter and whiter with strain and fatigue, Malcolm Straight urged King Nocturnal to proceed with caution. "Don't act hastily," were the words that came straight out of his mouth. "Why would anyone wish to shatter the age-old peace on Dalilennon?" asked Straight.

During the uncomfortable pause that followed Malcolm's words of reticence, Ms. Sylvia Smitharomance, no longer a naive prom queen, began addressing the heat in the room by slowly, methodically unbuttoning her lavender cotton blouse. Beneath it was a skimpy black silk top and some ample cleavage. Then, receiving unabashed attention from every man in attendance, which amounted to everyone except herself, Ms. Sylvia took the opportunity to verbally respond to Mr. Straight's query.

"There are many countries in this world jealous of Dalilennon's long history of peace and contentment," she said. "The very length of that history and what it stands for is in itself a threat to the revolutionary governments and terrorists of our time."

"Bravo," interjected Norbert Nodahead, clapping his hands thunderously with his eyes focused on Ms. Smitharomance's breasts.

At that exact titillating moment in time, a hand-burning zing was heard by angels and a nearby dove, and a would-be priest, eavesdropping, fell two stories into a thick clump of wild roses. Muffled yelps and caustic expletives, although plenty audible at ground level, weren't heard in the good King's chambers above.

"No thorns go as deep as those of a rose," quoth Julian Knotsofoolista as he unrumpled his Zorro hat and gingerly limped back to his cave.

The meeting in the good King's conference room plodded well into the evening hours with Poncho McTea pressing hard for good King Nocturnal to affix his signature to the Eglicatan defense pact. Only Malcolm Straight's consistent counterarguments and good King Nocturnal's natural tendency not to make snap decisions enabled the Dalilennonian hierarchy, at least temporarily, to waylay Eglicata's underhanded, sneaky plot. After nine hours of hot, grueling, sauna-like arbitration, the good King signaled for an end of negotiations for the day, and scheduled a resumption of their discussions on the morrow.

Good King Nocturnal, last to leave the conference chambers, shut the hinged window after sticking his head through it into the night, looked upwards, and pondered why a limp, sisal rope was dangling there, obviously extending from a higher plane, possibly the roof of his cathedral.

A den mother tidying up, the good King then shut off the big heater and went home to the Mrs. King who was busy tucking away yet one more cream tart.

A Disadvantageous Night

It was on that same day, prior to the motorcade, that Poncho McTea had sent his wife and son, neither of whom had ever ventured off the isle for any purpose, to spend time with his wife's sister and her family in an adjoining village.

The McTea nuptials had come seven years earlier, shortly after Poncho's arrival on the isle of fancy, and been part and parcel to Poncho McTea's rapid climb in the island's political scene. A fair foreigner, a true catch for any Dalilennonian lass, Poncho had borrowed the tome 'A History of Dalilennonian Genealogy' from the public library the first day after securing personal lodging and ascertaining that there would be no thrilling chess matches to attend. With the tome, Poncho had researched which family he wished to marry into. It was a cold, insensitive approach to marriage, but had proven, for him, to be both effective and efficient. What surprised the cagey diplomat most was how close he'd come to his young son, Stem McTea.

It was late that night, after the nine-hour meeting, that a light knock was heard on the side door of Poncho McTea's home, and Ms. Sylvia Smitharomance and Manual McGetitdone were ushered inside by Mr. McTea. Ms. Sylvia had changed from her mini-skirt into a tasteful light-brown sweater and tight-fitting blue jeans.

"Nice place," said McGetitdone as he walked around the house, surveying the kitchen, living room, and bedroom to assure himself no one possibly could listen in on the diabolical scheming soon to take place on the premises. He noted an expensive display of imported Mediterranean furniture and Picasso-like arty décor hanging on dual-toned pastel walls.

"Thanks, but the sooner my family and I leave for Eglicata the better," said McTea selfishly. He knew full well the hardship leaving the isle of fancy would pose for his wife and Stem, but also believed, as most men of their homes assume knowing, that he knew what was best for all concerned.

Prior to stretching out on the lush leather sofa, Ms. Sylvia Smitharomance delivered an official message to Poncho McTea. "Your cousin, Herr McCoffee, sends his regards and hopes, as do you, that you again will be at his side in the days to come."

Then, she sprawled out on the sofa.

McTea's heart fluttered within his chest. Hopes of hearing such news had been an inner driving force for many years.

McGetitdone and McTea next sat in stuffed chairs, McTea somewhat miffed because McGetitdone had beaten him to his favorite rocker where Poncho had spent many blissful hours listening to the music of Bach and Bruce Springsteen. The two chairs now occupied by the male conspirators flanked the large sofa being commandeered by Ms. Sylvia.

"I can't tell how good King Nocturnal is going to rule," said Ms. Sylvia from her prone position. "He seems attentive to our overtures, yet highly reticent."

"It makes no difference," said Manual McGetitdone. "We will get the plant, loose the fowlawarfare, and the world will never know or care how Dalilennon's king cast his vote."

"It's not so easy," responded Ms. Smitharomance, looking her usual alluring self while stretched out on the sofa wearing her soft, cashmere sweater and tight jeans. "We can't handle Dalilennon with force without jeopardizing our overall plan. The nation of Dalilennon may be isolated and sleepy, but it has a host of friends. Not the least of which, God save me for even speaking the name, being Darius. We must retrieve the disadvantageous plant peacefully. Once safely back in Eglicata with the needed supply of disadvantageous, then Herr McCoffee will decide the fate of this island nation."

"Personally," interjected McTea, "I don't see any real jeopardy to the plan regardless of what good King Nocturnal decides. In forty-eight hours the plant will be ready to harvest under a full moon. All we have to do is cut it down, pack it in the wet gunny sacks you brought with you, and sail away to Eglicata."

Poncho said the final four words with wispy stars in his eyes.

"Do you plan to return with us?" asked Ms. Sylvia.

"That depends on what happens between now and then."

Poncho obviously had thought through the possible scenarios many times.

"If things remain peaceful, I may stay until the invasion force arrives. If not, I may journey with you." Poncho's words were hollow, distant, as if said not to communicate anything of truth to the Eglicatanese sleuths he was scheming with.

"And what about your wife and son?" persisted Ms. Smitharomance.

"They know nothing about this affair. They'll be safe with my wife's family until I decide it's time to leave, whether that's in two nights or later."

"Before we check the plants," said Ms. Smitharomance, the agent, "we should devise a strategy to work on the good king and Mr. Straight tomorrow. No sense going to forceful action when there's still hope for peaceful negotiations."

McGetitdone, without relinquishing McTea's favorite Bach-Bruce Springsteen rocking chair, lit a cigar he'd scored from Poncho, and forty-four minutes of hot negotiating prep-work followed. The defense pact itself was of secondary importance behind the need to confiscate a set number of bundles of harvested, thirteen- and-a-half to fourteen day-old disadvantageous.

Individual words and phrases stuck out like toes in threadbare socks during the course of those forty-four minutes of intense bargaining, intense manipulation.

"Disadvantageous … military might … fowlawarfare … midnight raid … treachery … treasonous … spiteful … scandalous …" and the like. All were muttered during the quiet living-room scene where Poncho McTea, though politely refraining from making a fuss, remained irked that McGetitdone, during the entire forty-four minutes, comfortably sat enthroned in his favorite Bach-Springsteen rocking chair.

After their discussion, about forty-five minutes after it started, Poncho McTea entered his son Stem's room and returned with a bright red lantern. He rigorously pumped its mantel, lit the wick, and led his co-conspirators out the side door of his house, through a swinging gate, and to the semilit street beyond.

It was midnight by now, and no one was about. The three wound down the narrow cobblestone street stoically, only the sound of heel scuffs echoing off enclosing stone walls denoting their movements in the still, quiet night.

Light from Stem's red lantern illuminated doorways as they walked. Empty milk bottles were stacked neatly in wire baskets waiting for the morning milkman to replace them with full ones. Plastic garbage sacks--black, bulky, and odorous--lined doorways for the purpose of being whisked away in the night before homeowners arose from a sound night's sleep.

However, what Ms. Smitharomance most noticed about the occasionally lit entrances to the homes they passed, and shuddered at, were the never-failing insignias of patron saints peeking out from, and protecting every dwelling and its occupants along their pathway. Our Lady of Sorrows, Saint Andrew, Saint Anthony, Saint Paul, and innumerable others stood watch at every doorway. A few of those saints were illuminated by night lights of their own, but most became visible only when light from Poncho McTea's lantern, or rather Stem McTea's lantern, pierced the moonlit semidarkness.

The culminating effect of so much Christian oversight made Ms. Sylvia Smitharomance uncomfortable, and she sighed in relief when the final house and, as far as she knew, final saint was behind them.

"I'll take you on a roundabout trail from here," said McTea quietly to the two following his lead. "It's longer, but the chances of encountering barking dogs are far less."

Neither Ms. Sylvia nor Manual McGetitdone had spoken since leaving McTea's home. Manual, being the man he was, positioned himself in the logistical rear and purposely tapped the fanny in front of him more than once, yet received no response from the alluring female we know as Sylvia Smitharomance.

Chunky beige stones impeded their progress and caused the three conspirators attentively to scan the ground beneath them. They walked in near silence. As you'd expect, it being a still Dalilennonian night, no birds or ground animals gave away their presence.

One unanticipated drop-off caused McTea to stumble, then caution the others. Still, Ms. Sylvia lost her footing at the same spot, and Poncho, ahead of her, reached out and broke her fall. Sylvia Smitharomance's perfume in their sudden closeness was intoxicating to Poncho's nostrils, and the double agent found his right hand positioned high on Ms. Sylvia's left thigh.

McTea helped the lady diplomat/spy to an upright position, and paused.

They still were touching when McGetitdone, navigating by the light of the moon, dropped to their level.

"You can almost see more by the moon alone," McGetitdone said.

McTea, reluctantly pulling away from Ms. Sylvia, said, "It's another two hundred meters or so."

He extinguished the light from Stem's red lantern and, indeed, the going was easier. Light from the moon allowed them to better see the light-colored stones, highlighting rock surfaces against a darker backdrop of dirt and grass. The path on which they traveled skirted around small rectangular fields ringed by waist-high stone fences.

By now, the outline of Dalilennon's only mountain was visible in the night. After a total of about fifty minutes of walking, the three conspirators arrived at a familiar high metal gate. The bordering stone walls, higher than the norm but not as high as the gate, were distinctive and shaded dark in the moonlight.

"I left the key at home so you'd be able to see how easy it is to get in without it," said Poncho McTea.

The two men collided in their eagerness to boost Ms. Sylvia atop the wall, but McGetitdone, as often was the case, won that battle. He relished the touch, the feel of the firmness of her calves, then muscled Ms. Sylvia into a sitting position on the top of the stone wall. Poncho cupped his hands and boosted Manual skyward, then experienced firsthand Manual McGetitdone's uncanny strength as Manual, in one continuous motion, reached down and pulled McTea to a position on top of the wide wall beside Manual and Ms. Sylvia.

Poncho McTea relit the wick to Stem's lantern, allowing the three of them to peer below and spot rocks to avoid during their coming descent inside the garden wall. They then dropped to the ground like Contra militia under the watchful eye of Lt. Col. Oliver North.

"This shit grows fast," said Manual as he scanned the garden plot teeming with disadvantageous. At the same site where McTea had strewn seeds haphazardly on the ground less than two weeks before now stood a nearly full-grown crop of the weed. "No wonder it uproots itself and falls on its belly en route to any wise, diligent farmer's fire."

The sturdy, plume-tufted plants already were five-feet high and laden with dozens of seedy fronds near the top of each stem. It was the prolific seeds that, once ingested into his sheep-filled alkaline stomach, could save the mighty fowlawarfare from a deadly, gluttonous fate. Only those seeds, weed seeds on Dalilennon, could digest fatty lamb tissue fast enough to keep Herr McCoffee's flying war machine alive and well long enough to author McCoffee's defiant brand of world peace; peace under the control of one man.

And that one man, if you might recall, might have had less than the best interests of mankind entrenched in his self-grandiosed heart.

The clusters of seeds on the fronds were so thick and heavy that the intruders now understood what they'd been told about the strange plant's propensity to uproot itself and topple to the ground a few hours shy of a fortnight after being sown. Let those seeds die, then resurrect in the ground without fire, and there's no telling what exponential havoc the next weed crop could bring.

"One plant must produce millions of seeds," said McGetitdone with awed respect in his voice. The three of them, like Midwestern American farmers, touched and investigated plants between their thumbs and forefingers.

"Herr McCoffee says fifty full gunny sacks will revive the beast enough for a trip from Eglicata to Dalilennon, where it can refuel, then fly on to Darius where the fowlawarfare's mettle will be tested," said Ms. Sylvia as she paced among and around the tall row crop.

Poncho McTea said, "I rented the land as a sharecropper to avoid suspicion, and spent a lot more time cultivating regular crops such as potatoes, carrots, cabbage, and rutabagas than I did disadvantageous. Of course," he added with a smile somewhat visible in the moonlight, "disadvantageous plants don't take a lot of nurturing."

As an obvious afterthought, Poncho added, "You know, farming isn't all that bad."

The three conspirators, under the light of a nearly full harvest moon, quietly conversed about their intricate, time-specific plan to harvest the disadvantageous and transport full gunny sacks of it to their large vessel waiting offshore, then sail to Eglicata.

"Two nights, and we'll be off this forsaken island," said Manual McGetitdone. "This place gives me the creeps. It's as if everyone here knows what I'm thinking."

"If everyone knew what you were thinking, Manual, we'd either be far away from this island or already in jail," said Sylvia Smitharomance. "Let's go."

Boosted back atop the tall stone wall, Ms. Sylvia caught her breath in surprise. For, directly beneath her pacing back and forth in obvious agitation was a large, strong, stout donkey looking up at her and snarling through its nostrils.

"There's a mad donkey out here," she submitted in a meek, feminine voice, as if her guile suddenly had been stripped away.

McGetitdone topped the wall next, paused to study the domesticated ass in obvious agitation, then offered his hand to Poncho McTea. When McTea joined them on top of the wall, Blokehead, for it could be none other, began an assault on the eardrums of mankind.

"Bray-y-y, bray-y-y, bray-y-y," roared the obtuse animal time after time. Blokehead's outburst rolled across the base of the mountain and pierced the previously quiet Dalilennonian night like a rumbling hot rod in a Norwegian steam bath or a braking log truck in a Muslim mosque during prayers.

"Shut up, you stupid donkey," yelled Manual McGetitdone helplessly as the tumult, like a loud, unceasing burglary alarm, continued roaring into the night.

Blokehead pranced angrily beneath the conspirators along the base of the stone wall, braying nonstop with his head tipped like a moon-silhouetted coyote or an early morning rooster.

Ms. Sylvia and Poncho McTea looked to Manual McGetitdone to rid them of this vocal problem. That was his role, after all, an area he normally exceeded in, and what they'd come to expect from the strong-armed diplomat. McGetitdone's revolver had been left behind on the boat, this being peaceful Dalilennon where he feared nothing, but this big donkey looked and sounded violent. What was to be done?

Minutes, loud minutes, the type of minutes that seem elongated because detection is moments away; those type of stressful minutes passed for the three conspirators before McGetitdone jumped to the ground on the inside, disadvantageous side of the wall to retrieve some large stones. He tossed the stones to McTea in hopes either he or McTea would throw them accurately and quiet the haranguing critter.

But, before McGetitdone again was on top of the wall and before any rocks were thrown, a high, piercing, cackling type of laughter, like that made by the wicked witch on Dorothy's perilous journey to Oz, rang into the night, and Blokehead went silent.

"What a pair to draw to," laughed Ms. Prissy Hampshire. "Important folk like you shouldn't be out in the middle o the night scarin' me gentle donkey."

She laughed again, heartily. After so many years of being abused by an insensitive bureaucracy, Ms. Prissy finally saw an opportunity to return the favor.

"Let us down, and we'll talk," said Ms. Sylvia, now sitting on the wall, facing Ms. Prissy, and wanting to drop to the ground. Blokehead responded to her request with another loud chorus of brays, and Ms. Prissy's creviced jowls shook with pleasure.

"You're one of ours and you're one of theirs," snipped Ms. Prissy, pointing first to Poncho McTea and then to Ms. Sylvia Smitharomance. "I'll bet good King Nocturnal would want ter know what brings ya out here at this time o the night," teased the craggy midwife who hadn't had this kind of sheer, wanton fun in decades.

Blokehead brayed even more vociferously when Manual McGetitdone, rocks in every pocket, was once more tugged, by McTea, to the flat, wide top of the wall.

"Ain't no end to the surprises," cackled Ms. Prissy.

"Listen, old lady," said McGetitdone in an intimidating voice. "If you and your stupid donkey aren't out of here in thirty seconds, I can't be held responsible for what I'll do to you. Consider that a threat."

Manual McGetitdone knew he meant it; Poncho McTea knew he meant it; and Ms. Sylvia Smitharomance knew he meant it.

However, Ms. Prissy Hampshire either didn't know he meant it, or chose to ignore McGetitdone's threat. Apparently, she was having too much fun pointing and jeering and being abusive to a stereotyped figurehead that, for once in her eyes, didn't appear to have the upper hand.

"Three powerful 'bassadors of peace held at bay by a donkey and a wrinkled ol' lady. What a farce," she snorted eagerly, knowing this would be a time she'd savor for the rest of her life.

Manual McGetitdone was livid by now, and used his extreme anger forcefully to end the scenario that, until he committed a sudden, violent act, had brought so much pleasure to Ms. Prissy.

With the calculated quickness of Magic Johnson driving through the lane, Manual leaped from the wall, caught his balance, dashed to the ex-midwife, and felled her with one mighty fist to the cheek. He then whirled to face the real challenge, the donkey, and saw that Blokehead's spirit had been broken. The instantly subdued donkey stepped past the angry pugilist armed with rocks and hate, and leaned down to study his fallen master, sadly and faintly moaning as if he'd been struck himself.

Manual helped Ms. Sylvia Smitharomance down from the wall, left Poncho McTea to fend for himself, and, after Poncho jumped to the ground below, the three of them retraced their steps into the night.

One question and one response were all that was spoken during their flight back to their respective lodgings: McTea to his home, and Ms. Sylvia and Mr. McGetitdone to their docked boat.

"Good God, McGetitdone, did you kill her?" queried Poncho McTea, knowing the stir a murder on peaceful Dalilennon would make.

"I hope so."

Roger Tries To Retreat

It was Julian Knotsofoolista who discovered Ms. Prissy the next morning. She was unconscious, but breathing with faithful Blokehead by her side.

J.K. had walked from his cave to join Ms. Prissy for breakfast and, along the way, found his friend crumpled on the ground at the base of a high, stone garden wall. Gravely concerned, Knotsofoolista was baffled at what had transpired, yet knew by seeing the ugly purple welt on Ms. Prissy's left cheek that she'd been struck in a brutal manner. And he didn't sense, but knew the harsh blow had come from another.

The "crazed" crusader, who really wasn't crazy, consciously wished Blokehead had the abilities of Balaam's donkey and could explain to him what had transpired, why and how his innocent, albeit ugly friend had been felled in the night.

Knotsofoolista eased the body of the limp, retired deliverer-of-babies across the donkey's rigid back and led Blokehead to Ms. Prissy's home, where he loosened her clothing and gently positioned her beneath the covers of her narrow bed. When Ms. Prissy's breathing approached a natural, almost comfortable state, J.K. slipped away to a neighbor's house and solicited aid.

Anyone living near Ms. Prissy cared more for the cantankerous ex-midwife than Ms. Prissy suspected, and the first neighbor woman Julian asked for help immediately dropped what she was doing and came running to help soothe the old woman's pain.

Gentle whispers and prayers by J.K. and the neighbor, offered on their knees beside the unconscious woman to a God Who certainly understood the score better than they did, preceded Julian Knotsofoolista's exit through Ms. Prissy's front door. The neighbor was left behind holding a damp, wet kerchief to Ms. Prissy's ancient, sweaty face.

Julian K. returned to the garden wall where he'd found Ms. Prissy less than two hours before and carefully paced the area, counting footsteps in the dirt. A spy by trade, if not advanced training, Knotsofoolista scoured the area for telling clues like Perry Mason or Sherlock Holmes or a young Maltese banker trying to make sense of a Washington state lottery ticket. He even scaled the high garden wall, hopped to the ground below, and found identical sets of footsteps--less Ms. Prissy's narrow, childlike prints and those of Blokehead--haphazardly formed in the red dust now pooching from beneath his even redder, dustier high-topped tennis shoes.

Then, Julian Knotsofoolista climbed back over the wall and paid a visit to Roger K. Rightjet.

"Why come to me and not the police?" asked Roger K. suspiciously of his black-frocked friend.

"They can't even catch tomato-throwing children," said Knotsofoolista. "No, we need to find the villains, gather complete evidence that even a Dalilennonian policeman can understand, then turn them in."

"What if Ms. Prissy dies?"

"Don't talk like that," snapped Julian Knotsofoolista. "She's too ornery to die that way."

"But neither you nor I is qualified to carry out a criminal investigation," persisted Roger K. Rightjet, who sensed a threat arising to his chosen peaceful lifestyle.

"I am."

The words were stated tersely, knowingly, from the mouth of Julian Knotsofoolista, and Roger K. believed to a point, but didn't want to.

"What are you saying?"

And J.K., anxious to enlist R.K.R.'s aid, quickly moved into a partial telling of his past; a life story, like almost anyone's in brief, that looks like a pale broccoli leaf, or even one of those hybrid purple ones next to the real thing.

No one has time to recount or listen to the myriad of smiles and hugs and trials and pains that make a person who he is. No one has time to communicate, in words, the human journey of selling hidden treasures in hopes of buying a field that person feels compelled to possess. How could Julian Knotsofoolista convey the true merit of his frocked, cave-like existence to another mortal when he only knew of it himself through the murky lense of blind faith?

And so, J.K. told enticing, meaty fragments of his story for the purpose of enlisting a worthy ally.

"I won't bore you with details, but after being raised on Dalilennon, I left my mother and my homeland for the lure of the sea," said Julian. "The trip was unforgettable with a crazy captain who set me adrift in a small dinghy. The heat and thirst swelled my tongue until fate bumped me back into the same inept captain.

"This time, however, he treated me like a savior, welcomed my presence, and we pooled our talents to discover whatever land we could find.

"At long last, we struck ground in a highly inhabited country called Darius. The unstable captain sailed on, and I, glad to be rid of his craziness, stayed. I wandered for days among friendly people I couldn't communicate with until I met a gentle, loving man who spoke Dalilennonianese. He, his wife, and their only son welcomed me into their home, taught me their language, helped me obtain a solid education, and treated me with more kindness and respect than I've ever known, before or since.

"But, I missed home and my mother.

"Still, how was I to return? My new family wasn't rich, and I had no money.

"But, my adopted brother, two years older than I, came to the rescue. He introduced me to people in the espionage … that means spy," Julian K. added purposefully for Roger K. Rightjet's edification, "business. And I've been living in caves here, wearing a discarded priest's frock and discarded red tennis shoes ever since.

"And I'm getting rich," J.K. chuckled in satisfaction. "I make reports on a monthly basis when a certain boat docks here from Darius, and they pay me accordingly. So, I save money spying on an isle of fancy where, until now, nothing ever has happened.

"Of course, I do sort of go crazy in my solitude. Thank God for Ms. Prissy, you, and those goofy orphan twins. I even like Blokehead."

Roger K. winced, taking the final four words as a personal offence.

"What do you want from me?" asked Rightjet as the two of them sat at his small dining-room table. A wickered oil lamp lit the room, casting their respective shadows on nearby walls like the undulating waters of time or rabbit ears hoisted by a jokester on a dark movie screen before the show begins.

"Help me learn who hurt Ms. Prissy," said Julian K. "That discovery undoubtedly will help us understand why Eglicata has diplomats on Dalilennon at this time."

"I'm not big on being a hero and sticking my neck out, you know," said Roger K. somewhat defensively. "Give me time to think on it, and we'll talk again about it soon."

At this juncture, Julian Knotsofoolista strategically chose to withhold information about lanterns and dark nights and intrigue. Too, he said nothing about a closed-door governmental meeting he'd overheard while dangling two stories above ground on a sisal rope, or about rose thorns that still made the act of sitting less than a pleasurable experience for him.

"I'll be back tomorrow," said Julian Knotsofoolista while gingerly rising from the padded seat of one of Rightjet's two dining-room chairs. J.K. started walking toward the back door, stopped in deep thought with his right hand cupped over his chin, then returned to where Roger K. Rightjet sat watching him, pondering upon his own distant, dark-lensed past.

Then, in the e-eery, sing-song voice that identified J.K. as the "crazed" crusader from the caves, Julian chanted, "For the Lord is a God of knowledge, and by Him actions are weighed."

Then, in a frocked bustle of energy, J.K. whisked out the back door and was gone.

"Why me?" grumbled the now solitary, would-be hero, looking to where his unusual friend had just exited. "He's the savior, not me."

Roger K. Rightjet, suddenly feeling more alone than he'd felt in years, dejectedly walked to his garden and looked upon the tiny Eden he'd created since buying his home: the transplanted lemon tree that flourished in the growth-conducive climate of Dalilennon; the green nettles that stung his skin, yet flavored and graced many hot soups;

the clover-like freesias that looked elegant and took little care; and the young pear tree that had taken so much loving attention and time, including the strategic application of wooden splints to strengthen branches seemingly overlooked by God's grace. Only recently had that special pear tree rooted firmly in the Dalilennonian dirt, and now was prepared for many banner seasons of healthy fruit production.

But mostly, in his state of melancholy, Roger K. Rightjet turned his eyes to the roses: the yellows and reds and salmons that literally ringed the garden plot that, as a whole, had contributed so much to the healing of his soul.

The love he'd shared with shovel and pruning shears, plus subtle hints of fertilizer all reflected back at him now; radiated the warm, colorful love Nature had for Her true keeper, Her gardener, Who, without ceasing, soothed seeking souls nonstop with water and sunshine and seasons and growth.

Roger K. Rightjet instinctively knew the garden wasn't his. He could be part and parcel of its current beauty, but he merely was a caretaker, one small component of an integrated whole. Even now, he wantonly could slash and hack the plants he'd nurtured for many years, and within the next ten years or so not much from today would have changed. The trees and bushes and nettles and freesias always would come back or die.

He had no control, only input.

"I'm no savior," Roger K. muttered audibly to himself while looking at his beloved pear tree that was ready to throw off its splints, its braces and live unrestricted, free to flourish and bloom, to seed and germinate under light blue, sea-misted skies.

"Why can't I find peace?" grumbled Rightjet to the thorn-guarded roses; the reds and yellows and salmons ringing the garden in a definitive pattern woven by his mortal hands.

He sat down on a stone bench, a heavy stone bench that only had reached his property through arduous labor on his part and on the part of distant friends who'd never been invited inside his home. Roger drooped his thirty-two-year-old face into calloused, blue-collar hands and remained motionless for several moments.

Roger K. Rightjet, beset by emotion, was torn between asking for guidance through the avenue of prayer and shedding tears. So, he did both.

"I'm no savior. Where do I go?" he sputtered miserably, his eyes continuing to water for the first time since he'd arrived on the isle of fancy.

Roger K. stood and wandered around the lovely garden for twenty minutes or maybe three hours. Without direction, he strolled the herbary God had loaned him for much of the past seven years, and then, with resigned conviction, re-entered the rear entrance of his home. Before going inside, however, Roger filled his nostrils once more with Nature's tangy garden fragrances. Then, he purposefully turned his back and walked away from the Eden where plants nurtured to life at the touch of his human hands were bobbing and pulsing behind him out of his view in a soft afternoon breeze. Roger K. strangely was unaware of the day's brightness, of the challenging hope he wished to ignore.

His mind made up, Roger K. Rightjet grabbed an oversized duffle bag and began stuffing clothing and toiletries inside it. The clock on the wall informed him he had forty minutes to reach the dock and book passage on a tramp steamer he knew was in harbor loading whatever goods gentle Dalilennon had to share with the world.

Roger K. felt pangs of sadness, yet was determined to move on in this seemingly meaningless world; to find yet another corner to settle in away from violence and demands for chivalry. He packed his bag, walked out the front door and front gate, and strolled toward the unchanging sea without looking back at his adobe home or his garden.

But fate has many turns, many junctures, many moods to share with those under her wing; and her means of relaying such are as diverse as the winds of winter or Nature's multicolored brilliance on a sunny day in paradise.

Just as surely as brave Ulysses was cast upon a remote island and held captive seven years before Zeus ordered him free; as surely as Abraham Lincoln, not necessarily wanting the American presidency, was gently, and sometimes not so gently pushed that direction until he knew his role in history as clearly as if a sorceress had spelled it out in his alphabet soup; and as surely as Elvis, the knee-flapping idol with crooning guitar and unforgettably energetic, yet soulful voice had died simply because he was unable to keep step with the fast-paced history he was creating ...

... just so it was that fate intervened to prevent Roger K. Rightjet from departing from Dalilennon, the proverbial isle of fancy, on that troubled, yet sunny day.

En route to the harbor, duffle in hand, Roger K. marched smartly, mode steadfast. Nothing could alter his decision, he thought. No change of heart, no wafting of sweet smells from his favorite pastry shop, no reconsideration of Julian Knotsofoolista's urgent report could change his mind on this wind-puffed day. Not even the pretty lady from church who walked past Roger K. on his march to the waterfront (Nancy gasped at seeing his duffle.) could alter his intent.

But fate, as she so often does, chose the final precious moment to intervene and change the course of history regarding the future exploits of our would-be hero.

For why, but for fate's decree, would Blokehead, the loyal donkey, leave Ms. Prissy's side when she needed him most, and now be standing, actually waiting at the gangplank leading to the vessel Rightjet was planning to board?

Admittedly torn by his decision to leave his beloved home of seven years, yet adamant, Roger K. Rightjet gasped aloud when he saw his arch enemy, teeth bared, blocking his admittance to a hastily planned, major change in lifestyle.

Blokehead, whether having been forewarned of Rightjet's purpose or not, immediately recognized the wanting-to-be non hero and, braying playfully, began the chase.

Obscenities, the most vile Roger K. could produce on short notice, had absolutely no impact on the charging donkey, and our would-be non hero "made tracks" back up the hill away from the dock as fast as his churning legs would carry him.

Puffing up the cobblestone road, Rightjet, still clutching his duffle, passed the lovely Ms. Droosha now returning after posting letters. She waved at him, flashed a big, warm smile, and Roger K. responded with a hasty one-handed salute in return; with Blokehead, the big, strong, playful donkey braying loudly in gleeful, hot pursuit right behind him.

Ms. Nancy watched the handsome, humorous foreigner until he zagged from view, finding refuge from his adversary inside the nearby church with a tall steeple. She laughed, tossed her head and hair in the wind, and then let her thoughts wander toward future dreams as she hiked back to work.

Dreams

Everyone was laughing cruelly. She couldn't see faces, but the laughter was near, abrasive, and wanting to hurt and ridicule. She felt shamed by who she'd become, who she was, and wanted to run away and cry in the arms of her long-lost mother; to cry, 'Why are they laughing at me? I'm doing the best I know how.'

Taunts without faces, without solid reasons, are taunts that most prick the heart.

The Mrs. King awoke with a start in her lonely canopied bed. She was sweating from the residue of a dream that dictated her mood. Her tender heart was downturned, as if loaded with dirt from a full, overflowing flowerpot. She felt burdened with shame.

Short kilometers away, another woman, Ms. Sylvia Smitharomance, was tossing in her sleep. She sweated more from her dream's content than from the isle of fancy's late-night heat.

Alone. She always was alone. No one had slept with her since her betrothed youth. Made love, yes; sex, yes; but never the night. She controlled the rules of that game.

"No. Not that. Don't judge that!"

Ms. Sylvia bit her cover and writhed in anguish. A tear of pain, a byproduct of her life's chosen all-encompassing path of solitude trickled from her eye, bearing witness to the vulnerability of strength.

Ms. Sylvia fully shuddered awake with a violent 'No,' a protest to the helplessness her subconscious self knew so well. She opened her eyes; wild eyes, then calmer as the surroundings she saw provided clarity and safety away from the realm of dreams beyond her control, dreams she now could escape and leave behind.

Another dream lost in the night. Her sweating body and palpitating heart were without recollection or memory of that dream's content, just fuzzy reminders of what apparently just had taken place within her soul.

Puzzled, Ms. Sylvia Smitharomance checked the time, lit a cigarette and, once she'd smoked it and taken its last puff, shut off the light once more, and lay back down until dawn.

Broken Protocol

The Mrs. King's dream was alive, painfully alive in her heart. She felt the taunts and the ridicule as if characters from a Shakespearean tragedy had come to her bedside the previous night and chanted hurtful dirges while she'd unsuccessfully pulled the covers over her head and tried to sleep.

Though fully awake now, the hurt remained.

The hurt translated into shame for her, the Queen of Dalilennon's, vulnerability to the sometimes controllers of dreams, the Machiavellian jesters who, in this case, graphically programmed the Mrs. King's remembrance of past offenses.

Suddenly, the Mrs. King's outlook for the day was changed. Lying in bed, she wondered if her routine, daily practices were indeed inconsequential; if her haunting dream rightly had challenged her daily exercises as laughable, without ontological merit of any kind.

In her spacious, lonely, multicolored bed, she thought about, truly pondered, her normal paces.

Protocol would find the Mrs. King arising at this hour and spending much of the morning selecting wardrobes and menus for the day. A company of handmaids ('they never did like me,' she thought,) would attend to her every whim; tugging and pulling and making subtle hygiene suggestions when her mood was right. They, too, regularly slipped her crumpets and cakes and teas to sustain her until the morning meal was served.

At noon, she'd routinely dine with good King Nocturnal who, of late, had championed a cause to make her happier about who she was. He'd even, in earnest, offered to grant her a wish of any magnitude, but the Mrs. King's sense of queenly humility had caused her to decline the offer.

"What more could I possibly ask for?" she'd said to her good King and husband.

Good King Nocturnal gladly would have informed her of current events on the isle of fancy, but the Mrs. King habitually expressed a lack of interest regarding such topics.

On the previous day alone, the good King, out of respect for his wife's noninterest concerning current events, had bit his tongue at lunch and said nothing about: 1) meetings with Eglicatan dignitaries; 2) the coma of Ms. Prissy Hampshire; 3) a morning meeting with Poncho McTea who'd practically demanded a quick signing of the proposed defense pact with Eglicata; and 4) news that the fool Knotsofoolista again was at the home of Roger K. Rightjet.

Good King Nocturnal was a well-informed king, and gladly would have shared all with his wife, but, frankly stated, what did she care?

And so, the heads of a tropical island nation routinely spoke during lunch of crumpets and cakes, of the unchanging weather outside and, frequently, of how hard the wind once had blown before they'd been married.

Afternoons for the Mrs. King normally were spent in the company of Ms. Patty Pickly and Ms. Frannie Finger. The three inevitably would lounge in the comfortable sunshine with servants catering to their desires. The trio often walked in the lovely palatial garden, ooh-ing and ahh-ing at this flower and that without stooping to smell the heavenly fragrances those flowers so wanted to share with them.

Mostly, however, they'd eat, eat, and eat from the best food stocks available on the island of Dalilennon: salted fish, cheese, and wine cakes; strawberries and chicken gizzards and nuts from all over the world; and puddings and sweets and much, much more. The Mrs. King always revered the sugared sweets that could lift her black moods for a spell and give the ceaseless bantering of the two she lounged with, at least for a few moments, an air of lightness and humor that otherwise was lacking.

But on this morning, the morning following her semirecollected, disturbing dream, the Mrs. King Nocturnal did what she hadn't done in the 26 (27?) years of her stay in the Dalilennonian palace.

She elected to remain in her canopied bed without food, drink, or disturbances of any kind. She chose to lie there and reflect on what had been, and what was to be.

When good King Nocturnal, readying for the noon repast with the Mrs. King, was informed of this unusual turn of events, he hurried to seek out his bride; hoping, as the good husband he was, to provide her with comfort and understanding. For, indeed, the Mrs. King still was a top priority in the good King's life.

At the door of the Mrs. King's chambers, however, good King Nocturnal's path was blocked by a craggy old maid who easily could have been mistaken for Prissy Hampshire's sister. The elderly domestic, Maid Blueskysic by name, had been a devoted servant to the Mrs. King for at least 26 years, and packed some weight, or, more precisely, carried considerable clout regarding the Mrs. King's affairs when she had a mind to.

And today she had a mind to.

Maid Blueskysic, in unmistakably authoritative tones, matter-of-factly informed the highest ranking figure in Dalilennon, its good King, that there absolutely was no way he could see his wife of umpteen years on this given day. The frail old lady bodily blocked the entrance to the Mrs. King's chambers, and threatened the good King with a wrestling match, a mud wrestling match if he was man enough to step outside and grapple in earnest, were he not to heed her strict warning.

The good King backed off.

"Me thinks she's a pausing' ter study the merits o life, Yer Excellency," said the elderly spinster, and the good King, knowing the merits of a strategic retreat, left Blueskysic by the door and went to dine alone and 'study the merits of life' by hisself.

Tender shark meat, steamed carrots, frog roe, and a delicate home-grown red wine comprised the light noon meal that day as the good King, in solitude, pondered.

Nothing good had happened since the Eglicatan diplomats had set foot on Dalilennon. He couldn't point a finger and ipso facto their participation in any wrong doing, yet the facts spoke of unheard unrest since their arrival.

The unsolved incident during the motorcade, the blow to Ms. Prissy Hampshire, and now the Mrs. King's unusual behavior … Where would it all end?

One seriously had to question the 'merits of life' so easily defined short days before.

Poncho McTea, too, was becoming a source of worry for the good king. He seemed obsessed with the proposed defense pact with Eglicata. This seemed unlike the rational advisor good King Nocturnal had grown to know and trust.

Good King Nocturnal toyed with his white, flaky shark meat and sipped his wine.

On impulse, he rang for a servant.

"Tell Mr. Straight I wish to see him at his earliest convenience," said the good King to the servant upon the servant's arrival at the good King's table where he, in solitude, had been pondering and puzzling.

"Yes, Your Excellency," said the olive-skinned native dressed in white and scarlet.

Good King Nocturnal finished the boneless shark dish, picked at the roe, and gulped down a second glass of wine.

He thought once more of Poncho McTea and how the foreign-born diplomat had risen in his favor so quickly.

They'd first met nine years earlier when McTea, recently landed on Dalilennon, had gained a position as a writer for the isle of fancy's sleepy newspaper. McTea quickly had lined up an interview with the agreeable and approachable king. Much discussion had transpired during that first meeting, including a thumbnail sketch of McTea's past.

What he told the good King that day--what we who've been closely following this stark revelation of true fiction know to be a bold lie--in rough paraphrase, equated to:

Born of moderate-income parents in the distant landlocked country of Huligata, verified by his passport no less, (the verification coming in regards to his citizenship and not the economic status of his parents,) Poncho McTea had progressed to the position of staff reporter at the largest newspaper in that nation's capital city, Huli. His views had strayed along a divergent course from those of the military government ruling Huligata at the time, especially regarding one trade issue with democratic Darius.

According to research McTea said he'd conducted, textbooks, fair textbooks, could be imported into Huligata from Darius at half the cost of home-drafted, militaristic Huligatan textbooks.

However, he'd cried wolf too loudly, and a subsequent raid on his home had cost the lives of his wife and infant son. Knowing his own life, or its ensnuffment thereof, to be a Huligatanese governmental priority, Poncho McTea, with urging from his loving parents, had slipped away from Huligata to find a new home. After some travels, that new home had become Dalilennon.

From that first meeting between fictitious Huligatanese ex-patriot Poncho McTea and the good King, a cordial relationship had been established; a relationship that would benefit both of them for years into the future.

For good King Nocturnal immediately had turned to the foreign journalist to champion, in eloquent style, any media releases the good King felt worthy of circulation. Poncho had the innate ability to write skillfully, purposefully, and even forcefully, and the good King used McTea's pen and willing accessibility to "educate" Dalilennon's relaxed populace on matters of consequence to the good King.

Within less than a year of implementing such useful propaganda, however, the owners of the linotype-produced newspaper, the Dali Sentinel, approached good King Nocturnal (gingerly, of course,) about the propriety of the King Nocturnal-Poncho McTea relationship. The good King concurred with their assessment of the situation, and promptly made McTea the first foreign-born member of any Dalilennonian king's staff in memory. Of course, most folk didn't remember much more than the previous king's name anyway, as politics always had been a silent art on the peaceful isle of fancy.

Maybe too silent, thought King Nocturnal as he waited at his dining table and stared with disinterest at what remained of his frog roe.

"Mr. Straight says he'll be here in two hours," was the report from King Nocturnal's olive-skinned servant, and the good King elected to spend the interim walking the white-stoned, cobbled streets of his beloved island nation.

For at least the past twenty-six years, the good King had implemented a plan to close the gap between the general populace of the remote island and their good King. He did this by walking the streets, as he did now, every six months or so and selecting one unsuspecting constituent to grant a wish to. The scope of the wish only was limited by restrictions regarding personal monetary gain and, of course, that the wish be confined to good King Nocturnal's ability to grant it.

An elderly block layer had started the trend when he'd asked for, and received a stately, professionally built block residence of his very own.

Many unusual requests had followed.

One lady in her fifties had used the wish from good King Nocturnal to import rabbits and start her own rabbit farm. She now stocked several local restaurants and groceries with rabbit meat, and was known as the mother, or sometimes as the great, great grandmother of Dalilennon's growing rabbit problem.

One young married couple, much in love, jokingly had asked for a green-needled evergreen tree to decorate each year when the Savior's birth was celebrated. At no undue hardship, King Nocturnal had delivered a twenty -two-foot-high potted Douglas fir that now was visible in the happy couple's back yard. It was striking from a distance like a landlocked lighthouse because, for some unknown reason, it had cottoned to the island's dry, red soil like the Tree of Life in Eden, and now was the island's tallest landmark; 'cepting the isle of fancy's one mountain, of course, and St. Andrews Cathedral.

One child age nine, a gnarled-looking little boy who looked much older, more tired than his years should have allowed, first asked the good King to find the father he'd never known, then compromised by making a more achievable wish, asking good King Nocturnal for something the good King never previously had heard of--a skateboard. That wish had proven to be good King Nocturnal's most frustrating assignment.

"Why couldn't he have asked for a Maltese falcon?" had asked the good King more than once over the course of the ensuing years. Good King Nocturnal, however, did find a skateboard after five years of diligent searching, but by the time he went to deliver the roller board to the boy who'd made the wish, the boy was gone to sea, and the boy's opaque mother had passed on to another world, or not to another world depending on where she went.

The skateboard, a shallow-looking plastic toy with steel wheels, even now rested, unused and rarely seen, in the island's dusty, boring national museum.

A strange wish that he'd granted, one that forced King Nocturnal to rethink the merits of his wish-granting program, was to a queer character who desired and received a small sailing vessel stocked with provisions to enable him to sail in search of 'a land to be saved.' That unusual captain, who'd sailed and never been heard from again, in retrospect reminded the good King of a second Julian Knotsofoolista, someone with bizarre (distorted?) Christianity, whom, at best, was misunderstood by the mainstream of humanity.

On this day, the overhead sun pelted the good King with soft rays, accenting the beige pastels of Dalilennon's square block buildings and highlighting the reds and yellows and greens of the ever-present wildflowers and grasses.

In a small park--nicknamed 'Tree Park' because it afforded a near view of Dalilennon's only full-size evergreen, at least all but the base of the stately imported tree that reached high above a stone-hewn back-yard fence--King Nocturnal spotted a young lady, an attractive young lady with chin tucked within her thumbs exhibiting a glum, downturned, sad appearance.

And so the most powerful man in that part of the world plopped beside her unannounced, and the young lady instinctively, like Esther from Haman even prior to learning his ploy, slid away from the good King to the far end of the bench without looking to see who'd arrived next to her.

The good King studied her beauty, her fair complexion, and was moved by her sadness. Filled with empathy and the unconditional love he held for his constituents, the good King opted to offer assistance.

"My name is King Nocturnal, and I'd like to grant you one wish," said the gentle good King, who'd admired this particular lady's beauty from a distance on more than one occasion; being why Ms. Nancy, against her wishes, had been recruited to participate in a recent motorcade.

Nancy started. She'd heard of the Dalilennonian king's wish program and, like most island subjects, had pondered her reply were such an opportunity offered to her. But now, for real! The King of Dalilennon was sitting next to her on a park bench, smiling, and offering to grant her a wish.

Ms. Droosha's moodiness slipped from view like a Rocky Mountain elk on the opening morning of hunting season. Gone, without a trace it ever had been there.

"But I'm not a naturalized citizen," she offered as a safe opener.

"No matter," responded the good King. "You've become a Dalilennonian citizen and I love you just the same."

The subject's beauty allowed for such verbal freedom, and the good King really did want to grant her a wish and make her happy.

"Why were you so glum? One wish could take away your frowns."

Good King Nocturnal, who was a good King, had a gift for drawing others into his confidence, especially subjects childishly deciding which wish to ask for, deciding how to refine fancy into realism. He had the innate ability to speak gently to one's inhibitions without offending, without violating trust with harsh intrusions into tender areas. He could sense when to stop probing and begin laughing, when to pry a locked door or gate open with sensitivity.

And so, as they talked in the sunshine on the bench, Ms. Nancy Droosha poured out her aspirations and her fears.

Good King Nocturnal listened without interruption for some time, then responded, "Well, if you don't take the first step to wipe away those fears, you may be doomed to live with them forever."

He sounded like a gifted high school counselor or even Jeremiah trying to encourage the displaced to return to Jerusalem.

"You're not living by the precepts you profess. You would have others make approaches to you that you aren't willing to make toward them."

"But …"

"But nothing, my dear," continued the good King with a gentleness rarely witnessed outside Mr. Rogers' Neighborhood where Mr. Rogers always, at least on Tuesdays, wears the same blue, long-sleeved sweater. "The church you attend teaches you how to relate with others, with love in the spirit of gentleness, and that's not something you should keep to yourself."

By now, Ms. Nancy's current aspirations had focused, had run the gauntlet from fancy to real, and were centering on one concrete, humble wish. It was a wish, without demands, that could open doors to her future. Not permanently, just enough to nudge the future in a direction she wished it to go; to open doors of communication with a man she wanted to love.

"You're certain that's all you want?" queried good King Nocturnal as their conversation waned beyond the request of an actual wish. "I could just as easily command six such luncheons, even a dozen."

"I can't trap him into a relationship," said Ms. Nancy. "I mean, I don't want to do it that way."

"You don't know if you want to trap him or not," said the good King slyly. "If you did, you would, and be happy with the results. What you want to have happen is for him to take a subtle nudge from you and try to win your hand. You want him on the ice instead of you."

"You really are a wonderful king," said Ms. Nancy while impulsively giving a warm hug to the isle's leader without a thought of impropriety. "Now, I'd best get back to work."

"And remember," Ms. Nancy added as she stood up to leave, "he mustn't suspect a thing."

The good King felt warmed inside as Ms. Nancy Droosha bounced down the hill toward her work. He'd raised one person's mood, her happiness quotient by a visible fraction, and maybe she'd pass it along to others.

It was a good world.

His desire was to stay and bask in the warm sunshine, to revel in his success with Ms. Droosha until the sun's warmth gently dulled his senses, but Malcolm Straight soon would be at the palace to discuss matters of grave importance.

So simple, it seemed, to touch one soul with love and let its domino effect follow behind. So complex, however, to stop the inertia-like effects of evil dominoes from toppling significant causes and events in their wakes.

Good King Nocturnal sensed that Dalilennon was approaching a time of crisis, and his steps grew heavier as he neared the palace. For a time, whimsical fantasies had been placated thanks to an island beauty, but now the realities of an impatient world required his attention.

When he arrived at the spacious building that served as government headquarters--the same building in which the island's public recreation department was housed with racquetball courts, pool, and spa open Mondays and Fridays to citizens ages two to nineteen; Tuesdays and

Saturdays to citizens ages nineteen to forty-nine; Wednesdays to citizens fifty and older; and Thursdays for family uses--the good King entered by a private doorway and greeted his beloved advisor warmly.

"You have been waiting long?" asked the good King, pounding Malcolm Straight's shoulders with affectionate briskness.

"No, Your Excellency. Less than fifteen minutes."

Straight's face exhibited a haggard hue, a look of diminished sleep with tired, lined eyes and an absence of color along normally healthy cheek lines. His voice, though, remained as strong and unbending as ever.

"I'm glad you called, my good King. I have some serious reservations to express to you regarding our foreign visitors."

"First of all," said King Nocturnal in a voice that dictated their meeting had begun officially, "take your seat and know the subjects spoken here aren't to be revealed to anyone. In fact, I'd like as few people as possible to know we're even holding this meeting."

"Done, Your Excellency."

Good King Nocturnal turned and walked to sit on his throne, a bulky, oversized seat that dominated the room with its detailed glitter and purposeful pomp.

Then, the good King began addressing one of his top advisors.

"As you know, Mr. McTea openly has voiced his support of the Eglicatan defense pact. He thinks such an agreement will teach us how to better grow our crops from the red soil, plus teach innovative ways to better care for our aging and ill. He claims the world has passed Dalilennon by, and that a pact with Eglicata would thrust our nation into the modern world. He claims more automobiles, including convertibles, quickly could be imported to Dalilennon. Too, the objects of which we've heard but not seen, televisions, soon could grace our isle.

"In these matters, I have no doubts," the good King continued.

These final seven words, added following a lengthy pause, caused Malcolm Straight suddenly to sit upright in his chair, his back no longer supported and his feet almost leaving the floor. Had anyone other than the good King articulated those words, Malcolm Straight would have been on his feet stating strenuous objections.

Yet, aware of the wisdom of maintaining a demeanor of self-restraint, Straight held his tongue.

Another elongated pause followed as good King Nocturnal groped to find appropriate words to express his feelings.

Straight's stomach churned as if he'd just swallowed and activated a General Electric corn popper.

"The proposed pact," continued good King Nocturnal slowly, deliberately, "most likely would have these effects on Dalilennon. Whether, as a whole, they'd prove beneficial for the good of our people is the foremost question to be considered.

"Still, it's the final Eglicatan argument as to the safety of our nation with or without the implementation of this pact where I disagree with Mr. McTea. Hundreds of years of continual peace are legacies not to be tossed around lightly, as the Eglicatanese delegates are want to do. Joining with Eglicata, I'd think, would more likely make us a target in her wars."

King Nocturnal's closing inflection of finality changed the tempo of the two-person meeting, its flavor.

"Knowing you as I do, Mr. Straight, I'm certain you have some thoughts to add to this conversation. Now would be the time to do so."

Malcolm Straight then rose to his feet, freeing himself from the vinyl-covered or cloth chair he'd been sitting in, and began strutting around the good King's throne room to the pulse of his own voice. In fact, the good advisor had rehearsed so thoroughly for this moment that even the good King was obscured visually from his consciousness; as if a major soliloquy, a Shakespearean soliloquy, were to be delivered on the spot.

"Your Excellency, there are few times over the years when I and Poncho McTea have agreed on anything. At times, I'll admit, I've been guilty of choosing a side to defend solely on the basis it contradicts the views of the man who's become my rival.

"This is no such time," said Malcolm Straight directly to his one-person audience, good King Nocturnal, after spewing his preliminaries equally between stage left and stage right. "In my lifetime on the isle of Dalilennon, I've yet to encounter any plan, nay, any series of plans that carries more potential harm to our beloved homeland."

Hamlet himself could have been pacing, gesturing, and presenting his case before the good King.

"If we were fortunate, only our pleasant way of life would be changed permanently. If we were unfortunate, our beautiful island could lose some of our precious young men to fight another's war they'd neither have helped start or be able to comprehend our involvement in the first place. If we were extra unfortunate, war would come to Dalilennon! And what would we gain? Their protection? From what?

"Dalilennon hasn't been at war for hundreds of years and has no known enemies. The technologies we'd gain in trade? Ha! What do we have, other than our peaceful life and our freedom to give Eglicata in exchange for these technologies? Rest assured Herr McCoffee didn't create a powerful nation overnight by giving away technologies free of charge to tiny islands like ours."

Flaunting about the throne room like the Sugar Plum Fairy to strands of The Nutcracker, Malcolm Straight was getting emotionally charged, wound up, and intensely warmed to his vocal task when the good King cut him off short with a quick, halting arm command. (Just goes to show that even the best of soliloquies loses impact when the man in charge has heard enough: loosely akin to the proverbial tree falling in the forest when there's no one to hear it, although that analogy makes absolutely no sense in written form.)

"Enough, enough," cried the good King with a smile of approval on his royal lips. "And what is your opinion of the three Eglicatan diplomats?"

Mr. Straight, much to his credit, made an immediate transition from Hamlet and the Sugar Plum Fairy back to his accustomed role of concerned advisor to his good King.

"Quite frankly, Your Excellency, I don't trust them."

"And the nature of that distrust?" asked King Nocturnal.

"A lot of small factors trigger my concerns," responded Straight, "but nothing truly to find fault with."

"Mr. Straight," said the good King while readying to say a good thing, "I agree with your counsel and will see that the Eglicatan delegates are asked to return to their homeland in the morning."

Malcolm Straight was pointed to the door shortly thereafter, sporting a broad, patriotic smile.

King Nocturnal broke the news of his decision to remove the Eglicatan delegates from the isle to his other ranking advisor within the hour, and that advisor, Poncho McTea, took the good King's words childishly, totally forgetting who was in the position of authority. McTea ranted and raved at the good King for five minutes before good King Nocturnal decided he'd had enough of the man's trash talking and, with help from sleepy palace guards, physically had McTea removed from his royal chambers.

When McTea, under protest, did exit under escort, both he and the good King knew this chapter in the story between the two of them was unfinished.

Poncho McTea, with crazed tears of indignation and anger streaming down his face, broke the news to the Eglicatan delegation minutes later. Having ignored any semblance of spy protocol, Mr. McTea, after his eviction from the good King's presence, had walked directly to the large, well-equipped Eglicatan motorboat moored at the dock. It was the same motorboat Norbert Nodahead had kept at a safe distance the night Manual and Ms. Sylvia, with an assist from a skilled oarsman, had plunged into the surging sea and black rocks to first meet a lantern-swinging Poncho McTea.

The docked motorboat now offered refuge to the visiting emissaries, giving them space to plot and plan without interruption.

"He says you have to leave the island in the morning."

Nodahead and McGetitdone temporarily were unnerved by McTea's words, while Ms. Sylvia Smithromance, fresh from the sheets, smiled with a look of cat-like determination in her eyes.

"There's absolutely no way we'll leave Dalilennon without a harvested crop of disadvantageous," she said.

"Keep in mind, Ms. Sylvia, that we don't wish to sever ties with Dalilennon too soon," said Nodahead. "Any warring acts against Dalilennon now will be noticed in Darius, which is the only country capable of stopping our disadvantageous ploy by halting this boat while it's carrying the noxious crop on the high seas."

Norbert's mind worked best under pressure.

"Well, this boat isn't moving for twenty-four hours," stated Ms. Smitharomance.

McTea spoke. "Maybe I could plea for another day as an act of courtesy. I could argue that you have come too many kilometers to head back without more discussions."

"He won't buy that," retorted Manual McGetitdone, showing no respect for a fellow countryman who successfully had weaseled his way into Dalilennon's hierarchy.

"I have a plan," said Norbert Nodahead in his halting, nervous fashion. "This boat will be incapable of carrying us or anyone else abroad by the time the sun rises tomorrow morning. I'll misadjust the motor. The good King won't like it, but he won't have anyone who can fix it, either."

The other three exchanged looks of pleasant surprise. Times like this made them remember why Norbert Nodahead, the sometimes foolish-seeming member of their entourage, was of value to the Eglicatan cause.

Sylvia and Manual went to the sack; McTea walked home; and Norbert Nodahead, with tools--and under surveillance from a distance--went to the ship's engine room where he tinkered and clinked into the night.

To remove a tiny Welch plug inside the main metering jet of the carburetor was his focused objective.

Roger K.'s Reminisce

Many intense, introverted hours of thought followed Roger Rightjet's aborted attempt to quietly steal away from the island of Dalilennon. He found himself still there, on the isle of fancy, primarily because a strong frigging donkey didn't want him to leave.

Surely the signs were no different now than they'd been when he'd abandoned his homeland nine years earlier, or been chased from one island to the next after that. The symptoms, maybe, and maybe his views about those symptoms, but the signs again pointed at major changes for the worse.

In Dalilennon, where he'd spent the past seven years, an outside force was lighting the fuse. In Eglicata years earlier, an inner force, a so-called revolutionary force, had stricken Roger K.'s peaceful homeland with the tenacity of a trained pit bull. One minute a leashed pet, an ally, and one minute later the unchained pet was slashing the throat of a robust nation with its sharp, pierced teeth.

The end result for this tiny island nation, he felt, likely would be no different: an immediate loss of the sedentary, peaceful lifestyle Roger K. Righjet so cherished.

Why was life so complicated? Why was it not possible to live on the most remote and peaceful of islands without the troubles of the world relentlessly seeking one out?

" ... love one another with brotherly affection ... " was the thought that harmlessly fluttered through Roger K. Rightjet's mind. With it, too, came visions of a memorable smiling face that reflected warm thoughts of love. That vision of a Dalilennonian secretary triggered memories of a recent sermon, plus memories of that same frigging donkey.

Roger K. walked to his favorite chair, a rocker, to pause and reflect.

Again he asked himself why life was so complicated; so cyclical?

In his early 20s, Roger K.'s career and future had seemed secure. He'd been a respected, sought legal advisor for the high-ranking officials of his storied homeland of several million people and preparing to marry the daughter of a noteworthy Eglicatan diplomat whose influence had helped pave Roger K.'s pathway to prominence.

Such selective marriages ordinarily were distasteful to the romantic ideals held by the young lawyer, but in this case he was in love madly. The lady was his equal in diplomacy, tact, and intelligence, and quite picturesque with a beauty to make any man, especially Roger K. Rightjet, proud. Too, she exuded realms of gentleness and sensitivity well beyond the norm, was graced with smooth, cool skin from her toes to her temples, and puffed moist, shapely lips that caused Roger K.'s knees to chatter in anticipation of another blissful kiss.

Like many men in such positions, Roger K. Rightjet had gone blithely through that portion of life giving all to his work in the daytime, and all to his love in the night. And, like many peaceful, patiently ambitious young men in similar positions, Roger K.'s work demands became greater and greater, sometimes creeping well into the nocturnal hours.

This went on for more than two years, during which time the competent young lawyer became more and more involved with work and, though not consciously, less and less involved with love. This subtle migration toward work and away from the woman he loved was, in itself, a contradiction in values because, were the scales consciously tilted at any moment, the young man gladly would have tipped them in love's favor. As time passed, however, Roger K. began to play a mind game with himself, trying to justify why his professed top priority no longer occupied the bulk of his time.

She, too, though certainly not of her own volition, began turning more and more toward her work and, during those brief years, became as competent a diplomat as the nation had.

It was about this time when Roger K., with their time together reduced to half what it once had been, began noticing subtle, undesirable changes in the lady of his dreams. He noticed she no longer was willing to compromise on little arguments or disagreements, even when he, the capable lawyer, could matter-of-factly prove she was in error. She'd then toy and tease, never straying from her goal, until Roger K. Rightjet, often in heartfelt disagreement, would verbally say she was right; acquiescing to her stubbornness solely for the purposes of promoting peace and hastening their return to physical love.

But peace purchased at less than truth is less than peace, and their once picturesque romance began to erode, to crumble away piece by piece like wood to sandpaper or rock cliffs to the sea.

The final blow to their marriage plans paralleled the clouds of unrest that arose suddenly, then hovered menacingly over the nation of Eglicata.

At that point in history, the country was torn between its long-standing sedentary existence of peace and calm, and a new wave for change, for modernization. For several decades Eglicata had proceeded in a shell of contentedness, giving little notice to the fast-evolving world it reluctantly was part of. For years, people from the sleepy giant- of-a-nation had raised coffee, taken afternoon naps, and thought little beyond the multi-colored, peak-tipped sunsets that brought whole families together regularly, in humble silence, to view Nature's beauty.

A powerful figure behind the new movement for change was a brazen young man named Max McCoffee. From the ranks of a middle-income mercantile family, the young McCoffee excelled early in studies made available to him, and with the help of a sacrificing father, had been sent to continue his education overseas--an honor attained by few Eglicatanese students.

McCoffee spent four years studying abroad where he majored in science. He also picked up the equivalent of a second degree in politics, using every free moment to pour through college libraries and quiz students of like interests from every other tribe and nation. He studied what worked and didn't work politically in countries around the globe, both past and present. Of special interest to him was the powerful democratic nation of Darius. McCoffee expressed disdain for Darius's government, criticizing the time required to make effective changes there, yet grudgingly admired the ideals Darius professed to have.

The impact of Max McCoffee's foreign education shocked both his family and much of Eglicata when, short weeks after returning to his homeland, McCoffee and four former Eglicatan classmates of his chained their bodies across the main gate of a large coffee processing plant in the nation's capital city. Their expressed cause was higher wages and better health conditions for workers inside the plant.

In retrospect, it's easy to see that the demonstration made by McCoffee and his four comrades, aptly covered by the local news media, was a publicity stunt to give the young activists recognition for a rising cause. The demonstration accomplished nothing for the workers at the plant but, after a brief stint in jail, McCoffee emerged as the folk hero he'd envisioned.

What followed was a series of public speaking engagements and demonstrations that, not discounting a few minor jail stops, quickly moved McCoffee within striking distance of Eglicata's quiet, slow-moving power structure. Eglicatan officials who'd battled nothing more trying than traditionalism suddenly were forced to pay attention to the young revolutionary's unwelcome rise to prominence.

But not close enough.

And it was Max McCoffee's sudden seizure of power that ultimately spelled the demise of Roger K. Rightjet's love affair with his bride to be, by name Ms. Sylvia Smitharomance.

The lovers heatedly argued regarding McCoffee's potential worth to Eglicata's future: she singing his praises and Roger K. sounding the alarm.

Ms. Sylvia tried many womanly persuasions to gain Roger's acceptance of her political priorities. In the middle of the night, for they did find occasions discreetly to sleep together, she'd gently awaken Roger K. by massaging the base of his stomach. Still, Roger K.'s aversion to McCoffee's political aspirations would know no compromise.

"No," he'd say after feigning sleep as long as practical before his eyes would burst from inert anxiety, "I honestly feel he's a threat to all that's good and decent."

They'd argue then and, inevitably, Ms. Sylvia Smitharomance would arise in a huff, dress without a word, and stomp from the bedroom, slamming the door behind her. Roger K. loved instances when such rows took place at Ms. Sylvia Smitharomance's home, for in time she'd always return, drop her clothes to the floor with sleek, long-limbed torso silhouetted before curtains in the window, and return to bed with no additional mention of the revolutionary named McCoffee.

Two of the coffee-plant gang stayed with McCoffee in his sweep to political power. By name, they were Manual McGetitdone and Norbert Nodahead.

The two remaining upstarts were too vocal when McCoffee, without remorse or hesitation, had abandoned the plight of the coffee-plant workers they'd protested for. And they'd paid dearly for their dissent.

One of the two, Johnny Saddenista, hung himself on the day Max McCoffee became Herr McCoffee, leaving behind him a damning note that McCoffee found and torched before the scribbled epistle was seen by anyone who might have asked questions and attached meaning to Johnny Saddenista's premature death.

The final radical, a quiet, studious type who really never fit the mold of the coffee-plant gang, was banned to a distant country for life. Manual McGetitdone, who had few friends, bordered on mutiny before this man's life was spared over objections of Herr McCoffee to the contrary. McGetitdone stood his ground in defense of a friend, and in doing so gained a pardon that cost him dearly in concessions of future power.

Hence, even the manliest of men can make sacrifices for true friendship.

The coup d'état in Eglicata had been orderly, unanticipated (who'd think to topple the nation's long-standing government of peace and tranquility?) and efficient. McCoffee never organized more than three-hundred supporters, and armed even fewer.

And so, with only a handful of lives lost because the populace saw it more like politics as usual, and nothing impacting their daily routines, Max McCoffee became the Herr of Eglicata.

This rapid transition of power forced a frightening situation for Roger K. Rightjet. The lady he loved was welcome to stay, in fact had a real future in this new movement, while he, an up-and-coming lawyer days before, now was an enemy to his homeland, a threat to the stability of McCoffee's stilt-legged government.

When the restrictive nature of the new regime became evident, a very old practicing lawyer took Roger K. aside to offer him the best advice his eighty-plus years had to offer.

"Leave," he told Roger K. Rightjet. "Don't stay around waiting for a time when you may again practice law freely and openly. It will take too many years out of the heart of your life. You are a very talented, honest lawyer Roger Rightjet. Don't stay here until you become a mediocre lawyer, afraid to speak out like all the rest.

"When I was a young man," the old lawyer had continued, "I, too, was a good lawyer, and my government changed like the one Herr McCoffee will impose. I waited for a reversal of that change and saw my skills deteriorate, lessened by a predetermined knowledge of who would win and who would lose each court case. After thirty years, I pulled away and found new life, a new zest for truth here in Eglicata. Don't deny yourself those thirty years. Leave now, Roger Rightjet, and be free to share your gifts."

The truth and sincerity of the old man's words touched Roger K. deeply. He made the decision to leave Eglicata, but needed to make one last plea for his love to leave with him.

His answer came outside her door that evening, a harsh answer that meshed anger, pain, frustration, and helplessness in one brutal slash of reality. Herr McCoffee's personal limousine was parked in front of Ms. Sylvia's home, two armed bodyguards standing watch beside it. Upstairs, as the naïve lawyer watched, an embracing silhouetted twosome in Ms. Sylvia's bedroom was plunged into a darkness that blackened both hope and trust in Roger K.'s heart.

"Fate, oh fate, why do you do this to me?" cried Roger K. Rightjet from his favorite rocker in the Dalilennonian home that, at least for a time, had replaced his bitter past in Eglicata.

" … with love in the spirit of gentleness … "

"Where'd that thought come from?" mulled Roger K. with disinterest, rising and walking once more to his garden, to the colorful blossoms of flowers he so loved. It was the grace and compatibility of the plant world that man needed to emulate, he thought.

The night, as usual, was peaceful and quiet.

Knock, knock, knock on the front door, within hearing distance of where he stood in the garden.

Roger was startled from reminiscing back to reality. No one had knocked on that door for years, before he'd moved in. Knotsofoolista was Roger K.'s only visitor, and he always came to the rear, less visible entrance.

Knock, knock.

The sound definitely was real.

Roger walked back into the dwelling and to the front entrance with a mixture of amazement and trepidation in his heart. Had someone connected his past with recent rumblings in peaceful Dalilennon?

Roger K. peered through the tiny glass peephole in the wooden portal and saw three official-looking bodies somewhat disfigured by the oval bubble imported from Malaysia along with the teak door years earlier.

"What do you want?" asked the most righteous of Rightjets through the door. "I'm sure I can't help you."

"We don't want anything," responded a straight-sounding voice. "We wish to extend an invitation for you to lunch with good King Nocturnal."

It sounded suspicious to Roger K.

The invisible little people like himself--the unseen, faceless majority--rarely were seen by the ruling class, let alone named to luncheon guest lists. They were going to take him to jail, he knew it.

"Friggin' donkey," growled Roger K. under his breath, remembering the ship that had sailed without him. Running was useless. The best he could hope for would be to hide with Julian Knotsofoolista in the caves, and that didn't sound too appealing. Any idiot, even members of the Dalilennonian police force, could stop someone from leaving the isle of fancy. Watch the docks. There was nowhere to hide now, he thought. Like Custer, he'd dallied too long.

Knock, knock, knock.

"Mr. Rightjet, may we speak with you?"

Roger K. reluctantly fumbled with the doorknob. Feeling he was without viable options, he opened the door and, while hopelessly looking at the floor by his feet, invited the envoy into his home.

"I didn't know good King Nocturnal knew I existed," he muttered.

"You'd be surprised what good King Nocturnal knows," said Malcolm Straight as he, Officer Oliver Ogilvie, and a red-and-white clad servant accepted seats on a bench in Roger's small living room. "He often surprises his constituents in many ways."

The conversation, hardly begun, halted abruptly when the front gate to Roger K.'s yard screeched open, then banged shut. Then, an excited, high-pitched child's voice cried in a loud, sing-song voice, "Roger Rightjet, Roger Rightjet. Come quick."

Roger flashed a weak, embarrassed grimace toward his guests, shrugged dumbly, then retraced his steps to the teak front door with its bubbled peephole. Though somewhat distorted, he saw a young boy approaching his door entrance and a young girl at the gate with her arms wrapped around the neck of his hated adversary, Blokehead.

The nearest child, the boy, pecked at the door and demanded Roger K.'s presence. "Please, Mr. Rightjet, this is very important."

Before responding, Roger K. glanced over his shoulder at Malcolm Straight, crack Officer Oliver Ogilvie, and the servant as if seeking guidance on how he should react to the child's urgent plea.

"You'd better talk to him," said the uniformed officer seated next to the servant in red and white apparel who meticulously was devouring the contents of a glassed tray filled with cracked nuts.

"Don't eat them all," muttered Officer Ogilvie as an aside to the hungry servant.

Roger K.'s face flushed warm from the excitement, the uneasiness of what might transpire. Then he opened the door partway.

"I'll come out on the porch and talk with you only if that, that, … " he paused so as not to employ, in the presence of children, the negative, descriptive words lurking on the tip of his tongue, " … that beast is out of my yard and a good distance away."

Jean Paul trotted to Mary, spoke quietly in her ear and, within moments, the little girl and Blokehead were standing at a distance of fifty meters directly beyond Rightjet's front gate, from where they studiously watched Jean Paul and Roger K. through its metal bars. Except for Blokehead, of course, whose studious looks of interest soon digressed toward washed tufts of semigreen grass.

Roger K. thought he pulled the teak door closed, not knowing Straight had blocked its intended closure with his foot, leaving a crack open so Straight and Ogilvie could overhear the conversation between the little boy and Roger K. Rightjet. The servant, with no one to slow him, took the opportunity to dig for and consume more macadamia nuts.

Jean Paul, standing on the porch with Roger K., then excitedly began to deliver the private message that had prompted his, Mary's, and Blokehead's visit to Rightjet's residence.

"Quit chewing so loud," snapped Ogilvie in a harsh whisper.

The youngster's rapid-paced spiel, which Roger K. tried to slow on at least three occasions, indicated that he and his sister, Mary, had been looking for their dog, a fun-loving bitch named Mizzi, late the previous evening, when they'd spotted the Dalilennonian governmental official who'd earlier been spattered with tomatoes. He'd gone to visit the foreigners on their big boat, and later Jean Paul and Mary had watched as one of the foreign leaders, "the fat one," had tinkered at length with the boat's engine.

"That's nothing to report," returned Roger K. Rightjet. "Besides, why come to me and not the proper authorities?"

"Ms. Prissy, Ms. Prissy," exclaimed the excited urchin in a tone indicating that his patience with this adult was wearing thin. "That's what we came to tell you. We didn't know what to do with what we'd learned, so my sister Mary and I again went to visit Ms. Prissy and found her awake. She wants to speak with you, Roger Rightjet!"

"And where is she, Jean Paul? Where is she staying?" Roger K.'s voice evoked new compassion, new interest.

"She says to meet her in St. Andrews Cathedral on Roman Street at half three," said the tiny messenger whose hasty, trusting actions belied his young, tender age.

"So be it, Jean Paul."

And, suddenly, Roger K. Rightjet abandoned his intentions to leave Dalilennon: a country whose virtues exceeded the reaches of one's garden; the bravery of small children and a gutsy former midwife; went beyond the sands of her white, oft-touched shores; and approached the essence of saints whose personifications graced almost every doorknocker.

Roger K. stayed on one knee, watching as Jean Paul rejoined his sister and the beast, Blokehead. Roger watched their exit from view with a renewed glow in his heart, a glow of love for what suddenly had been rekindled in his soul.

Then, as he rose back to his feet, Roger K. wondered if the change was meaningless, if, indeed, the king's men had come to take him to jail.

"I now can answer the question you didn't have time to ask minutes ago," said Malcolm Straight as Roger K. stepped back inside his home. "A luncheon is to be held at the request of an admirer of yours, whose name must remain anonymous. She was granted a wish by good King Nocturnal, and asked for a luncheon date with you, the good King, and his top advisors. From what we've overheard as reported by Jean Paul, we shan't be shy of meaty topics to discuss.

"I needn't confirm your acceptance for today's noon luncheon," stated Straight, knowing Roger K. Rightjet had no option in the matter.

Roger Rightjet watched the trio walk out his front gate, then re-entered his house. Without thought, he reached for an empty glass tray that previously had held macadamia nuts. Then, for possibly the first time since seeking refuge as a gristmiller on Dalilennon, Roger stood up straight to his full height and said, "No, you needn't confirm."

Queens on the Mend

Mrs. King Nocturnal found her twenty-four-hour sleepathon, thinkathon, in-bedathon, or whatever-a-thon one wished to call it, to be quite refreshing.

A new sense of personal worth had kindled inside her during that one day of seclusion. Not public worth—the kind accented daily by courtly pomp—but instead the inner kind that allows one, queen or not, to look another in the eye and speak with confidence of worthy topics.

The transition from nose picker to a woman of etiquette and grace wasn't complete, mind you, as Saint John hadn't visited her in the night with his overriding message of unconditional love, yet directional thoughts over the past twenty-four hours had sown seeds of what she could aspire to be … as a human being, and as a loving person and queen.

And those seeds did more than hint that change was needed.

She waited that following morning for the rising sun to grace her big, canopied bed. Even at a slant, the sun felt warm, filled with life.

The change in Mrs. King Nocturnal's lifestyle wasn't preplanned, but decidedly abrupt.

Her servants raised eyebrows hardly eight words into the day.

"I don't wish to select wardrobes this morning," she said; and next ordered grapefruit, orange juice, and the very smallest of cherry pies for breakfast. Moderation.

Seven times that morning Mrs. King Nocturnal, out of habit, reached for her nose. Six times she corrected the maneuver with her fingers arrested in midair, and even the seventh effort wasn't a total waste. On that occasion, she consciously controlled her action in time to double her finger and rub the exterior of her nose, not its interior.

After all, the healthful benefits of nose rubbing must in some way parallel those of nose picking.

The good Queen felt better about herself, and about life as a whole by the time she checked in for lunch that day. She was anxious to see the good King and discover if he would notice the changes in her, the changes for the positive that were, for the first time in years, warming her heart from its core.

Before meeting the good King, she checked the menu with a kitchen maid and expressed surprise in regards to the meal's magnitude. A bountiful pot roast with clean-cut carrots and potatoes in white sauce; skewered rabbit; fresh baked buttermilk biscuits with raspberry preserves; a garnish tray of celery, raw cauliflower, sweet pickles, and cracked nuts; a gelatin-cottage cheese salad, its sides dripping after being yanked from a plastic mold; hot asparagus spears; and desserts of pies and tarts were being prepared for the noon repast.

She sought out the good King and, in her mind, found him to be stronger and more handsome than ever. For a moment, she paled considering her own bulbous physique, but soon was comforted when she saw the unmistakable love his eyes held for her.

Good King Nocturnal then explained the meaning of the huge feast, summing up his words by saying, "Ms. Nancy Droosha is the pretty lady's name, and Roger K. Rightjet the name of the man she wishes to trap."

"Isn't 'trap' too harsh of a word to use, dear?" asked Queen Nocturnal.

The good King laughed.

"Advisors Straight and McTea will dine with us as well. My, but you do look pretty today," he added, and the good Mrs. King Nocturnal blushed like Zipporah probably blushed when she and her sisters first encountered Moses at the well.

Good Queen Nocturnal felt both silly and good for doing so.

"Messer's Straight and McTea," announced the stuffy butler King Nocturnal often had thought of replacing. He simply was too efficient.

"Thank you, Hans. Show them in."

Straight and McTea hadn't lunched with the royal couple for many moons, and felt slightly awkward; especially Poncho McTea, whose recent tirade hadn't been forgotten. Still, Poncho's nefarious thoughts went beyond that altercation as he mentally tried to visualize what a fowlawarfare would look like hovering over the shores of Dalilennon, what he would wear at his homecoming party thrown by Herr McCoffee's court in Eglicata, how he would break the news about their move off the island to his wife and son …

"The child said Ms. Prissy Hampshire regained consciousness … "

"What?" came McTea's awkward, involuntary response to Malcolm Straight's straightforward (could there be any other type?) accounting of events, aka report to the good King. "What did you say about the old lady?"

"She's awake," stated Malcolm Straight smoothly, firmly, noting the discomfort his news brought to McTea, "and she's asked for a meeting with Mr. Rightjet. Though why she wishes to speak with him is a mystery to me."

The Ms. King motioned servants to make certain tea was placed before her early guests, and offered them premeal tarts and cakes. Both declined the sweets.

"Has Officer Ogilvie been dispatched to question the old hag? We need to know what she remembers as quickly as possible," said McTea nervously.

"Not yet," responded good King Nocturnal. "We don't know for certain where she's resting."

The same efficient butler returned to the spacious dining chamber, this time introducing the beautiful blond secretary of foreign birth, who followed at his heel.

"Ms. Nancy Droosha," Hans intoned with the precise pomp of Camelot, or the feigned rigidity of a bit Shakespearean player bent on making his mark with three words.

"That will be all, Hans," said the good King, rising against protocol to meet and introduce his new arrival. "Ms. Nancy Droosha, I'd like you to meet my wife, the woman whom makes Dalilennon the wonderful place it is, Mrs. King Nocturnal."

Already unnerved by such elegant surroundings, Ms. Nancy flushed crimson as the Mrs. King extended her limp right hand and wrist toward her. Nancy didn't know whether to touch or even kiss the royal hand offered in friendship; she felt paralyzed by the indecision confronting her. Nancy's blush spread from high on her cheek to the collar of her sleek, silk dress. Her one-inch-high heels, though not visible to the others, quaked with enough energy to propel Dorothy back to Kansas.

The good King laughed with pleasure, introduced the two advisors--who remembered the wonderfully dressed beauty from a recent motorcade, perhaps before--and granted her a temporary seat next to the Mrs. King in her golden throne.

Ms. Nancy remained quiet, anxious. How would Roger K. Rightjet react when he learned why he'd been called to luncheon with the good King? Was it too late to cancel, to retreat to the anonymous safety of her work, her sedentary life where risks were worlds away, and warm comfort the norm? It sometimes was lonely, but …

"Who's seen the old lady since she regained consciousness?" asked Poncho McTea.

The good King deferred the question to Malcolm Straight.

"As far as we know, only the two street urchins have seen and talked to her. They are the ones who delivered the message to Mr. Rightjet," Straight said. "But, there could have been others."

Her blush subsiding, Ms. Nancy Droosha took an immediate interest in the conversation. Her sensitive blue eyes attentively skimmed from speaker to speaker. Ms. Prissy, whom she'd been told had been injured, was awake and wanted to speak with Roger K. Rightjet? Where did he fit in?

"Come with me," said the Mrs. King to Ms. Nancy Droosha while rising from her queenly throne. "We shall go to the garden. There are things about this luncheon you must know." At the doorway, with Ms. Nancy at her side, the Mrs. King turned back to good King Nocturnal and said, "Please call us when Mr. Rightjet arrives."

Through one courtyard, then a second did they walk until an arched portico led them, in late-morning light, into the royal gardens of Dalilennon.

Nancy gasped. "It's beautiful."

Ringed by ten-foot-high adobe walls, thick and weathered, the interior Walgreens-sized plot teemed with colorful flowers from all over the world. Ms. Nancy recognized some varieties of flowers from what she'd learned while working in the importing/exporting trade, and others from Darius of old where visual recognition, at least in Nancy's memory, often exceeded botanical names, even common names. Still, many other varieties of flowers in the palatial garden were totally foreign to Ms. Nancy; as if they'd crawled through time, through a crack in a distant, old-world temple and now existed only in this one garden on this isolated isle of fancy.

The rainbow was represented thrice over in flowers, and Nancy Droosha, like a child, was thrilled at the brilliance radiated by the tiniest of aqua-marine flower petals, and laughed at the drooping stupor of tall, bright-yellow sunflowers.

They walked by budding roses, of course, and petunias and phlox.

"This is what I wanted you to see," said the Mrs. King, pointing to the only plot in the entire garden barren of any semblance of beauty or color; barren of apparent life.

Although Ms. Nancy's curiosity was kindled, she said nothing. Instead, she waited.

The Mrs. King stopped in the pebbled walkway that divided the many flower beds and reached a dead end in front of the barren plot.

"I want to tell you something, Ms. Droosha. It's in regards to Mr. Rightjet. Please don't ask me how I know what I know, or why, but I know more about Mr. Rightjet's tenure on this island than almost anyone could guess; even more than the good Mr. King knows. And I believe in my heart that Mr. Rightjet is very much like this barren section of garden."

Nancy waited wordless as the good Mrs. King again pointed to the brown, bleak section of garden, so barren and drab next to the brilliant colors and hues radiating without constraint from the vibrant, fresh flowers growing all around it.

"Don't misunderstand, Ms. Droosha. The plot I'm pointing at is seeded with flowers that come up every other year. When these seeds do arise through the surface of the ground as flowers, those flowers are every bit as beautiful and last just as long, if not longer, than any of the colorful blossoms you now see all around you.

"The same is true of some human beings, Ms. Nancy. Only, instead of physical beauty, it's a spirit of greatness, a gift of leadership that surfaces periodically, then almost always at the individual's choosing, returns to a subterranean existence. Yet, much as that person may wish to remain out of view underground, his or her God-given gifts inevitably will draw them, sometimes with feet planted in protest, back to the public's eye in meaningful ways.

"I'm convinced your Mr. Rightjet is one such person, and that's why I'm addressing you on this subject now. Humans aren't flowers. They don't have to dive back into the dirt and lie dormant. They can have a much longer, productive life cycle. The key for a man is a good woman, like you or I, who can make that man strong enough to utilize his gifts every day and make the world a more beautiful place in which to live.

"But this isn't what you expected to hear in the royal garden, was it?" asked the Mrs. King with a warm smile. "As we walk back, I'll tell you what I know about what this luncheon will entail, especially for your Mr. Rightjet."

As they prepared to leave the garden and its beauty behind, Mrs. King Nocturnal said," Please pick some roses for your table."

And beautiful Ms. Nancy Droosha bent at the waist with a slight breeze nudging through her hair and picked three from among thousands of colorful roses gently nodding in the wind, each one from among those thousands hoping she'd pick them.

While the Mrs. King and her new friend were leaving the garden, walking back to chambers where the feast was to be served, the arrival of Roger K. Rightjet, by the same stiff butler, was announced to good King Nocturnal and his party.

Roger K. looked around him with apprehension as if he were a proud, stalked wolverine. At the invitation of the good King, Roger K. sat uncomfortably in a high-backed, hand-crafted Mediterranean chair, and waited for what he knew not.

Then, he watched as the Mrs. King and Ms. Nancy Droosha returned from the royal garden.

"Are you all right?" asked good King Nocturnal to Roger K., the latter's face having lost all color at the sight of Ms. Nancy Droosha who, in the company of Dalilennon's queen, was smiling at him and carrying three bright roses in her right hand.

"You're as white as one of the roses Ms. Droosha is carrying," laughed Malcolm Straight.

Roger K.'s heart fluttered unnaturally. He saw black spots float across his line of vision as the fragrance of fresh-cut roses triggered memories of a long-lost love every bit as beautiful as this smiling, loving creature standing before him. She stood three meters in front of him cradling three clipped roses breast-high against her white dress: a deep red, a salmon, and a spotless white.

The red rose triggered painful memories and somewhat clouded Rightjet's ability to focus upon the beautiful woman before him; a beautiful woman who watched him intently with sensitive, loving eyes.

Roger Rightjet wanted to bolt from the room, to at least retreat and think. He felt his thoughts of confusion existed corporeally in the eyes of the others, as if posted on a chalkboard in front of a classroom. He earnestly wanted to apologize to Nancy Droosha before he'd made an offense: to say, "I'm sorry most beautiful, but I'm no good. I've failed in the past, and … "

"Hans, please bring us a small potted vase for Ms. Droosha's roses," said the Mrs. King. "And don't forget the water."

Good King Nocturnal signaled for all to take seats around the slate-topped dining table. He waited until Ms. Droosha, next to Roger K., and the Mrs. King, between Ms. Nancy and himself, were situated in their seats; saw that Straight and McTea were seated as well; said a short prayer; then signaled for numerous domestics to begin serving the sumptuous meal.

And it came in legions. Paul Bunyan himself never could have left such a plenteous Dalilennonian luncheon wanting to consume more food.

Only the Mrs. King, at her leisure, was allowed without objection to curtail the volume of repast she chose to eat. Kings can exhibit an inordinate amount of "peer" pressure when it comes to coaxing dinner guests to eat beyond their limitations, but that authority doesn't apply to queens on the mend.

Nancy timidly picked at creamed carrots and skewered rabbit while the good King's advisors, at length, grilled her guest, Roger K. Rightjet, on the subject of Ms. Prissy Hampshire.

After regaining his natural color following the shock of seeing Ms. Nancy Droosha carrying roses in the company of Dalilennon's king and queen, Roger K. handled subsequent questions with the aplomb of a season diplomat; as if Roger K. Rightjet had frequented the homes of royalty prior to stepping ashore on the isle of fancy.

Ms. Nancy admired the man more and more as his many gifts began to surface. The Mrs. King had been absolutely right about him.

Yet, Ms. Nancy and Roger K. hardly spoke to each other. Maybe a few "please pass the butter's" and "please pass the blackberry pies", but nothing of substance. No, "I came from Darius and immediately went to work for the import-export company. Where are you from?"s. Or no, "I've never been married, have you?"s.

All that transpired between them was a mountain of loving tenseness, many awkward smiles, and numerous darting looks that communicated Ms. Nancy's willingness to empathize with Roger K. Rightjet's obvious state of confusion.

Nancy felt shamed, even guilty, because she wanted to turn the conversation away from the haggard midwife to a different topic where she could speak with authority and impress Roger K. with her mind as well as her beauty.

Mrs. King Nocturnal sensed what Nancy was feeling, and chose not to intervene. A near murder on peaceful Dalilennon was a true national priority, well above any foreplay of tentative, potential, wholesome lovers.

"I'd best be on my way," stated Roger K. Rightjet, looking for permission to be the first to rise and leave the luncheon. "If I'm the one chosen to hear Ms. Prissy Hampshire's report, I'd best be on time. Seems a lot of people are interested to hear what she has to say."

"Where are you going to meet her?" asked Poncho McTea innocently enough.

He'd pumped many questions toward Rightjet in the past two-plus hours. Some that triggered warning signals in the lawyer-turned gristmiller's brain; and they weren't subtle warnings. Like Julian Knotsofoolista's recent sighting of a light flashing where a light shouldn't be flashing, Roger K. Rightjet sensed something was amiss.

That was Roger K.'s thinking at this point of time regarding this advisor to the good King. He was reluctant to proceed, to trust Poncho McTea until more data was made available to him.

And so he lied.

"I'm to meet Ms. Prissy in her home at the base of the mountain."

Malcolm Straight started involuntarily. What was going on? A bold lie was being uttered in the presence of the good King?

On his feet, and stuffed to the kneecaps, Roger K. extended appropriate thanks and adieus to those among the small gathering. He finally turned to Ms. Nancy and promptly got lost in her deep, caring, blue eyes; the sight of which he'd consciously tried to avoid throughout the duration of the meal.

"Thank you for having me," he heard his own voice say. "We'll have to do it again some time."

"When?" she asked smoothly, neither trying to ply on his obvious state of weakness or cover her sincere eagerness to pursue another encounter with this gentle man.

Then, without warning, Roger K. Rightjet was lost, adrift without a conscious thought in his head. His voice abandoned him then, and the spots again were floating between him and anyone or anything he looked at. Too, all color quickly drained from his face.

Roger K. tried to bolt away from the table, nearly knocking his heavy Mediterranean chair to the floor, then reached out and caught the chair before it could topple. Everyone was looking at Rightjet and smiling.

Everyone, that is, except Malcolm Straight.

Without premeditation, Roger K. swooned to the little vase centered on the slate-topped dining table. "May I have one?" he asked, and plucked out the wine-red rose--not the white one or the salmon one--with his pale, sweaty fingers.

Then, with one last heart-yanking look toward the radiant beauty whom earlier had picked three roses with him in mind, Roger K. Rightjet sniffed the red rose's small, open bud, smiled stupidly, and strode with noisy, eager steps out of the good King's dining chambers.

"My God," he exclaimed to himself, trying to suppress an idiot grin with mock self-reproach, "I'm in love." He wanted to dance, to run, to step outside and roll in the red, alkaline dirt.

"Rightjet!!"

Malcolm Straight pursued Roger K. down the hallway outside the dining chambers seeking answers.

"I don't know what you got going, buddy, but you'd better give me some answers fast. What you did in there is an unpardonable sin. Even if you do have stars in your eyes because of that sweet little woman, it's no excuse to state a bold lie in the presence of my good King. Of your good King, as well.

"What's gotten into you, Rightjet? You're not in Eglicata or Darius or any other country where intrigue is the norm, where one answers a question according to whose ears are listening. You're in Dalilennon, a quiet island nation with a good King who often walks unaccompanied through the streets. He fears no one and no one fears him. And do you know what makes this possible, Rightjet?"

Roger K. was too frightened to venture a guess.

"Trust.

"Dalilennon isn't a perfect country. And we Dalilennonians are far from perfect ourselves. Maybe you think us simple, Rightjet, and maybe we are. Yet, we are a nation that has avoided war for centuries, and we are a people who, for the most part, are content with who we are and what we have.

"And the main reason for that contentment is our ability to look each other in the eye and share the truth. We have too much reverence for our Maker to do otherwise. Then, you state a bold lie in the presence of our good King and get away with it.

"I'm giving you fair warning, Roger K. Rightjet, don't ever taint the air around my good King again, or you'll have me and all of Dalilennon to answer to."

Malcolm Straight, apparently no longer interested in answers, pivoted and clomped away at a brisk pace, kicking Roger K.'s fallen red rose aside as he went.

Rightjet watched him leave, then did the same in the opposite direction with new emotions pounding in his chest, heart, soul, and brain.

Would-be heroes are kin to heroes in many ways, especially in their ability to absorb another's anger and put the energy generated by that anger to good use. But there are differences, too.

Whereas a true hero consciously would have accepted Straight's firm reprimand for what it entailed, perhaps learn from it, yet still known full-well that his outright lie was in the best interests of Dalilennon; would-be heroes like Roger K. Rightjet, following such curt reprimands, silently dwell on personal pain and the unrighteous burden of guilt they have to bear. Rightjet sensed the gravity of his guilt, his lie, and felt motivated to make future amends to good King Nocturnal and Malcolm Straight.

But that's where the primary difference between a hero and a would-be hero best comes into focus. Whereas a hero would do right and know he'd done so, a would-be hero would do right and know he'd done so only after fate continually prodded him in the direction he needed to go.

Roger K. left the good King's chambers early enough to walk two kilometers to St. Andrews Cathedral and arrive with plenty of time to spare. And the therapy provided by sweet-smelling sea breezes as well as the stroll itself were heaven-sent. Along the way, Rightjet passed through rows of unkempt blackberry vines and wild roses that formed a corridor along an alley he traversed angling toward Roman Street.

Before Roger K. knew it, he was in the shadows of the massive Catholic landmark known as St. Andrews Cathedral. Only the mountain loomed higher on all of Dalilennon. Even the fast-growing evergreen on the opposite side of Tree Park wouldn't eclipse St. Andrews' height for many years to come.

Roger would have felt vindicated for telling his lie had he known at that very moment that Manuel McGetitdone, after receiving word from Poncho McTea, was off to tend to unfinished business at Ms. Prissy's empty house at the base of the mountain.

The would-be hero eased through a gigantic metal-framed wooden door and stepped into the cavernous reality of St. Andrews Cathedral.

Frescos and icons of great detail virtually were all around him; seemed to grace every stone wall, both low and high, plus the domed, arched ceiling above. The ceiling was highlighted with a stained-glass skylight through which the afternoon's golden sun now filtered streams of colored light. Literally thousands upon thousands of loving hours had been spent handcrafting the huge church's interior, changing reddish-yellow stone and common plate glass into infinite beauty.

The high ceiling at the far end of the church, opposite where Rightjet entered--beyond the sloping row of curve-backed, imported wooden pews and directly above the elevated pulpit and candelabra stand--boasted the massive stained-glass replica of the born-again Christ. Not many Easters before, Julian Knotsofoolista had made his presence visibly known to Dalilennon's faithful by his Tarzan-like antics outside that heavenly work of art.

"You are Roger K. Rightjet," said a frocked figure emerging from a door to the front and left of the empty pews. "Priest Darrell Precious at your disposal," said Priest Precious, offering an unexpected, courtly bow. "Do you prefer steak or air? ... football or hope?"

Priest Precious laughed a wide-mouthed laugh as he approached the perplexed foreigner. "Apologies, apologies, old man. But, I've heard so much about you. Only the particulars remain."

He smiled again, and in so doing inaudibly challenged the grister to speak.

"Nice teeth," said Roger K., and both men laughed comfortably.

"As happens so often in life, Roger, I paid the price. Promise me that you'll come again for a true visitation, and I'll lead you to Ms. Hampshire. You're an interesting man who's received high marks from some of my favorite people. Unless you protest loudly when next you come, we won't talk through a slatted hole or stop at a tumbler of wine."

The precious priest remained handsome in his 50's, even youthful in a slightly marred body that hinted of adventure. A slight scar curled from his forehead and disappeared beneath a full crop of gray hair. He was clean shaven.

"I'm surprised you know so much about me, Your Grace," said Roger K. "I pride myself in solitude. I will come again to test your sources."

Priest Precious, clad in a white frock and gold belt, lifted his eyes to the frescos and icons telling hundreds of stories of man's history, man's growth, man's pain. The jocular priest of moments before suddenly drew away, slipped from view as if remembering the reason Rightjet was there and that the Lord was life's only stronghold in times of trouble. Only a halo was lacking to complete a radical transformation from broken-toothed jokester to loving Catholic Father.

"Come, Mr. Rightjet. I have a wounded parishioner who believes in the same sources. She's been injured badly, but will recover. You may speak to her alone, but I urge you not to stay long. She's very weak."

Roger K. followed Priest Precious through the side entrance from which the ordained man of God had emerged moments earlier, through a second doorway, and up a slight flight of stairs to a room with chalkboards, shelved books, and small, wooden chairs.

Priest Precious pointed Rightjet to a low doorway in an alcove of the classroom.

"She's resting there," said the priest. "You may wake her gently if she's sleeping, but please don't tire her more than necessary."

Then, the priest with gray hair turned and exited, his feet quietly pattering out the classroom's open door and down the short flight of steps.

The day's frenzied pace suddenly overtook Roger K. like fatigue to an octogenarian planting a garden in midday sun. Streaks of sunshine angled through a window above the low doorway he was to pass through, highlighting Rightjet's tired feet and exposing yellow specs of afternoon dust rotating in slow, circular motions.

The fatigue Roger K. was experiencing was the culmination of a day filled with visits and luncheons and political advisors and anger and love and pain and hikes and friendships; a day that didn't include rest or an explanation regarding a fallen rose. Still, Roger K. needed no Blokehead to nudge him forward. He sensed there would be other times on Dalilennon and elsewhere to withdraw and restore energies.

Rightjet took a deep breath and plunged through the opening of the alcove into the unknown.

Once inside, he found himself on a small balcony overlooking the church floor. The slanting rays of sunshine he'd witnessed moments before while standing at the cathedral's lower level—the level where devout Dalilennonian church parishioners humbly bowed and prayed each week--now radiated at Roger K. through the same high, clean panes of stained glass near the head of the born-again Christ. Yet, those rays couldn't be expected to survive more than a few minutes more before the ongoing earth's tilt would illuminate saintly wooden icons above the alcove's doorway.

That's just how the universe works.

The firm handrailing around the balcony was ornate, carved in dark, expensive imported wood. Like boxed space for the rich in a fancy nineteenth-century theater, the curved extension above the church floor had been built to hold eight to ten patrons.

Now, it held two.

To the left of the balcony's entrance was a small two-foot-high cot cradling a sleeping woman tucked beneath what appeared to be a warm patchwork blanket.

Rightjet gasped.

Ms. Prissy, on her back with feet pointing toward the grister, opened her eyes, then gauged Roger K. Rightjet. Her face was a worn mat of loose skin and wrinkles, with warts and curly black hairs independently jumping from a network of round black moles. The left side of her face seemed to weep through a purple mask of bruised pain, reaching from a rumpled beginning at midcheek, then expanding in an oval that encompassed the perimeter of a blood-red eye.

'Older people hurt more,' thought the would-be hero inwardly as yet another strong emotion, compassion, surfaced during this bizarre day on the isle of fancy.

"I'm sorry," he stumbled quietly.

Ms. Prissy's eyes, even the bloodshot one, sparked to life then; looking as if his pity had flicked a disharmonious circuit breaker in her soul.

"What's ther matter, bloke, ain't ya never seen beauty afore?" she asked, and cackled a pain-stifled laugh that startled Roger K. into laughing along with her, then wince in unison with Ms. Prissy from the obvious physical discomfort generated by her jocularity.

"Don' kiss me, though, er I'll turn to a frog." And Ms. Prissy cackled again.

What source of power possibly could fuel those eyes, her spirit, and make this woman want to laugh now? … even want to survive?

"Ms. Hampshire … "

"Prissy. Prissy's ther name," she pronounced lightly, her wrinkles flexing inside the purple-stained wound as she spoke.

"OK, then." Roger K. Rightjet smiled. A swell of admiration suddenly surfaced in his heart. What an incredible woman!

"Ms. Prissy, I don't wish to stay long, but I need to know. Why me? We have never met, and you asked me to come to your bedside. Almost everyone on Dalilennon wants to hear your story. Why did you ask to see me?"

"Cause yer a real looker," she spouted toyfully, regaling in laughter that triggered a coughing bout that doubled the midwife, ex-midwife, in pain.

Roger calmed her, and offered water from a glass sitting on a small stand near the cot.

He asked again, and Ms. Prissy seemed to retreat, to draw her spark from view. Then, there was silence; and nothing is as silent as an introspective cathedral.

Roger K. looked up beyond the balcony. The golden rays so visible through the skylight when he'd entered the church now were focused elsewhere.

As he thought of leaving, to help reserve her strength for the ordeal she faced, that was when Ms. Prissy Hampshire reached for his hand. They touched, and the coldness, the pallor of her clutched fist gripped his heart with anger toward the unknown source of this woman's pain.

"Please, no questions," she said in a serious, stronger voice. "I know what needs ter be said.

"A good friend 'tol me all I need ter know of 'a you. To most folk hereabouts he's a crazy man. But he's not. He's the best friend an' lover an' sorta priest a hag like me could hope to know. Julian's a godsend," emphasized the battered woman, rocking forward on pinpoint elbows.

"He 'tol me you'd be the one to talk to, so here goes … "

She talked then, her head resting on a pillow at the end of the cot nearest the balcony's western railing, and Roger K. Rightjet listened. Her eyes, one surrounded by wrinkles and the other gnarled and swollen, never strayed from the attentive face before her, watching Roger K.'s reaction as she relayed the only available first-hand account of Dalilennon's biggest intrigue in anyone's memory.

Ms. Prissy laughed when she told the grister about late-night diplomats standing on top of a garden wall, afraid to proceed because of a braying donkey.

"He knowed he had 'em, too, 'cause I ain't never heard Blokehead make that much ruckus," she said, with the mystifying sparkle of life radiating from her eyes.

"I give'd 'em the raspberries fer a minute or two, too. Told 'em how silly they looked, world leaders an' all, being scared to death by a harmless donkey. Ol Blokehead makes some noise, but he don't hurt nobody."

Roger Rightjet wasn't convinced, but held his tongue.

"Then, the strong one from that eggie sorta country jumped to the ground and smacked me a good one. Ya know, the whole thing was wrong. In ther first place, a big man shouldn't hit a woman. In ther second place, he shouldn't hit an old woman. And in ther third place, he shouldn't hit anyone et' all on Dalilennon."

Then, Ms. Prissy showed her teeth, yellow and crooked as would fit the mold, and capped her story by saying with a smile, "Guess that's why he caught me with my guard down."

"You be quiet, Ms. Prissy, and get some rest," said Rightjet. "I'll do what I can to help from the information you've given me, but what you need to do is be still and patient because your body needs time to recover. And I don't recommend that you go home. I have no doubt that the same people who did this to you know where you live and will stop at nothing to prevent you from sharing what you just told me."

Roger K. reached his right hand to the wounded face of the ex-midwife and gently guided one, then the other eyelid to closed positions.

"Me man was right about you," her tired voice said peacefully. She opened her eyes again, grinned, winked one ugly, bloodshot eye, then closed both her eyes once more, her face creased by a contented grin amongst the wrinkles and pain.

"I'm no hero," Roger K. said to her lightly, almost inaudibly, and turned to go.

At the low doorway leading away from the balcony overlooking the cathedral, Roger K. Rightjet paused to glance at the massive stained-glass window on the front wall of the risen Christ. He pursed his lips as if to speak, then thought better of it. Would-be heroes get direction whether they ask for it or not.

Only Priest Darrell Precious saw Roger K. Rightjet leave the cathedral; Priest Precious and a small flock of yellow finches dining nearby on a round, white mulberry bush. The birds rose as if tossed in a blanket, then settled lightly back on the bush as Roger K. strode by in the late-afternoon shadows.

J.K.'s Near Demise

McGetitdone was angry when he found no one at Ms. Prissy Hampshire's cottage at the base of the mountain. Unfinished business bothered him. He should have killed her that night and, for the life of him, didn't understand why he hadn't. He remembered the crushing blow he'd delivered and how she'd crumpled in the dirt like a dead pheasant.

How could she still be alive?

The trained saboteur searched the cottage for clues to her whereabouts. He found bloody bandages reiterating what he already knew, that she was alive, but nothing to hint as to where she'd gone.

Manual McGetitdone wanted to dishevel the place, to tip and scatter every piece of furniture and everything of value. But he refrained. He was a professional, and knew his top priority was the fast-growing disadvantageous crop, and nothing else.

He left Ms. Prissy's home as he'd found it, exited through the back door, and then returned to the boat.

"She's gone," he reported to Ms. Sylvia Smitharomance, "and she hasn't been there for several hours."

Ms. Sylvia pondered for a moment, then said, "Because Rightjet told Poncho she was at her home, it means they not only suspect us, but Poncho as well."

"When it gets dark, Norbert and I'll go check the crop," said McGetitdone. "I'm too antsy to sit here and wait."

"Make sure no one sees you," she said. "Our free time on Dalilennon is growing short, and no one must know why we're here."

And so it was, a couple hours later, while closely peering around them in every direction like Dick Tracy on the prowl or a teenage girl sneaking at night out her bedroom window, that two Eglicatan dignitaries--McGetitdone and Nodahead—embarked on what they assumed would be a safe, elongated journey from the boat to the walled garden plot where disadvantageous, aka fowlawarfare food, was growing at a fast rate.

With the assistance of Poncho McTea's key, they entered the garden plot through the stout iron-barred gate and were shocked at the phenomenal growth of the coveted disadvantageous weed. The plants now dwarfed the human intruders, reaching in excess of seven feet in height. Spindly stalks of fibrous green already were bent by heavy clusters of matted disadvantageous fronds that would keep reproducing seeds until the combined weight of fronds and seeds would snap stalks, plummeting all to the ground in heaps of disconnected potential life. From among the seeming countless seeds scattered on the ground, only the healthiest would spring to life, courtesy of rapid germination, to perpetuate the species.

The disadvantageous plant truly is an oddity, a platypus of the plant kingdom. From the moment of its pollination, when pollen from its anther is transferred to the stigma of the plant's flower by one of a myriad of willing insects, optimum growth takes slightly less than fourteen days.

A typical disadvantageous cycle, where abnormalities are few, sees rapid growth until, at almost fourteen days following pollination, Nature marvelously breaks stalks, tumbles fronds to the ground, and from them bursts forth healthy seeds seeking moisture and germination that will repeat the hasty cycle.

It's easy to see why disadvantageous is a noxious weed!

Still, it was the catalytic properties of the ungerminated disadvantageous seed that could solve the sheep-eating digestive disorder threatening the life of Herr McCoffee's second and final flying fowlawarfare.

By now, night, under a slightly less-than-full moon, prevailed in the garden.

"Between six and seven more hours and these puppies will be ripe for the taking," said Norbert Nodahead. "Hopefully, we can complete the harvest and get the crap on the boat by daylight."

"Sh-s-s-s. Someone's coming," said McGetitdone. "Too late to climb orange trees. Hide in the shadows. Damn moon."

"The shady trees cover him with their shadow; the willows of the brook compass him about," came Julian Knotsofoolista's eerie, haunted-house voice as he clambered atop the rock wall and peered below him toward the thin-trunked orange trees that provided negligible cover for pudgy Norbert and stout, hard-faced Manual McGetitdone.

Manual reacted to the situation in character.

Not one to let a frocked adversary get the last smile, at his expense or not, Manual McGetitdone pulled his snubbed revolver and fired a shot in the dark.

Then, everything happened at once.

Occasionally on planet earth, events prove so cataclysmic, so mind-staggering, that time, that indefinable element that leads one hastily or not so hastily through each day, literally stands still.

And that very thing happened at this moment when Julian Knotsofoolista's body recoiled from the pistol shot and plummeted several feet below into a giant purple-plumed cactus plant on the outside of the stone wall.

"Dammit," growled Norbert Nodahead while clutching several fronds of disadvantageous. "Two wrongs don't make a right."

"It's done," snapped Manual McGetitdone with iced anger in his voice and veins. "He makes no difference. We're committed to Herr McCoffee's plan for peace and can't afford to be stopped now."

Nodahead made no comment, but was first in line to exit through the high iron gate and head back to the Eglicatan boat; McGetitdone following in his wake.

Outside the garden wall, Knotsofoolista's body had thumped hard on the cactus, then on to planet earth. Zorro's brim was dented, and no movement was to be seen nor sounds heard from Julian's still form.

Why is life so cold, so futile, that even this strange, caring soul had to be snuffed into obscurity amongst none but his enemies? Why are the misunderstood so prone to fall alone in the dark? What is God's plan?

Enough! One must wipe away one's tears and return to fancy.

Like Manual McGetitdone's blow to Ms. Prissy Hampshire's temple that failed to secure her permanent demise, so was the snubbed revolver bullet that pierced Zorro's laced black hat, then went spinning harmlessly into space.

The shock of the projectile's nearness had caused Julian K. to faint and collapse outside the wall, landing seat first on the purple, spiny succulent. He was jolted from the pain of his rude arrival on the cactus, moaned in familiar resignation, then lapsed into unconsciousness with red tennis shoes elevated on a rock as if a Registered Nurse was treating him for shock.

The moon was rising.

"Six hours and five minutes from now and we can begin the harvest," noted Nodahead as he led he and Manual's retreat. "Let's get out of here. No need for them to discover our prize now."

As the two criminals--for, indeed, they now looked the part--cleverly outwitted Dalilennon's sleeping police force and headed back to the boat, Roger K. Rightjet, coming from the east, angrily approached the same garden plot with the high wall around it. Had his steps not been tainted by anger, and maybe been moments quicker, possibly he'd have heard the receding echo of villain footsteps, or noticed a frocked hump laying next to a spiny cactus just outside the twilit, mostly moonlit wall.

After grabbing the horizontal bars on the gate and pulling himself upward, Roger K. climbed over its top and dropped down to the ground. He now was inside the same wall from which McGetitdone had jumped to batter Ms. Prissy Hampshire. Roger K.'s current goal was to learn what had been of interest to bring McTea, McGetitdone, and a third Eglicatanese conspirator to the garden plot the night the aged ex-midwife and Blokehead had stumbled upon their doings.

Plants were divided into numerous sections by low rock fences, plants familiar to Rightjet. Low, well-tended grape bushes … a cabbage patch with two wiry, gnarled olive trees along one side … what looked to be a long, narrow potato bed to grow the tiny new bulbs that were main staples of the Dalilennonian diet … some scraggily looking carrots that probably were planted to replace nutrients as much as glean a harvest … a space near the high wall densely cluttered with the disadvantageous weed … and probably the corner receiving the best morning sun that boasted a larger-than-average row of orange trees.

A man who loved gardening, Roger K. was impressed with the care and beauty of this particular garden. However, the large patch of disadvantageous puzzled him, seemed out of place, and made him want to cut the weed down before fronds toppled and new seeds began to sprout.

As he puzzled and walked and thought, Roger K. Rightjet heard a sound originating outside the wall and determined someone, on this mostly moonlit night, wished to join him inside the parameters of the garden. With little cover available on short notice, the unwilling hero, who slowly was becoming more and more willing, elected to crouch in the shadows behind one of the orange trees.

Roger K. Rightjet, looking across a shadowy distance of less than thirty meters, had never before seen the man attempting to climb the high iron gate from the outside. The grister carefully gauged the newcomer's nonthreatening size, and readied himself to subdue the intruder once he reached the ground inside the gate.

The tempo of Roger K.'s heart, already beating faster than its norm because of the anger he was feeding upon, tuned to new levels. It had been many years since Roger K. Rightjet had scuffled atop the high plains of anger; still, excitement was overriding fear.

Roger K. calculated when the new intruder would reach the top of the gate and commit to jump down into the cabbage patch below. At that point in time, he, Roger K. Rightjet, planned to attack before the culprit got his bearings after landing at ground zero.

Rightjet readied himself, dug a foothold in the alkaline dirt to ensure a fast start, and watched as this alien being pulled himself up to the top rail of the gate.

The eyes of the most righteous of Rightjets were focused, exhibiting a flare of cohesive concentration beneath attentive, fluffy eyebrows.

Like a one-hundred-meter sprinter leaving the blocks too soon, Roger K. could rein his energies in no longer and swiftly broke into a run toward the gate one split second before the unknown man headed earthward. Had he waited that split second longer, Roger K. could have avoided that dash altogether because his chosen rival lost his grip at the top rung and tumbled to earth once more on the OUTSIDE of the high iron gate.

As quickly as he'd begun to charge did Rightjet screech to a halt and retreat once more to the orange trees.

He needn't have hurried.

His foe, if indeed he still was man enough to step into the garden arena, was gasping for air, rubbing his backside, and rolling eyes unable to focus in the moonlight. Too, the man's eyeglasses had landed, unharmed, a short distance away.

The mysterious invader gathered his glasses and began studying the gate once more; not to determine how, but rather if he should try to scale it again.

Norman Expedience, for that was the man's name, needn't have bothered to furrow his brow in thought, for throughout history it's been proven over and over again that such decisions, in the end, often aren't made by the clumsy invader, but by fate.

Enter Blokehead.

Let it be said that Blokehead hadn't always taken to the task of harassing strangers: those he disliked and Roger K. Rightjet. But, since the serious injury to the elderly ex-midwife who fed him and provided his lodging, Blokehead had developed somewhat of a sour disposition. That was especially true of anyone fitting either of the two categories mentioned in the last half of the first sentence of this paragraph … if, indeed, one solitary hero in the making can be categorized as a category.

Suffice it to say that Blokehead charged, the intruder climbed, and Roger K. sprinted through the cabbage patch.

And what a nighttime battle ensued!!

While Blokehead brayed his dislike of both pugilists from outside the iron barrier, the two warriors inside the gate, standing amongst the cabbages, engaged in a fray much harder to describe than envision. 'Twas like the fights of black & white western movies where two worthy combatants, with nary a drop of blood spilled, trade swift, clean blows to the head and body, recklessly fall to the garden turf (alas, no tables to shatter as a good western would want,) and quickly get up for more. A mighty battle it was, with the young intruder, ala Clark Kent, tossing eyeglasses aside at the outset and nobly defending his purpose.

Blow upon blow was exchanged until, exhausted, the regularity and severity of those blows decreased like sunshine at the outset of an Antarctic winter.

Neither of the pugilists would quit, however, and what had been a boxing match became a slow wrestle. Eventually, the last of Roger K.'s anger was extinguished, and he pulled away to assess the new man he'd battled with while catching traces of energy from the air he so noisily gulped.

Roger K., now on his knees, ducked a slow haymaker from his weary opponent, and the stranger fell, face-first, on the torn floor of the cabbage patch.

"No more," gasped Roger K. to a foe too weak to respond as the moon dipped behind a wispy cloud. In addition to the gasping of the two men, yellow-throated birds of slight stature warbled unseen from branches of the orange trees.

Neither man wished to take the initiative and explain his purpose for their quiet brawl that, as far as anyone other than the two of them knew, never had taken place.

Seeing they were getting nowhere, the stranger flipped a coin with the loser to introduce himself and his intentions first, the winner second. A brief seminar on the ramification of coin flipping ensued. Since flipping a coin to determine an important matter was a new concept to Roger K., the stranger patiently explained the rules and it was agreed that the hometown warrior would make the call while the coin was in the air.

He didn't

Rightjet made his "5", or "cross" call only after the coin was in the other's hand, hence a foul was called. A peek showed that Roger K. would have lost, and a second flip ensued during which, while the coin was airborne, Roger K. called "cross," and won.

With apparent fair play adhered to, the newcomer introduced himself as Mr. Norman Expedience, an agent of espionage for a country he wished not to name who'd just arrived on the island to determine what it was the country of Eglicata was seeking on Dalilennon. He went on to say that he was a bachelor, lived in a city Roger K. never had heard of, and enjoyed swimming, squash, and playing various card games.

Roger K. Rightjet next gave his own biographical sketch, omitting any mention of his Eglicatan past. Without batting an eye, or at least not doing so unnaturally, Mr. Rightjet, a true hero in the making, asked the young spy, for indeed that would appear to be the proper term to apply to the newcomer whether he was spying on the home country or another, what had brought him to this particular garden immediately after landing on Dalilennon.

Norman E. took Roger K. Rightjet into his confidence after checking his Dalilennonian driver's license and proceeded without hesitation to share information given to him by an unnamed Dalilennonian contact. That information proved to be strikingly similar to the puzzling facts that had brought the gristmiller to the very same garden plot; enough data to implicate the garden in the Eglicatan ploy, but nothing of enough clarity to reveal the nature of said ploy.

Since it was dark and the new, young spy had no place to stay, Roger K. invited him to clean up and rest at his house, hoping his lawyer-like intellect would entice Norman Expedience to reveal more of his role in this mind-boggling affair.

As Roger K. scaled the gate to exit the garden, Norman Expedience, standing in the shredded cabbage patch they'd scuffled in, lightly dropped a Dalilennonian "paper 5" note to the ground, one he'd borrowed from Rightjet, to help repay the garden keeper for undue damages.

When Norman reached the top of the gate, on the first try this go, the new arrival to Dalilennon paused to purse his brow and ask, "Whose frigging donkey was that, anyway?" He next dropped to the ground and followed Roger K. Rightjet into the night, feeling more bruises and aches than protocol should have warranted for a new arrival on the peaceful island of Dalilennon.

And, as they left the garden behind them, the clock started once more for another central character in this tale of fanciful thrills ...

... for that's when a rumpled mass of thwarted priesthood, with a new bullet hole in Zorro's brim, groaned back to life.

Julian Knotsofoolista rubbed his butt, gathered his wits, and grumbled thoughtlessly, "Yet, let no man strive nor reprove another: for thy people are as they that strive with the priest."

Clarity slowly was beginning to overcome the darkness in his head, and J.K., rubbing his wounds, said for his own benefit, "I guess it's better than being clubbed by a tetherball section."

As Knotsofoolista tentatively gained his feet, adjusted his cloak and hat, and decided life would proceed as usual, the caped crusader lilted in his best raccoon voice, "I'll be better, doc, I'll be better soon as I am able," then groggily walked away humming obscure tunes about Strawberry Fields and Yellow Submarines.

And the disadvantageous plant within the gate behind him continued to grow rapidly, fast approaching a planned harvest some four hours away, give or take an hour or three.

Strolling and Pacing

An hour or two earlier by the moondial, integral pieces were beginning to fit into the complex puzzle facing Malcolm Straight. After much introspection and soul-searching, Malcolm S. decided to approach good King Nocturnal concerning his doubts regarding the loyalty of Poncho McTea. The child's report to Rightjet and Rightjet's unwillingness to disclose the site of his planned rendezvous with Ms. Prissy, specifically avoiding Poncho McTea's direct question, hinted at a pattern of connivery and mistrust.

Yet, Malcolm arrived too late.

By the time Malcolm Straight returned to the palace to express his concerns about Poncho McTea, the good King had retired to the steam rooms and given strict orders that he was to be disturbed by no one. What's more, an attendant to good King Nocturnal informed Straight that the good King intended to proceed directly from the steam rooms to the palatial garden to commune with Nature. And then, for the first time in several fortnights, good King Nocturnal planned to enter chambers with the Mrs. King and remain there until morning; all to be accomplished without interruptions of any kind.

Advisor Malcolm Straight was exasperated once he heard this unwelcome news, yet saw no recourse other than to wait until morning to address the good King. Due in part to his inherent indecisiveness on major issues, good King Nocturnal, more often than not, stringently mandated that his minor decrees be carried out to the last letter, crossed T, and most minute detail.

And the sleepy Dalilennonian guards, likely unaware of indecisiveness at any level, were exceedingly glad to serve any wish the good King might express.

For several hours, Malcolm Straight distractedly walked around government grounds. He only left once to sip wine and a second time to spy on Rightjet's home and learn if Roger K. had returned there from the cathedral. Like his initial visit to meet with the good King and his trek for wine, the latter trip to Rightjet's, too, provided no release from the worries building up inside him. Roger K. Rightjet was not available to be spied upon.

By now, about the time McGetitdone was firing a revolver shot at Julian Knotsofoolista in the previous chapter, night was well established beneath a healthy moon.

Mr. Straight checked his timepiece by the moonlight and, with a sudden burst of renewed energy and direction, headed with confidence and authority to the home of a good police officer whom, though the officer and Straight merely were acquaintances, was familiar with Straight's prominent position in the hierarchy of Dalilennon.

A good distance away, in a tiered tropical courtyard, good King Nocturnal paced his premises. He imagined, though not based on a shred of factual data, that many urgent messages had arrived since he'd secluded himself from the outside world.

He suspected Ms. Prissy Hampshire had informed Roger K. Rightjet of the worst of possible fates awaiting Dalilennon, then plunked over in death. He imagined a bright star had fallen through the roof of the nation's large cathedral and, at that very moment, was destroying everything in and around the church; that a ploy was afoot to capture he and the Mrs. King, then take away their sovereignty; and that a message soon would arrive that fish swimming in the sea, in waters ringing the isle of fancy, soon would be poisoned with oil.

All these frightening possibilities and more thought the good King within the confines of his head, and he simply didn't know what to do about any of them. 'So important to have good advisors,' he thought internally.

When not thinking the direst of thoughts, such being a mental burden Nature occasionally insists on appeasing with pleasant alternatives, the good King thought warm kudos about his bride, the Mrs. King, who'd shown a new spark for life, a glow shining through her eyes in the past twenty-four hours. The thimble-sized things she suddenly was doing such as talking with Ms. Nancy Droosha without exhibiting signs of boredom; adding well-thought, verbal input to general conversations; and not picking her nose at the dinner table all had been noticed by the good King.

Definitely, the Mrs. King's resurgence toward etiquette and joy were pluses on the ledger, yet the unrest of recent days with Eglicatan dignitaries on the isle always would return to perplex and worry the good King as he strolled and paced, and paced and strolled within the reaches of the quiet palatial garden.

Even small birds, for all birds are small on Dalilennon, took note of the good King's problems and opted to honor his plight with silence.

As the moon rose over the sea, the good King chose to nix his problems temporarily, and walked with decisive steps to the chambers of the Mrs. King where a lively evening of tea, a meal, and wine was graced with warm, pertinent discourse that fell on the most compassionate of ears.

When the royal couple took to their bed that night, and more so the next morning, each knew they'd experienced a Dalilennonian night long to be remembered.

A Grisly Nighttime Harvest Goes To Sea

As the clock ticked toward 2:37 a.m., a pudgy man holding the Welch plug to a nearby vessel's carburetor impatiently paced between the rarely used fireplace and the opposing wall of Poncho McTea's villa.

The wall to the right of the front entrance featured a doorway leading down a short hallway to the unit's master bedroom, off of which a "loo" was located. Another hallway to the right of the fireplace led to the McTea family's kitchen; which included a deep sink for washing laundry as well as dishes, plus high, wooden cupboards.

The dignitary's rental home with Mediterranean furniture and Picasso-like wall hangings probably included more comforts than Herr McCoffee would have approved of for his cousin's place of residence. That view clearly had been defined in a seldom-seen proclamation the Herr had made on a Saturday in May during his second year as the leader of Eglicata. That proclamation, now buried on a dust-laden shelf in a county library rented to store a fragment of the government's plethora of rules and regulations that couldn't be contained under one roof, stated that any Eglicatan emissary in a foreign land must live no better than median-level income earners of the country they were assigned to.

But, frankly, McCoffee was many kilometers away and Poncho felt the need to keep up with appearances.

Sitting in his favorite Bach-Springsteen chair, Poncho McTea displayed an outward calm he didn't feel. He'd chastised Nodahead more than once for Norbert's ceaseless pacing to and fro across the living-room carpet; with no results.

Apparently, the comfort pacing provided Nodahead outweighed the discomfort the same pacing afforded McTea, and Norbert continued to pace.

The two had grilled each other on various elements of the devious plan they soon would embark on until each felt assured the other wouldn't become a liability.

At 2:51 a.m., the four of them (Ms. Smitharomance and Manual McGetitdone currently being engaged in some nerve-calming sex in the next room,) would leave the villa with Nodahead heading to the moored boat and the other three to the disadvantageous patch. While Norbert repaired the disabled engine and watched over the vessel, McGetitdone would use a rusty scythe to cut down the nearly fourteen-day-old weed, McTea would gather and bundle the crop with lengths of wire cut especially for the occasion, and Ms. Sylvia would bag and seal the bundled disadvantageous in wet gunny sacks transported from Eglicata for that very purpose.

The wet gunny sacks, had said McDove, would keep the crop moist and help minimize major enzyme loss due to evaporation or dissipation.

Nodahead was to have the engine purring by the time the disadvantageous crew reached the sea with their cargo, then drive the getaway boat into the sunrise. Poncho McTea planned to be on board as they peacefully chugged away from Dalilennon: he, with a smug grin on his face, waving goodbye to good King Nocturnal and Nocturnal's fair island. From there, they'd travel by sea back to Eglicata and the foundering fowlawarfare.

Yet, sometimes the best laid of plans can go awry and, on this particular moonlit night when the good King and Mrs. King were "getting it on" better than they had for years, such is exactly what fate had in mind.

Complications arose from the outset.

When the foursome, Manual and Ms. Sylvia appearing more refreshed than the other two, emerged from McTea's villa at nearly 3 a.m., two sets of eyes were watching them from a distance with more than casual interest. Not those of a seven-year-old boy and his sister, these eyes belonged to Poncho McTea's arch enemy, Malcolm Straight, and the police officer he'd conned into joining him on this late-night act of vigilance. Crack Officer Oliver Ogilvie, next to Straight, waited in an alert crouch, unaware that good King Nocturnal knew nothing of his actions.

When the surveillants (which is a pretty heavy word for the isle of Dalilennon, so heavy, in fact, that it's not a noun in the author's dictionary,) saw the Eglicatan force split in two directions, Mr. Straight did the noble thing and followed the three, with Officer Oliver Ogilvie assigned to track Norbert Nodahead.

Initially, things went smoothly for the Dalilennonian cause as Straight, following in the dark, sneaked unseen to the garden with the high wall around it. After the others had used a key to unlock the gate and step inside, Straight, grasping horizontal bars of iron, pulled his body to the top of the gate, then moved sideways and positioned himself, still unseen, among tree limbs along the wall's interior, his weight supported by a natural toehold.

What he witnessed was beyond his comprehension. The three late-night invaders began harvesting, gathering, bundling, and bagging volumes of the noxious weed disadvantageous; the same weed most Dalilennonian farmers would have paid big bucks or exchanged unscratched lottery tickets to have removed from their gardens.

And what was more amazing to Malcolm Straight was they were doing it in the dead of night. Straight was dumbfounded by what was unfolding before him.

And it was exactly this perplexity, this source of wonder, that led to the downfall, literally, of one Malcolm Straight.

Some men, in the course of their years, consciously adopt "clever" traits and characteristics that, they feel, tend to enhance the image they wish to project. Some give their pants an upward tug when conditions call for such a purposeful gesture; some cup their chin between thumb and forefinger when such a pose might add a look of intense pondering; while still others may, with one motion and two hands, draw the hair on their heads straight back as if such an action will solve any dilemma.

Once these gestures pass from consciousness to habit, the need for premeditated thought is eliminated, and the action is as automatic as breathing is to a duck.

And so it was that the amazement Malcolm Straight felt at seeing this noxious weed harvested by desperadoes in the middle of the night on sleepy Dalilennon triggered an automatic, knee-jerk-type response from him that he'd consciously adopted when he was a teenager wanting to look cool and impress girls: he rubbed his forehead and leaned back.

The result, as you might expect, was disastrous, as the advisor to good King Nocturnal had the wind knocked out of him at the conclusion of his ensuing fall to earth. Worse, though, was the fact that Malcolm still was gasping frantically to catch his breath as his hands were being tied behind his back by an evil-looking Manual McGetitdone, whose facial scar now flared red 'neath the full moon.

Straight was yanked roughly to the iron gate, and tightly bound to it with rope. He watched as the grisly nighttime harvest continued.

By keeping his pounding heart in check and listening intently, Mr. Straight, once his head cleared, could discern the voices of McTea and McGetitdone apparently discussing his, Malcolm Straight's, future. Suggestions made by his arch rival for Straight's benefit, (was boiling him in oil a realistic option?) nearly popped Malcolm Straight's eyeballs from their sockets, while McGetitdone's calm voice in unknown dialect seemed to hint of a more civilized approach.

"He is a high-ranking diplomat. And much as I'd like to do otherwise," continued Manual McGetitdone to McTea in a language foreign to Malcolm Straight, "Herr McCoffee would prefer we take him hostage and not kill him."

It took two hours, including the Straight interruption, to complete the harvest.

Since their "haul" proved to be far bigger than what they could carry in one trip, and more than what was needed to unfounder the fowlawarfare, much of the disadvantageous was scythed, bundled in wet gunny sacks, and stored along the garden wall for their return to Dalilennon aboard the giant bird. It was from Dalilennon that Herr McCoffee planned to launch his attack on Darius.

And, having decided to pursue McGetitdone's plan to take Straight hostage, they untied him from the iron gate and latched heavy bundles of nearly fourteen-day-old disadvantageous to his back.

Yet, while the harvest is plenty and the laborers few, an even stranger series of events was unfolding aboard the ship.

For t'was destined to be the most unusual of nights in the annals of Dalilennonian history.

After leaving the company of Mr. Straight, good police officer Oliver Ogilvie dutifully tracked Norbert Nodahead to the Eglicatan boat and, when Nodahead stooped to repair the Welch-plugless engine, subdued the foreigner with a difficulty equivalency of .003 on a scale of one to twelve. Understandably startled, Norbert dropped the tiny circular engine part and looked to his captor as the vital plug rolled and circled like a plastic tiddlywink, finally settling beneath the rubber-coated steps leading from the covered engine room back up to the motorboat's main deck.

Norbert Nodahead may have been a scrapper in some ways, but the immediate threat of bodily harm had pudgy Norbert nodding his head in adamant agreement that, yes-sir, he was under arrest. Norbert then was tied hand and foot, gagged (to his vehement dismay,) and tucked away in the ship's hold … 'hold' being one of many nautical terms soon to be employed in this technical journal of intrigue.

Norbert covetously glanced at the irreplaceable Welch plug, was both tantalized and frustrated by its unreachable closeness, then, by crack Officer Oliver Ogilvie, was thrown like baggage into another compartment of the boat.

The good police officer still had absolutely no idea what was going on, but dutifully stationed himself between the ship's lifeboat and starboard bow to await what was to come.

He waited nearly three hours before anyone else came aboard.

Let it be said that neither Roger K. Rightjet nor Norman Expedience, the next two to grace the ship's deck, were of an inherent villainous nature. Neither of them ever had stolen a ship before, and neither had tinkered maliciously with the engine of a seafaring vessel.

They simply had arrived on the Eglicatan ship, admittedly late at night and expecting no opposition, to see if Mr. Expedience's mechanical prowess could rejuvenate the ship's engine; the engine whose lack of firepower had prevented the Eglicatan envoy's departure from Dalilennon the previous day.

After hearing Roger K.'s retelling of Jean Paul's story and more, Norman Expedience, sitting on Roger's front porch and munching on one of our sorta-hero's prize pears, suggested he might be able to help.

Yet, these facts weren't known to the good police officer hiding behind the lifeboat. For all he knew, these two new intruders could have been spies from abroad, or even the ones who'd popped Ms. Prissy Hampshire. For that matter, they could be doing almost anything aboard the Eglicatan boat. For crack Officer Oliver Ogilvie, crack officer whom he undoubtedly was, wouldn't have been able to pin a legal charge on anyone aboard, were he asked to do so. In point of fact, he was clueless on the matter.

Yet, Mr. Malcolm Straight, a great leader of men, had been adamant, if not specific, and crack Officer Oliver Ogilvie was on board to do his best for God, the flag of Dalilennon, and good King Nocturnal.

To the engine room went the new twosome, and close behind came the Dalilennonian police officer who'd never before used the nightstick he carried in his right hand.

En route to the engine room, behind Expedience, Roger K. stooped to pick up a peculiar rubber engine part and was tucking it into his front pants pocket when Ogilvie struck him with the nightstick from behind. 'Bop' to the back of Roger K.'s head, and out he went. And, for the second time in his few hours on Dalilennon, Norman Expedience was called upon to fight.

Now, it may be that the earlier battle with Roger K. had taken much out of Norman's storehouse of energy; possibly Norman's televised John Wayne tactics were ineffective against this officer of Dalilennonian justice; maybe the police officer simply was a tougher dude; or it may be a combination of all the above, but the end result was that Norman Expedience lost quickly.

In less than a minute, in fact.

But this time the damage was far greater to Norman Expedience. He ended the short fray with a painful, bloody proboscis that caused his eyes to water relentlessly, especially when Officer Ogilvie less than gently slammed Expedience's eyeglasses back on his nose.

But the plot was thickening.

A short distance away, Poncho McTea, sauntering ahead of his disadvantageous-carrying peers, heard grunts, curses, and thumps aboard ship and, deducing that Norbert likely wouldn't be making such noises were he alone, sensed something was amiss with their plan.

Poncho returned to the others in the moonlight--Straight being pissed because he had to carry the heaviest load--told them what he'd heard, then cautioned Ms. Sylvia and their captive to wait behind while he and Manuel McGetitdone reconnoitered the situation.

All four of them retraced their steps to a stone bench at a safe distance from the vessel, and dropped their bundles of disadvantageous to the ground. Then, McTea and McGetitdone, in sneak formation, began stalking their own Eglicatan boat.

Stealthily, with the craftiness of true villains, McTea and McGetitdone, the latter's scar once again flaring red in the night, approached the docked ship and crept aboard unnoticed as a somewhat bewildered Dalilennonian police officer pondered what to do with the three captives he'd secured with ropes.

No matter what else can be said about Poncho McTea, no one can or would want to argue that he's anything but a crafty, cunning man.

After sizing up the situation and cautioning McGetitdone to stay out of sight, McTea walked from shadowy darkness onto the same moonlit deck where Roger K. Rightjet moaned motionless with "lights out" against one railing; Norman Expedience quietly sat tied some meters away from Rightjet, sporting a sore nose; and Norbert Nodahead, his head bobbing agreeably at the sight of McTea, sat bound with his back against the wooden lifeboat.

The crack police officer whom McTea personally had dealt with on more than one occasion, including an assignment to catch the cave-dwelling perpetrator who'd once annulled McTea's winning full house of jacks and twos, stood watching over them, still wearing a perplexed look on his face.

"I'm sure glad you're here, Mr. McTea," Officer Ogilvie said in earnest. "I've got three of these blokes tied up and, other than Rightjet, don't know who they are, what they've done, or what to do with 'em." Then, he added, "Thought Mr. Straight would've been along 'afore now."

The latter words completed the puzzle for the cunning double diplomat and, following a few direct questions to determine what the capable police officer did and did not know, Poncho directed Officer Oliver Ogilvie to call it a night.

Cautioning the crack officer to absolute secrecy regarding the evening's events while extending his best Shirley Temple smile of appreciation, Poncho McTea praised Officer Ogilvie for a job well done and sent him home.

And well the good officer should be praised. For, thanks to Ogilvie's timely intervention at Mr. Straight's insistence, Poncho McTea once again could become tight with good King Nocturnal.

Poncho was well aware that the good King had isolated himself from the outside world the previous evening and hadn't sanctioned any nocturnal exercises.

Poncho might have to miss that ship after all.

Officer Oliver Ogilvie left the moored Eglicatan boat and headed up the hill away from the waterfront, slightly disappointed that he'd been cautioned to silence. Such a story he could have told his many friends; a story that would have stretched the parameters of belief. Yet, the officer's loyalty to Dalilennon was at stake and, save any unscheduled tussles with that imported drink tequila, nothing short of an edict from good King Nocturnal himself would part Officer Ogilvie's loyal lips, at least as far as this night's events were concerned.

While walking up the hill away from the boat, Officer Ogilvie took scant notice of an attractive figure mechanically plodding toward him on the opposite side of the narrow stone street. With a beer for himself and a bear hug for his wife foremost on his mind, that chance sighting, something crack officers regularly are tuned to acknowledge, barely grazed his consciousness.

And, absolutely, there was no conscious thought propelling the individual walking downhill across the street; instead, an unmindful mission of love.

The sight truly was extraordinary.

While Dorothy's love of unending caliber carried her through the eye of a whirlwind, through the heart of a tin man, and on to Oz before being reunited with Auntie Em; and sweet Juliette elected death before life without her love; so it was equally obvious that the unconscious mind of Ms. Nancy Droosha had noted a painful blow to the head of her would-be lover and, without bothering to awaken the beauty, stood her on her feet, dressed her, and, foreseeing the future as few unconscious minds can, packed an overnight bag in preparation for a somnambulistic jaunt down a slight Dalilennonian slope to find Roger K. Rightjet.

Ms. Nancy, sleepwalking, passed the normally adroit, but tired police Officer Oliver Ogilvie on the opposite side of the street, approached the seashore, and boarded the Eglicatan vessel before the unbelieving eyes of Norbert Nodahead, who'd already been completely unsettled before being ungagged and untied. Also watching Ms. Nancy's unanticipated arrival, exhibiting flairs of amazement, were Poncho McTea, Manual McGetitdone, and a foreign agent already two fights into his first day on the island.

Norman Expedience, hands tied behind his back, thought to himself that nothing could surprise him in this strange land.

Nancy Droosha plumped down at the side of Roger K. Rightjet, laid her head on his shoulder, and continued in a blissful, love-filled sleep. At her non-Rightjet side was her night kit: undergarments, a toothbrush, and a copy of Pilgrim's Progress inside.

The Eglicatan agents put their heads together, pondered the situation, and concluded the voyage soon must be commenced, even if the number of hostages was greater than the number of their captors.

Norbert, though certain he knew where it should be, couldn't find the missing Welch plug to activate the disabled Eglicatan vessel, but the villains only were slowed momentarily.

The seaworthy SlipSparrow, Dalilennon's main connection with the outside world, was moored only two slips away.

Norbert Nodahead and Manual McGetitdone hastily agreed that Poncho McTea--with Rightjet, the man who'd spoken with Ms. Prissy, and Malcolm Straight both out of circulation as captives on the boat--would be more effective for the Eglicatanese cause if he stayed longer on Dalilennon.

Hence, their team of conspirators on the stolen ship SlipSparrow would consist of Ms. Smitharomance, Mr. Nodahead, and the strong man with the scar, Manual McGetitdone.

Held in ropes during the journey would be Rightjet, Straight, the lady McTea knew as Ms. Nancy, and the foreign man about whose identity, or lack thereof, would have left the Eglicatanese delegates clueless, had they so much as cared who he was.

By the time all personnel decisions had been made, a reasonable amount of time had elapsed, and Ms. Sylvia Smitharomance, still waiting on the stone bench with a bound Malcolm Straight sitting with her next to several gunny sacks full of disadvantageous, had seized the opportunity to share no small amount of physical pleasure with her bound captive. It wasn't the form of pleasure Mr. Straight normally cottoned to outside his own bedroom, but a man whose fate is up for grabs can't be too selective when it comes to personal gratification.

And, he had to admit, the temptress was good at what she did.

Once notified of the change of plans at the dock, Ms. Sylvia, following a corporate decision to leave the bundles of disadvantageous in place until daylight, boarded the SlipSparrow for the first time and gasped in surprise when she saw her betrothed from years earlier conked out, or shall we say comatose, with a beautiful woman resting her head on his shoulder.

Although Sylvia Smitharomance may have evolved many miles in womanly skills since her youthful, passionate days with Roger K. Rightjet, those days always were remembered endearingly, especially late at night when she was alone and feeling empty.

As she looked upon her former lover, the injured grister for the first time since being bonked on the head, managed to produce a sound beyond a feeble moan. Then he opened his eyes, saw Sylvia Smitharomance standing over him with tenderness he couldn't comprehend, and promptly said, "Oh, shit."

A quick, painful glance to his side revealed the presence of a second beauty, Ms. Nancy Droosha, blissfully sleeping on his shoulder with love radiating off of her face. Roger K. managed to flash a feeble, silly smile, then promptly slipped back into unconsciousness.

At daybreak, Poncho McTea and Manual McGetitdone retraced earlier steps to retrieve the bundles of disadvantageous by the stone bench and, once there, McTea, in front, let out a horrendous holler.

"Get out of here, you frigging donkey," he screamed.

It seems Blokehead--possibly when Ms. Smitharomance had been entertaining Mr. Straight and not tending to the flock, or possibly later when the bound weed had been left unattended--had taken a liking to the scythed crop, and was grazing freely on its contents. With his belly filled to the max, Ms. Prissy's domesticated partner offered no resistance as the two Eglicatans, in two trips and without one kind work to Blokehead, took what remained of their cache of disadvantageous to the boat they were about to steal, then inventoried their situation.

Not wanting to return inland to the garden plot in daylight, and calculating they did have enough disadvantageous to revive and propel the fowlawarfare to Dalilennon, the unusual crew of sailors cast off with neither McTea nor a sizeable chunk of the desired crop for which they'd come, most of that being in Blokehead's contented stomach.

As the SlipSparrow churned from the harbor and into the ocean, Norman Expedience--still bound, gagged, and tied to the lifeboat's stanchion--managed a slight smile of confusion as he looked inland and saw, high on the isle's only mountain, two lighted lanterns waving them out to sea.

Hotline to Heaven

Good King Nocturnal sloshed jam on his bread without thought as Poncho McTea relayed the events of the previous evening; or rather the version he chose to tell. The good King could understand, since he'd expected as much, the nighttime exodus of Eglicata's unusual delegation, but the defection of no less than three of his loyal subjects, especially that of Malcolm Straight, took the good King aback.

In fact, he was shocked by what McTea had to say.

"And we still don't know the real reason they chose to visit Dalilennon in the first place?" asked the good King as he tipped some hot, imported coffee to his lips.

"No, Your Excellency," responded McTea. "I began having reservations regarding the foreign diplomats yesterday, so followed them to the boat where they met up with Mr. Straight, Mr. Rightjet, and Ms. Droosha just before the SlipSparrow left harbor. You can imagine my feelings of despair and helplessness, Your Excellency, as I watched a force of that many calmly securing, or rather stealing the only true sailing vessel in all of Dalilennon."

To keep his tale on a simple, believable level, Poncho intentionally omitted any mention of the final passenger, the unknown foreigner, fearing such an honest revelation would threaten any semblance of creditability his own concocted story might otherwise have.

Apparently, the good King accepted what McTea told him on face value because, after complaining about Dalilennon's lack of international telephone or telegraph service, the good King outlined a plan of attack. Good King Nocturnal told McTea he'd write a letter to Herr McCoffee in Eglicata, using no less than the official seal of Dalilennon to emphasize the gravity of the matter. That letter, good King Nocturnal told McTea, would question the actions of the Eglicatan envoy to Dalilennon and demand the immediate return of the SlipSparrow and all Dalilennonians aboard the vessel.

Turning his back to the good King to gaze at the palatial garden through an open window, Poncho McTea inwardly laughed at the ludicrousness of drafting such a letter. Not only would Dalilennon be under the control of Eglicata before any mail-carrying ship could return with a response to such a letter, but the thought of miniature-size, nonwarring Dalilennon demanding anything of anybody was, in itself, a joke.

"Thank you for your report, Mr. McTea."

Poncho nearly was through the partition archway leading out of the good King's chambers when good King Nocturnal called him back, then promptly sideswiped the double-diplomat's mood of exuberance.

"I will begin proceedings immediately to replace Mr. Straight's advisory position," he said.

Poncho frowned, but said nothing.

Once McTea had exited his presence, good King Nocturnal called a servant and instructed that servant to bring to him one of the tiny nation's best police officers.

Having just arrived at work and still tying his wrinkled, black tie following a late night of confusing investigative duty, the same police officer who'd subdued Norbert Nodahead, bopped Roger K. Rightjet into submission, and outfought the most foreign of foreign agents short hours before was informed he'd been summoned to meet with good King Nocturnal.

'Good news,' thought crack Officer Oliver Ogilvie to himself; for he, indeed, was the police officer the good King had summoned. Officer Ogilvie was anxious, even excited about the possibility of recounting the noble deeds he'd rendered the night before for good King Nocturnal and his country. Maybe, too, the good King would shed some light upon this tricky affair that had given him a headache rivaled only by the migraines experienced during the garbage collector's strike seven years earlier. At that time, Ogilvie and other patrolmen had been forced to take up the slack of the strike by meeting the stench head on.

But, if crack Officer Oliver Ogilvie suspected his headache would subside after meeting with good King Nocturnal, he couldn't have been further from the truth.

For, without asking for any feedback about the previous night's activities, King Nocturnal gave Ogilvie a new assignment that sent what remained of Oliver's grasp of reality into a tailspin.

He was instructed by the good King to watch and report on the comings and goings of Poncho McTea.

"Next thing you know, the good King will have defected to a distant, foreign land, and Ms. Prissy Hampshire will become king," mumbled the befuddled functionary. His thoughts, or whispered words, were in no way intended to express irreverence toward his good King, simply confusion on his part.

Earlier, good King Nocturnal had noticed the side-to-side jumping of Mr. McTea, and was a far cry from the fool McTea might think him to be.

'It's not familiarity that breeds contempt, but the assumption of knowledge,' had once said the best of the Brits, and the recollection of that phrase, for the good King had read a book or three in his day, gave him strength and direction about how to proceed beyond he and Dalilennon's current situation.

Next on the sovereign's list was the need to name a new close advisor to his administration. Pickings were slim.

By lunch time, good King Nocturnal had patrolled the palatial garden many times in ponder mode and, save breaks to stoop toward the ground and smell the many bright flowers, had little of merit to show for his efforts.

One possible solution would be to hold a national lottery with the winner becoming his new advisor. Fair to be sure, but the thought of a Julian Knotsofoolista pulling the right lot and being promoted into a key cabinet position could prove humbling, if not crippling to the king of any nation, large or small.

When the Mrs. King joined her husband for the noon repast, filled with her obvious renewed zest for life, her mood soured when the morning's revelations were made known to her.

Still, the Mrs. King didn't hesitate to suggest a Straight alternative.

"Priest Precious," she said unabashedly, and went on to itemize a list of virtues that would more than qualify the good priest for administrative, government duty.

When the Mrs. King mentioned " … a hotline to heaven, …" the good King was convinced.

And so, armed with an arsenal of counter-arguments should the good priest prove reluctant to serve his good King, at good King Nocturnal's request, Priest Precious was sent an official invitation to dine at the palace and discuss high-level diplomatic matters on a royal scale.

A Coming-Home Party

An odd assortment of allies, friends, and compatriots met that very day at the rural home of Ms. Prissy Hampshire. It was dubbed a coming-home party for the elderly spinster with wrinkled face, and each in attendance had distinctive ways of expressing their pleasure in her victory over death.

Julian Knotsofoolista wished to make the affair wholly one of lightness and love, so constantly was in sight and out of sight trying to upgrade the event's overall mood. At any instant, he may hang, upside down, and peer through an exterior window; squat atop the low reefer in the high-ceilinged kitchen; dangle, with only red high-tops in view, inside the unlit fireplace; or simply Russian toe dance about the premises.

Jean Paul and Mary lent mirth in different ways, exhibiting large grins and infectious shrieks of laughter. Too, each delighted in untying Mr. Julian's Mickey Mouse shoelaces, causing the Russian toe dancer to stumble and fall repeatedly as J.K. and the children laughed until their eyes watered with tears of joy.

The impish quickness of the little ones in itself was a pleasure to Ms. Prissy who, not healed totally, spent much of the festive occasion watching, laughing, interjecting, and simply flashing warm, craggy smiles toward those she loved. Having such mirth and happiness in her often lonely home buoyed her spirits beyond compare.

Ms. Prissy's pain mostly was history now, yet spells of dizziness persisted, forcing the leathery old hag to spend more time lying down than she would have liked. In her thinking, it wouldn't bode well for her to faint now and worry her friends.

Another close friend, and possibly Ms. Prissy's most devoted ally, stood peering through one window, displaying a glassy look of bliss.

Blokehead hadn't been particularly active this day, and one look at his overfed stomach explained why. He occasionally brayed to reiterate both his presence and pleasure at seeing Ms. Prissy on the mend. Still, for all practical purposes, the stuffed donkey mostly relied on immobility as he maintained his position outside the open window.

Jean Paul and Mary earlier had hopped aboard Blokehead and urged the stout critter to give them a lift, but the donkey's mind was firm on the matter and, regardless how hard they tried to wheedle and coax, Blokehead, the oftentimes fun-loving donkey, refused to step out in play.

Food for the occasion was furnished by the frocked Knotsofoolista who brought ample supplies of fresh lemons, pears, and herbs to accent the large fresh fish he'd caught that morning. Lively Julian K. took time from his entertaining antics to cook a swordfish soufflé, and the happy household filled their bellies and souls with food, camaraderie, laughter, and unconditional love.

Blokehead, for readers to better understand what was about to happen, possibly was the finest of his line, at least on the isle of fancy, but occasionally did overeat to a degree that, for obvious reasons, required an absolute minimum of movement. Content beyond belief at this point in time, the pooched donkey stood at the window by the hour seeing and hearing little beyond the immediate.

This wasn't at all natural for such an animal normally adroit and active with wit, attentiveness, mischief-making, and inherent protective juices comparable to those of a four-year-old Shar-pei.

And so it was--with a stuffed Blokehead smiling through the window and the atypical foursome of Julian Knotsofoolista, Jean Paul, Mary, and the aged, recovering ex-midwife enjoyably eating their fill—that an unannounced guest with less than noble intentions within the confines of his self crept unseen upon the immediate Dalilennonian countryside outside Ms. Prissy's home.

Since Ms. Prissy had such an array of guests, the unannounced intruder, whom we know as Poncho McTea, quickly surmised that now wasn't the ideal time to approach the troublesome hag. Instead, he'd have to wait until she was alone, then perform an act of whatever diabolicalness was in his heart. It was only a streak of luck, he sensed, that Ms. Prissy hadn't yet connected the face and name of Poncho McTea with the beating she'd received and, though he only was an accomplice that night, relayed such information to proper authorities.

McTea felt the need for patience, but not much patience because the more she talked with people about what happened along the garden wall, the better the chances were that his role in the messy affair would surface.

McTea stole away as he thought he'd come: unseen. Moments later, however, the same vantage from which Poncho McTea had viewed the party was filled by another onlooker, crack Officer Oliver Ogilvie.

"I'll be nuts in a week," mumbled Officer Ogilvie as he left this new, bizarre sight inside and around Ms. Prissy Hampshire's home to resume his strange assignment from good King Nocturnal to track the comings and goings of one of the good King's most trusted advisors. Indelibly locked in crack Officer Ogilvie's memory was the sight of laughing, mischievousness children; the frocked crazy man wearing red high-topped tennis shoes visibly Russian toe dancing (he did dance with spirit, thought Ogilvie,) through the window of Ms. Prissy's cottage; and the immobile donkey watching them.

"Just maybe," Ogilvie mumbled aloud as he turned to again follow McTea, "maybe good King Nocturnal is playing a joke on me, and soon he'll slap me on the butt and send me home with a six-pack of Michelob Light to share with my wife."

However, the good King never did.

Sextants and Baggy Britches

Once the good ship SlipSparrow was out to sea and the ropes of the captives tested and found secure, Manual McGetitdone set about the task of training Norbert Nodahead in the business of seamanship.

To be able accurately to pilot the vessel during daylight hours was the instructor's goal for pupil, but complications arose quickly.

For starters, poor Norbert's equilibrium found the adjustment from walking on land or the formerly engine-powered Eglicatan vessel, now in dry dock for lack of a Welch plug for the main metering jet of its carburetor, quite different from his state of equilibrium on the SlipSparrow's wind-driven decks. For, if the pudgy Eglicatan agent allowed his head to follow his roller-coaster like steps, as any good seaman understands, the results invariably were futile. Without fail, Norbert Nodahead lasted between zero and four minutes before his head and stomach would lead the miserable bloke to the ship's railing where, as seamen are want to say, " … he fed the fish …" on a regular basis.

Now, this turn of events pleased Manual McGetitdone not a whit because his plan was to thin the ranks of their captives and, with Norbert at the helm, spend many an hour below deck frolicking with Ms. Sylvia Smitharomance, who'd again jostled his hormones.

Since Nodahead obviously couldn't be at the railing "upchucking" and guiding the vessel at the same time, Manual alone was left as the vessel's only qualified, or even minimally qualified pilot.

Ms. Sylvia could learn quickly enough, he reasoned, but she at the helm would negate the highlight of his scheme.

As any seaborne or oceanborne upchucker can attest to, such is an extremely humiliating, debilitating, and weakening experience. Soon, no longer strong enough to make the necessary trips to the ship's railing, Norbert placed a bucket by his below-deck bunk and moaned over and over like a Haitian wind or a tired flue pipe in an abandoned wilderness cabin.

Ms. Sylvia took it upon herself to tend to the needs of the captives randomly strewn about the SlipSparrow's deck, strewn with as much cohesiveness as Porta-Potties at small college football games. She tried as best she could to shield the captives from the bright seasonal sun, and issued cupfuls of life-giving water from their bounteous onboard supply. Food for the voyage, however, had been stocked with far less than seven people in mind and had to be portioned out sparingly, if at all in the case of the four last-minute captives strewn about the deck like … oh, you get it.

Strong emotions pushed a lump into the throat of Ms. Smitharomance as she tended to the needs of Roger K. Rightjet and the lovely young lady who gazed upon Roger's every movement with doting puppy-love eyes.

Roger K., on the other hand, looked at Sylvia Smitharomance and involuntarily was moved by a desire to explore feelings and doubts long since buried, but not forgotten. Both Roger K. and Ms. Sylvia instinctively knew that their respective roles in the universe had been intertwined for a purpose, though neither had a clue what that purpose was.

At the other end of the spectrum, Malcolm Straight was madder than hell about being held captive with no charges filed against him. He ceaselessly voiced loud outbursts of profanity for everyone within earshot to hear, which pretty much included all on board and one low-flying albatross. Malcolm loudly cited some international nautical rule that said stealing a seaworthy vessel was akin to treason and downright disloyalty to good King Nocturnal, but his words carried little weight.

By late afternoon of that first day, Manual McGetitdone's nerves, dulled by Straight's ceaseless railings, were shot. And so, in a fit of bestial rage, McGetitdone bolted from the helm of the ship to where the loud Malcolm Straight was crying for justice, removed Straight's constraints, picked up the Dalilennonian advisor over his head, then held him beyond the ship's railing. At that precise moment, neither McGetitdone or, to an even greater extent, Straight, knew if the strong Eglicatanese diplomat was bluffing, or indeed would begin the process of thinning the captives right then and there.

Ms. Sylvia Smitharomance watched the entire scene without moving, interfering, or speaking. She sensed the experienced, scar-faced saboteur was too good of an agent to chuck the high-ranking Dalilennonian to the sharks, but was aware Roger K. Rightjet or any of the others might experience a different fate.

With Straight's objections suddenly reduced to a mere whimper, McGetitdone lifted the Dalilennonian advisor back on board ship and, again, tied him up.

As darkness began to fall on day one, Norman Expedience, still bound, summoned the Eglicatan lady with tight slacks and high heels, (Don't ask me why Ms. Sylvia Smitharomance was wearing high heels aboard a seafaring vessel, I'm just telling the story.) and quietly shared some thoughts in her attentive right ear.

She nodded, thanked him, and said his message would be relayed. Immediately, Ms. Smitharomance walked to where McGetitdone was manning the boat's sails, and a long discussion ensued, she repeatedly gesturing toward Norman Expedience.

Manual McGetitdone furrowed his brow in thought, pondered on her words long after Ms. Sylvia walked away, and tried to reflect on what needed to be done. Although tougher than nails, McGetitdone knew his masculinity had limitations, such as the need for sleep, and the information imparted to him by Ms. Sylvia Smitharomance offered a feasible option to his current dilemma.

And, once again, the plot thickened.

The stars overhead shone brightly that night, as they often do in warm climates, and a slightly less-than-full moon cast a yellowish-orange reflection on the trench-filled sea. As persons living near large bodies of water can attest to, celestial entities like the moon and off-hours sun can cast their brilliance toward the viewer with straight lines of reflected light: narrow, then wider like a Fiat's headlights; like the charted vision of an ancient, wise eagle; or even like what's witnessed through the slanted eyes of an octogenarian shaman.

Rocky Wilson

Such wondrous sights could have been appreciated by Manual McGetitdone early the next morning at the helm of the SlipSparrow had he been awake to see them.

Weariness of such magnitude rarely is forgiven at the wheel of an auto, where loud, crunching noises often accompany one's folly, sometimes after it's too late to rectify the damage. But, on a sailing vessel in calm weather, the damage is minimal, only adding to the amount of time needed to reach one's desired port, or destination.

Ms. Sylvia, seemingly undisturbed by Manual being asleep at the wheel, gently shook McGetitdone's strong shoulders and, when he opened his eyes, Manual was rewarded with one of Ms. Sylvia's rare smiles. They conversed quietly, then went separate directions to bring Norman Expedience and Norbert Nodahead to the ship's wheel. Once there, McGetitdone quizzed Mr. Expedience about the intricacies of sea navigation, found him an apt pupil, and turned him loose to guide the ship under the armed supervision of Norbert Nodahead, who professed to be feeling much better.

Then, an unusual thing happened that altered the course of this unusual sea voyage. Tired as he had to have been, Manual McGetitdone still was ready for some quick below-deck play, and grabbed Ms. Sylvia to join him. Hadn't she been acutely attentive to his masculine needs since leaving Eglicata, and even before?

But, as ALL know, women will be women, and, with her first true love aboard ship and in peril, Ms. Smitharomance informed the strong man with a scar on his face that she wasn't "in the mood" for such a tussle.

Now, if women are to be women, how much more so is it true that virile men are inclined to be proud? Much. And so it was that an unruly row developed between the two where masculine Manual was tempted to grab Ms. Smitharomance in an aggressive manner, somewhat like he'd done earlier when dangling Mr. Straight over the ship's rail, and forcibly get done what it was he wished to get done.

And yet, something trumped his desires, and that something was the very woman Sylvia Smitharomance was. For, instantaneously, with no coaching, Manual McGetitdone--by no means dull--sensed that during the many times she'd allowed him to possess her body, Ms. Sylvia never had abnegated any rights to her mind or soul.

Enraged, Manual McGetitdone stormed to his bunk, while the attractive temptress, unperturbed by Manual's outburst, went to take one more look at a sleeping Roger K. Rightjet

Then, she pattered away to sneak some a.m. z-z's of her own.

At the forefront of the vessel, Norbert Nodahead found comfort for the first time since coming aboard, and promptly fell asleep.

The plan had been in his thoughts for some time, so once Nodahead nodded off, Norman Expedience set about the intricate task of retooling each of the ship's many navigational devices to determine one's location at sea.

The sextant was first.

Since north was at point X, McGetitdone's charted destination was point Y, and the place Norman wanted to land the boat was point Z, all he had to do was move point X further skyward the equivalent number of degrees between Y and Z, move all the subsequent markings the same number of degrees, then sit back and calmly watch Manual McGetitdone guide the ship where he, Norman Expedience, had programmed it to go; not to the little port on Eglicata's north shore where a truck would be waiting to transport the bundled disadvantageous to the ailing fowlawarfare.

One has to admire the brilliance, the sheer ingenuity of Mr. Expedience to derive such a plan, for what could make more sense than allowing the culprits the opportunity to drive themselves to the jail? Or, as the would-be famous saying would go, had anyone thought of it and wished to verbalize it louder than a whisper, allow the culprits the opportunity to "stew in their own juices."

So, while Norbert Nodahead healed his weary body through the miracle of sleep, the sextant and all other miscellaneous nautical devices of a similar nature were altered, changed, and rearranged until only the crafty Norman Expedience knew when and where the ship would reach land. Or, at least he had the best guess. Those damned leftover parts and wires troubled Norman a bit, but he knew deep down that he'd done his best.

On the morrow, Manual McGetitdone complimented Norbert for his watchmanship, noted that the ship still was on course (according to the instrument panels,) and took the helm once again. In spite of his consuming anger when he'd gone to bed, Manuel had slept refreshingly well and, with favoring winds behind them, hoped to push the old tug hard enough to sight land by nightfall.

Still, Manual was more than a trifle troubled about the large number of folk on board, and, by using what to him was pure logic, determined Roger K. Rightjet was the first person in line for elimination. Straight, of course, must be kept alive or Herr McCoffee very well would make certain Manual would prefer he'd never returned from the voyage at all. And, in the case of a sudden storm or any other unforeseen event that might extend the duration of their sea voyage, the nautical-wise stranger could prove useful.

The woman? Let it be said that, as a whole, Manual McGetitdone was a firm believer in equal rights for women, and had no qualms in regards to throwing a female overboard. Yet, like many with a virile nature, the temporary captain was willing to make special allowances for such a woman as Ms. Nancy Droosha. Her inherent beauty, at least for Manual, added an element of desirability that superseded the common sense of a villain.

And so it was Roger K. Rightjet, and only Roger K. Rightjet who met Mr. McGetitdone's criteria for gangplankmanship. Or, as the late Capt. Hook would have said had Roger K. Rightjet had the misfortune of being teleported into Peter Pan's supposed presence at the worst of times, "I guess you'll have to do, Roger K., apparently Peter's not available and it's time to walk the plank."

Manual's elimination plan, however, didn't meet with immediate approval from his peers, let alone Roger K. Rightjet. Norbert advocated leaving Rightjet aboard without sharing any food or water rations, and Ms. Sylvia stated throwing Roger K. overboard would constitute a senseless act of power that soon would come before the ear of Eglicata's great leader, aka Herr McCoffee.

Please remember, it only had been hours earlier when this strong-willed, impulsive man--Manual McGetitdone by name--had been denied on another front of importance to him, and it was time, he felt, to let everyone know once and for all who called the shots on the seaborne world of the SlipSparrow.

And so, only a drum roll and gargantuan audience of boisterous, greasy-skinned pirates would have made the melodrama thicker as Roger K. Rightjet, the good guy, walked the gangplank with hands tied behind his back. Ms. Nancy was crying and sobbing profusely from an excellent viewing vantage, Mr. Straight vociferously was cursing McGetitdone for his non-Geneva Convention tactics, and Norman Expedience's nimble mind was racing posthaste trying to unshelf a workable plan to foil this diabolical scheme.

Roger K., apparently without alternatives, heroically was stepping forward to, shall we say, cast his fate to the wind; and Manual McGetitdone, who normally wasn't quite this evil, joyfully was prodding Rightjet ahead with a sharp stick, telling Roger K. not to worry because Roger's mother would love him no matter how he died.

McGetitdone laughed long and hard, sort of like Snidely Whiplash, but in a serious, noncartoonish manner.

Oh, it was a frightful time for those aboard the SlipSparrow and, had it not been as real as a reality television series, only could have been more scary had dozens of hungry, snapping crocodiles been in the water beneath the plank gazing upward to slash and fight for their next meal.

As McGetitdone ridiculed and chided the noble gristmiller, aka Roger K. Rightjet, and Ms. Nancy, God bless her soul, was graced with a fainting spell; as the future of our would-be hero was up in the air (or would that be out on a limb?) as few in this world have lived to tell of; while all this was in motion, Ms. Sylvia Smitharomance added one more piece to a plan of her making. Having earlier authorized Nodahead to move elsewhere to steer the craft and avoid the unpleasantness of witnessing the ordeal, Ms. Sylvia stole to the side of the rope-bound Norman Expedience, whispered in his ear with warm, steamy puffs of air, untied one of his arms, and repositioned herself at the rear of the boat.

Fast-forward precious seconds to the very instant Roger K. was jabbed in the butt one last time and, hands bound behind him, plummeted toward the ocean to what one would presume to be unavoidable death, with or without crocodiles.

It was a time average poets and novelists like to commemorate by saying 'time stood still,' but it didn't.

Instead, several events happened almost simultaneously.

With Malcolm Straight's near-hoarse voice spewing new levels of obscenities, Norman Expedience, positioned only ten meters from

McGetitdone, threw a knot of rope that struck Manual in the middle of his back. McGetitdone shifted his attentions from Roger K. and, in the exuberant thrill of victory, heartily laughed at a man foolish enough to blow his cover with only one hand free.

And so, you'd think that the bound body of yet one more of life's many would-be heroes would have drifted off to sea without a memorable act of true heroism, or even a fruitful venture in love to his credit.

And yet, the difference between "would have" and "did" is a variable, either huge or small, of universal magnitude and, in this particular instance, at fate's decree, it happened that the "would have" "did not."

A dormant love of some seven or eight years, about how long Calypso held Odysseus in her Gozitan cave--which is a rabbit trail we'll avoid at all costs because who knows how time was measured in the era of Greek mythology?—Ms. Sylvia, she being that dormant lover, fetched Roger K. from the sea at the end of a gaff hook and, once aboard, embraced him with warmth that had waited years for its release.

However, the embracing came easier, much easier, than the gaffing.

Not a lady of profound gaffing experience, Ms. Sylvia Smitharomance had the forethought to fish early and often for the fast-sinking almost hero. Her first gaff, for Roger K.'s bound hands annulled the possibility of him grabbing the pole, missed entirely, and the second grazed his head. Frantic, as Roger K. was heading downward, Ms. Sylvia made a mighty swipe in her final 'go' and nearly popped the eyes from R.K.R.'s sockets as she cleanly pierced the crotch of his trousers without the slightest of wounds to his person.

While being drug aboard upside down, the mechanics of which was no mean feat of accomplishment for a woman of such lovely, sometimes feminine stature as Sylvia Smitharomance, Roger K. swore never again to complain about baggy britches.

As it was, or should have been stated earlier, Ms. Sylvia loved him, untied him, and had Roger K. Rightjet crawl beneath the ship's wooden lifeboat, promising to bring provisions and water to him if he'd only stay put.

Since he really didn't have anywhere to go, Roger K. stayed under the lifeboat as promised.

And time continued to move forward.

The sun's rays aboard a seaborne vessel, especially in latitudes akin to where the SlipSparrow now was sailing, often are sources of intense heat compounded by warm reflections off a ship's white ashen deck. As the sun passed due overhead the SlipSparrow, sweat beaded on every brow.

Ms. Nancy was the only captive given provisions from the ship's dwindling food supply, and she needed it. Her strength waned as she moaned and wailed for the believed loss of her would-be lover, uncontrollably blubbering as if to expunge Roger K.'s memory through repeated gasps of grief and despair. To make things worse, other than occasional light relief when the ship's billowing sails would blot the sun temporarily, there wasn't much shade above deck, and even Ms. Nancy wasn't given permission to go below.

Not more than fifteen meters from the mourning Ms. Droosha, however, was the very man she mourned for and believed dead. By midday, Roger K. thought the wooden lifeboat he was under had transformed into a hellish sweatbox, and wasn't convinced the dramatic saving of his life had been with his best interests in mind.

Norman Expedience, at least on the surface, quickly acquiesced to McGetitdone's position of power, while fellow captive Malcolm Straight continued to vocally espouse, though not as loud, his opinion of the existent state of affairs on the SlipSparrow until he was gagged, as well as bound.

With McGetitdone at the helm, the two non-navigating advisors to Herr McCoffee moved below deck to get their rest. Nodahead would be called again to watch the foreigner guide the ship if land wasn't sighted as soon as Manual hoped.

The winds were favorable, and Manual continuously sought the horizon to spot rocky shores. But, as the afternoon progressed with no land in sight, McGetitdone, puzzled, began reviewing the charts. Something was amiss.

By sunset, McGetitdone's state of quandary had tilted toward anxiety. If indeed they were adrift, as it was beginning to appear, the amount of food aboard was insufficient to keep the six remaining passengers (for Manual didn't know of Rightjet's presence under the lifeboat where Roger K. had "stripped for gym" to combat the heat,) alive for long.

McGetitdone pondered who next must be pared from among his shipmates until Norbert Nodahead arrived to take the evening watch.

This sighting, were Manual McGetitdone a Christian, (though we've no evidence to support such a thought,) could have been construed as providential in Manual's eyes. Was Nodahead's arrival three minutes before he was scheduled for helm relief a sign from a higher realm that Norbert Nodahead, while McGetitdone was pondering this grave matter, was the precise answer to the question troubling Mr. McGetitdone?

McGetitdone grinned at Norbert, a man who hadn't reached his position of prominence without being a likeable fellow. Outgoing, the Eglicatan with the plump body had learned to deal with many, many people, always nodding in agreement at the proper times and lending his attentive focus to the vanities of aristocratic society. Through people he'd met and impressed with his agreeable mindfulness, Norbert, even before Herr McCoffee's bold, empowering coup, steadily had climbed upon the social scene of Eglicata; taking every opportunity along the way to, with a nodding smile, add coins to his pockets.

For it was the lure of riches that gave the little man impetus, and it was only through a byproduct of learning that he still was in Herr McCoffee's cabinet. That byproduct was his personal epiphany, something that seems natural to most, that political power truly provided Norbert Nodahead a lucrative avenue to add to his fast-growing golden coffers of wealth and prosperity.

Norbert was valuable to Herr McCoffee's inner circle because he met everybody and remembered what each of them had said. Plus, much to the powerful Herr's delight, Norbert had no real political aspirations of his own. His loyalty only was to money; and the quieter his role in obtaining that money, in Norbert's eyes, the better.

As Herr McCoffee had turned more and more to the alluring world of power, warfare, and intrigue, the Herr increasingly was surprised at just how effective the little nodding round man could be.

Still, Norbert didn't like political intrigue and began to desire more and more money for the jobs he was asked to perform. Unlike those he worked with, Norbert was an independent businessman, with no government pension, who was well paid for duties he excelled at.

Each time Norbert's asking price went up, which was becoming a common occurrence, Herr McCoffee's eyelids were beginning to rise accordingly, as he, too, had a direct interest in monetary wealth.

The last time Nodahead's asking price had been elevated, and McCoffee's eyelids done the same, Manual McGetitdone secretly had been called in for a session with the Eglicatanese national chief. He'd been told, in so many words, that the death of Norbert Nodahead--whose mind carried far too much knowledge to even consider the possibility of a pat on the back and a pink-slip into retirement--in the line of duty would be less than a calamity for the nation of Eglicata.

Their conversation roughly was akin to one held thousands of years earlier between King David and Joab in regards to Uriah the Hittite, although McCoffee and McGetitdone's desires to kill Norbert Nodahead had no known ties to Bathsheba.

And so, with the memory of that meeting with Herr McCoffee fresh in his mind, McGetitdone took special note of the timely arrival of Norbert Nodahead that night at the helm of the SlipSparrow. It was as if Norbert had arrived in answer to a prayer Manual McGetitdone never submitted. The thought of prayer evoked a chuckle from the moody strongman who, the question of whom next would be sacrificed being resolved, need now devise a plan to achieve his ends; or, more precisely, Norbert Nodahead's end.

Norbert was instructed by Manual McGetitdone to study the ways of a seafarer under the tutelage of Norman Expedience, his thinking being that the activity would keep the two of them occupied as he went below deck to awaken Ms. Sylvia Smitharomance to discuss the imminent demise of Norbert Nodahead. For, even with all his brawn and brutality, Manual McGetitdone was a wise man who needed the competent lady advisor to Herr McCoffee as a future ally; not only at this time aboard ship, but upon their return to Eglicata when the popular Nodahead's death would be discussed at length.

During the earlier secret meeting between Manual and Herr McCoffee, McGetitdone had held firm in his belief, if the need arose, that Ms. Sylvia be taken into confidence. McCoffee had argued the point, only relenting when the underlying logic of his henchman's words came through to him.

Norbert Nodahead indeed was a more popular public servant than McGetitdone, at least in part because of Manual's disdain for public consensus, and without corroboration on the story to be told of Norbert's death by someone of such stature as Ms. Sylvia Smitharomance, the pudgy advisor's death might look exactly like what it was to be: murder.

Now, on an elderly seagoing vessel such as the SlipSparrow, or at least on the SlipSparrow itself, there exists a long tube running from the captain's quarters below deck to three locations aboard the ship. This system of communication had been installed many years earlier to allow the captain, whomever he might have been at the time, to communicate elsewhere on the ship without leaving his all-important homey post where he could recline sipping brandy and watching NFL football on a color television set no one beyond the captain's inner circle of friends knew existed.

Traditionally, the communication tubes afforded the commanding officer power to impact the lives of all aboard ship at any time of his choosing, 24/7. The barked command, "Get your butt(s) up here," was a directive with such an ominous tone that chosen sailors hurriedly scrambled at all hours of the night to, with hearts pounding, tepidly seek admittance to the captain's quarters with light knocks to learn the reason for their summons. An equal number of sailors, however, awoke at night, soused in sweat from frightening, unrealistic dreams where, (in their dreams, mind you,) the same captain had called for an accounting of the sweating sailor's undisclosed deeds that the captain had no way of knowing about.

The tube, or rather series of three tubes branching from their source in the captain's quarters, led to two places in the general sleeping quarters and to the ship's helm as to where the SlipSparrow would next sail were put into practice. The original design called for the placement of a cork, or stop, at each of the four ends of the three tubes, and had been drafted by a Naval Academy engineer even more gifted than Norman Expedience.

In days of yore, the sailors who nightly rotated to sleep beneath the corks in the sailors' sleeping quarters knew that a conk on the head was forewarning that the captain--once he caught his breath, as popping the cork in itself required no small emission of air--soon would be demanding someone's posthaste presence in his, the captain's quarters; and it was the sailor beneath the cork's responsibility to awaken the summoned sailor, remind him quickly to brush his teeth, and make certain that individual reported to the captain in a timely manner.

As time went on, however, the third captain of the SlipSparrow surmised that his perpetual earaches were due to blowing on the confounded cork in his stateroom when he'd prefer watching the Steelers and Bills go at it. And so, he had the other three stops permanently removed, and his kept in place. New sailors to the vessel quickly learned that lightly knocking on the captain's door was far less painful than blowing on the captain's cork.

The ship's communication system evolved, and the word 'evolved' isn't used without premeditation, until it became like an intercom system in the most modern of secondary schools where sneaky superintendents listen in on classroom activities with no one the wiser. But schools, as a whole, have more of interest to listen to than the bunks of sailors, especially sleeping sailors, and, in time, the SlipSparrow's secondary communication system went out of use; meaning the tube in the captain's suite, as well as those by the sailors' bunks and ship's helm were plugged indefinitely.

That long-standing arrangement had been changed early during our current voyage when McGetitdone had popped the cork of the tube in Ms. Sylvia's sleeping quarters, the captain's suite, so her sleeping breaths could bedazzle him vicariously as he merrily guided the good ship forward from his position at its helm.

But, as is repeated o'er and o'er in the good Black Book, the actions of the lusty will be repaid one day, and it was on this very evening, while Manual McGetitdone spoke below with the alluring Ms. Smitharomance, that Norbert Nodahead made an accidental discovery that would change his life. Already bored with gawking into the moonlight; acquiring what, for him, was useless nautical information from an eager instructor; and keeping vigilant watch over a foreigner who showed no outward signs of dissatisfaction with the status quo, Norbert playfully pulled a plug at the extreme bottom left of the ship's nautical control panel, near three dangling, unattached wires, and was astonished not only to hear human voices, but his own name spoken as well.

Norbert's normally red face drained in color as the diabolical plot for his undoing was outlined for him to hear through the tube. He knew the foreigner at the ship's helm, too, was listening, (the system's sound quality being quite good,) and that gave him joy, because the man whom heretofore had been an enemy and a captive, suddenly was an ally.

The scheme, which Ms. Smitharomance voiced no objection to, was for the cunning lady with foxy legs to coax Norbert Nodahead into her bedchambers where, with stealth and swiftness, Manual McGetitdone would undo the pudgy man's life with nary a final nod from Norbert.

Oh, diabolical it was, with uncleanness akin to Lady Macbeth lurking in the wings. To be done in short order was the ploy, and McGetitdone went fast-aloft to replace his crew of two, explaining he couldn't sleep and was sending Nodahead below and Expedience back to the ropes.

An oft quoted phrase, most often quoted by the mediocre of mind, says 'great minds work alike.' Another phrase, though not quoted as often, might say, 'speaking alike is dumb luck.'

Anyway, as the alluring Ms. Smitharomance and Norbert Nodahead met in the hallway below deck, none of their four eyes reflecting much faith, each said independently, and jointly, "I'd better go, …" paused for the briefest of moments, then in harmony again began, "I need to go …"

Normally such instances are conducive to laughter, but t'was not a jovial moment, so Ms. Smitharomance said, "Screw it. I'll meet you back in my state room in a couple minutes," then walked directly to the women's loo. Nodahead thought she was on to something, and went to the men's bathroom to prepare as well for what was to come.

En route to their respective bathrooms, however, Ms. Sylvia paid a visit to Roger K. Rightjet, and Norbert a visit to Norman Expedience.

As is said, the lusty, the evil, the malicious will get theirs in the end, and the only one aboard meeting that definition, Manual McGetitdone, was moments away from a double dose.

The strangest of bedfellows, the long-legged Ms. Smitharomance and the ruddy-cheeked, pudgy Norbert N., met as planned, and went into action as Manual had arranged. As they went into action, and a mighty action it was considering Norbert's unimpressive stature, both Sylvia and Norbert, by nature and not design, forgot the perilous position the little man was in.

Yet, Manual McGetitdone, stealthily creeping down the corridor to Ms. Sylvia's stateroom, was not to get it done that eve for, armed with clubs, Roger K. Rightjet, loosed by Ms. Sylvia, and Norman Expedience, loosed by Norbert Nodahead, timed their bops perfectly, and felled the ruffian from either side with synchronized precision.

After tying Manual's wrists and ankles, Norman Expedience returned topside and Roger K. went to Ms. Sylvia's sleeping quarters to tell the Eglicatan diplomats not to worry, that all was safe.

Outside her door, however, Rightjet heard joyful moans of bliss and glee coming from within, and opted to back away and leave the frolicking couple to their devices until daylight …

… the same daylight that should return them within sight of Dalilennon, said Norman Expedience with pride sweeping upward from his shoe tops. For it was only then that he explained to his fellow travelers how cleverly he'd rewired the ship's entire navigational system without even referring to a manual.

Drafting a Priest

Priest Precious was taken aback when good King Nocturnal, not noted for his jocularity, solemnly proposed the priest's promotion to one of the most prominent posts in all of Dalilennon.

His reaction was anticipated.

The priest's: "I'm already lacking time to tend to the needs of my church. How could I possibly do justice to an added task? …" "Aren't the needs of the church and government oftentimes contradictory? What, in such cases, would I do? …" and "Would my people still come to me for confession, or see me as an arm of the good King?" all were parlays to thwart the good King's wishes that came as no surprise to good King Nocturnal; in fact, had been strategically anticipated by the good King many hours in advance.

And so it went: dinner being overtaken by darkness and the three of them, for the Mrs. King participated as a quiet observer and listener, huddled in the newly torch-lit palatial garden where they were graced by a gentle, warm breeze that wafted a curl of soft, flowing hair across the Mrs. King's forehead. That curl, in the good King's eyes, added an element of cuteness to the appearance of his bride.

Having determined earlier in the day that Priest Precious WOULD become his new advisor, His Excellency patiently waded through a torrent of priestly objections to his palatial proposal before beginning to present his case in earnest.

But, Priest Precious's objections to the idea had deeper roots than the good King had envisioned. When the good King said a healthy government provided the stage for a healthy church, the feisty priest retaliated by saying any time he dedicated to the government of

Dalilennon would negatively impact his church; arguing the point he was mortal and there was only so much of him to go around.

Many hours did they disagree, and many hours did Priest Precious hold his ground. He held it even more firmly as time elapsed, as the good King's initial volley of flattery dissipated into the night air.

The Mrs. King sat quietly through the discussion, only leaving once to seek a small cream tart to help curb the stress she was absorbing from their seeming inability to agree.

While she was gone, a tired-looking police officer entered and spoke quietly into the good King's attentive left ear. During that interchange between crack Officer Oliver Ogilvie and good King Nocturnal, a quiet interchange Priest Precious barely was privy to (what do you expect, he wasn't an advisor yet?) the priest did hear his good King, at the conclusion of that private discussion, commend the officer for a job well done and send him home.

Upon Officer Olilvie's exit and the Mrs. King's return, the previous discussion was resumed. Still, no progress was made.

Then, Priest Precious, acting nearer to being a tired politician than an ever-patient servant of the Lord, pushed the issue, and asked the good King if he even had a choice in the matter. Without waiting for a response, Priest Precious stated that if he did have a choice, he'd kindly thank the good King for the offer and remain in his current capacity with the church.

Let us reflect at this pivotal moment of our story.

History has recorded many an instance where the fairest of rulers have found need to enforce new levels of strictness when the affairs of state began heading into dangerous waters. Franklin D. Roosevelt was one such ruler, and Chairman Mao another. Whether each one's chosen level of strictness passed justifiability tests is left for God and the muses to ponder. Enough said that these two men of the past, in positions of power like good King Nocturnal, chose to deal with imminent threats by making edicts and decisions not necessarily understood or appreciated at the time.

Such a thrust of pressure was good King Nocturnal facing that evening in the cooling palatial garden. Not for at least thirty years, probably much longer, had Dalilennon's future been in such a precarious position, and to the good King's way of thinking, the help this one man could provide to Dalilennon because of his calm spirit and penetrating mind was of vital importance. In addition, of course, was the hotline to heaven thing that the Mrs. King had informed him of.

And so, after moments of quietness, good King Nocturnal audibly responded to Priest Precious's query about whether or not he, the man of God, had a choice in the matter.

"No, good priest," he said, "you have no options if you wish to remain on Dalilennon. From now until three months' time has expired, you will serve as an advisor to your King (since he was speaking of himself, the good King modestly refrained from using the adjective 'good'.) Once that time has elapsed, you may remain on staff or resign at your leisure. I expect full cooperation."

Promptly rising to his feet, Priest Darrell Precious asked to be dismissed.

He required time for prayer, meditation, and introspection.

Officer Ogilvie Stops a Grapefruit

It was midmorning when Officer Ogilvie arose. He kissed his wife, had breakfast with white coffee, dressed as Dalilennonian businessmen of the day were want to dress and, with the warm, bright sun beating down on his back, trudged, with somewhat less than decisive steps, back toward police headquarters.

His wife, good woman whom she was, had asked little about this new assignment that, contrary to anything he'd been required previously to perform for God, country, and the Dalilennonian police department, was keeping him out late at night. Mrs. Officer Ogilvie momentarily had wondered if another woman was taking his time, but only fleetingly in a 'not really interested' sort of way since marital unfaithfulness in church-conscious Dalilennon was a rarity. Besides, she thought, Oliver and I are quite content.

The police station was Officer Ogilvie's first stop and, as expected, the chief barked at length about Oliver's sudden inability to arrive at work on time. Crack Officer Oliver Ogilvie's orders were from none other than the good King and too confidential, aka secretive, for even the chief of police to know about. Hence, the highest ranking police officer on the isle of fancy lowered the guns on Oliver's tardiness.

Officer Ogilvie took it, all of it, like a man.

"Yes sir … no sir," he responded with timeliness and peacefulness until the chief of police temporarily had worked himself into a rage and back again, finally dismissing Officer Ogilvie with a tart, "Do you understand?"

"Yes, sir."

"Well, go about your business then," barked the chief in curt dismissal, eager to be done with Ogilvie's laxness and move on to his morning tea.

It would be safe to assume that the police chief had no idea Officer Ogilvie had an assignment from good King Nocturnal. In fact, one could bet a nickel the chief didn't know if Officer Ogilvie was working on any assignment at all.

Ordinarily, life at the station was so mundane that, other than keeping the premises spotless, the biggest events on a consistent basis came when local schools would bring children to tour the place of justice where law and order was upheld. On those occasions, most of Dalilennon's police officers would be present in their bright blues to tug up their pants in dignified manners and answer questions in deep, authoritative voices.

On days when children weren't scheduled to visit and learn first-hand just how important the police department was to the daily lives of the people of Dalilennon, the officers performed other critical tasks. Those tasks might include, out of the chief's view of course, lounging on the hard-backed stone bench in front of the main grocery store to watch tikes play in the isle's warm, spewing fountain; slipping into the rear of a darkened pub for a quick game or two of Crazy 8's or spades; or strolling beyond the downtown area on especially sunny, warm days to keep an eye on women and children spread out on blankets to gain suntans and play on the isle's sandy beaches.

These are samples of what the local policemen did best; calling it "visibility patrol" if the chief of police asked them.

But on this warm day, crack Officer Oliver Ogilvie's visibility patrol took him past the fountain, past the card games, beyond the city limits, and past the seaside bathers on a focused journey to the base of the isle's one mountain where Ms. Prissy Hampshire's house stood.

The only reason the local police force, skilled as they were, had failed to interview Ms. Prissy previously was their unwritten desire to avoid, at all costs, someone as ornery as the craggy Ms. Prissy Hampshire. Indeed, on more than one occasion, she'd expressed her disdain for both the Dalilennonian police department as a whole and its government that had "cheated" her, to use Ms. Prissy's wording, out of her rightful midwifery pension.

Recent events had made Officer Ogilvie accustomed to performing less than palatable police assignments and, at the request of good King Nocturnal himself, Ogilvie now was rightly prepared to visit the old hag in her home: unless, of course, that frigging donkey felt otherwise.

Blokehead moaned from an overdose of disadvantageous when the crack Officer arrived, so Officer Oliver Ogilvie walked unimpeded to Ms. Prissy's front door, and knocked.

Keep in mind that Ms. Prissy Hampshire may have been near death only days before, even bedridden at the moment of Officer Ogilvie's knock and verbal assent to step inside unseen, but the outright impertinence of a Dalilennonian patrolman coming to her home created an uprising within the wrinkled old lady that nothing less than a direct edict from the good King, if even that, could quell.

With the agility of a fifteen-year-old baseball player from the Dominican Republic, the aged crag was up and throwing, at Ogilvie, anything her hands could touch. Wall pictures, pillows, shoes, and pens; silver chalices, spoons, crayons, and glass wrens: all were cast once the kindly knock and creaky "Come in" revealed the personage of crack Officer Oliver Ogilvie at Ms. Prissy's doorstep.

When Ms. Prissy began moving toward her reefer preparing to resume the fight with a new arsenal of frozen-food-style weapons, Ogilvie's defenses waned momentarily and he was hit smack in the chest by a big pink grapefruit. Oliver gasped for air, and the wrinkled old lady emitted a loud cackle of pleasure.

At that point, crack Officer Oliver Ogilvie lost his cool and, bawling like a Brahma bull, charged the old hag. Within seconds, and not without receiving a long fingernail scratch along his back, Officer Ogilvie had the lady plunked to her bed and, as if by magic, acting her age.

Blokehead patronizingly smiled at what was transpiring before him, and Ms. Prissy said, "Y'er a real ruffian, you are. We might be friends yet," and laughed long and loud until Ogilvie's rage subsided like snow in sunshine. Ogilvie began to chuckle at the craziness that was happening; the craziness he now was part and parcel of.

Officer Ogilvie went about the cottage salvaging what he could after their brief, but animated, fracas, noting the confounded grapefruit that had struck him, on the floor by the door, wasn't even bruised. As he gathered miscellaneous items and restored the bare premises to its previous state, crack Officer Ogilvie told Ms. Prissy why'd he'd come, possibly revealing more than prudence required when he spoke to her about the man he'd been following, one Poncho McTea.

The name meant little to Ms. Prissy, but descriptions of title and appearance convinced the ex-midwife that Mr. McTea was the same man she'd warned Roger K. Rightjet about not many days earlier, the man who'd been on the wall the night she'd been "unjustly smacked" on the side of her face.

At the very instant these details were being shared between the craggy Ms. Hampshire and a police ruffian who might yet become a friend of hers, Blokehead's gorged stomach took a gastric turn for the better and, at long last, he again was free, at least gingerly, to move about. The donkey's suddenly retuned senses now smelled a scoundrel in their midst, yet Blokehead placidly remained contented and warm in the morning sunshine and, in spite of his new awareness of dangers afoot (ahoof?), was unable to perform any constructive acts of heroism to protect the unprotected.

Inertia, even for the most loyal of donkeys, if they are overfed, can be an overriding force.

Officer Ogilvie warned Ms. Prissy of the danger she faced from many unknown realms, and promised to help and protect her as best he could. Then, he left the cottage for a scenic hike back to town.

Poncho McTea, lurking in the shadows, watched Officer Ogilvie leave Ms. Prissy's abode. The conniving double agent knew the terrain along the base of the mountain better than most, and raced ahead of Officer Oliver Ogilvie with one thought, and only one thought on his mind.

Violence, once first inception is contrived within one's soul, is hard to step away from. It creates in villains and potential villains a vacillating vacuum between potential disclosure and self-destruction. And, to make matters worse, like a wayward dog killing sheep, normally it's only the initial kill that carries with it any residue of remorse.

And it was that difficult "initial kill" that weighted McTea's mind as he raced ahead of Officer Ogilvie. Or, more accurately, it was the additional time such a kill would buy the double diplomat who only needed to stay alive until Eglicata, armed with the disadvantageously fed fowlawarfare, took over the island and rewarded Poncho for his long, laborious service for country; and, of course, service for his mother, she being a healthy ninety-two-year-old who happily tugged down two packs of Pall Mall cigarettes a day back in Eglicata.

McTea ran ahead of Ogilvie, took a shortcut possibly few people other than himself and Julian Knotsofoolista knew about, then lurked and waited.

The ideal location for this planned act of self-serving espionage brought memories back to Poncho McTea; it being the same high, stone wall he, Manual McGetitdone, and Ms. Sylvia--"sweet" Sylvia, he mused, thinking of a long-ago, too brief encounter with the foxy lady in an Eglicatan Men's Loo--had stood upon when Blokehead and Ms. Prissy Hampshire had interrupted their late-night nefarious doings.

While climbing the grated gate that separated the outside world from the diabolically planted disadvantageous garden on this warm Dalilennonian day, Poncho McTea, the gardener responsible for the crops inside, wrestled a sizeable stone to the top of the wall. His ploy was to hang from the opposite side of the stone barrier, then scramble atop the wall once Officer Ogilvie passed. Since the path below paralleled the wall for some distance, McTea could pick up his stone, follow unseen from above on the wide rock wall, jump at a moment of his choosing and, during his descent, savagely whop the patrolman upon the head with the big stone. He knew his plan was fiendish, and might not meet the approval of his 92-year-old, cigarette-smoking mother, but it seemed a necessary next step to keep his role in this devilish Eglicatan scheme under wraps.

Besides, having attended a few Catholic services in his day, McTea thought his whole plot was providential when he discovered a near-perfect foothold to maintain his balance on the side of the wall opposite Officer Ogilvie's approach.

Time passed slowly on this day for the would-be assassin, and thoughts of every kind rambled through his mind. A memory of his mother slapping him on the butt for an early offense in school he never was sure he'd committed; a memory of the strange relationship between he and his cousin, the Herr, that always had been one of convenience rather than friendship or love; and a memory of the day he'd been caught romancing a lady t'was not his to romance and the following week's assignment "of an important, long-range nature" to Dalilennon that, after what seemed like eternity, finally was nearing the closure he'd dreamed so long and hard for.

These were the immediate thoughts on Poncho McTea's mind as he pondered, crouched, mused, and waited.

It was hot along the wall, and uncomfortable. A darting honeybee rode a heat wave close to Poncho's face, causing him to swear and swipe at the floating insect as if the bee's intent was to harm him, not simply to enjoy God's sunshine and explore new options during a short life. Tropical seashore bushes gently waved below him, hinting of the day's first breeze. Island birds, normally an ongoing source of music and merriment, were subdued; only chirping occasionally without enthusiasm.

Distant footsteps became audible, and Poncho McTea's adrenaline began to pump, pushing strength into his forearms as if he were Popeye seconds after tossing down a can of spinach.

… Only a few more seconds …

… and Poncho drew himself upon the top of the flat wall, picked up the rock in one sweeping motion, and began preparing for the kill. And it was at that very instant that the would-be assassin, poised to make his first kill, had the bottom drop out of his stomach, figuratively, as his diabolical intentions irrevocably were put on hold.

For, looking back up at him with the most irritating of grins was none less, nor any more, than Julian Knotsofoolista, who broke into a childish skip and began singing with one finger planted to his lips, "This little light of mine, I'm gonna let it shine, let it shine, let it shine, all the time."

Knowing crack Officer Oliver Ogilvie to be close behind, McTea promptly made the decision to abandon his preordained plan of attack on the adroit Dalilennonian police officer, jumped to the ground outside the wall near the merry, singing, want-to-be priest with what in McTea's eyes was an irritating grin, and hurried away to again ponder how to combat these confounded coincidences that consistently refuted the best schemes of devilishness he could devise.

Julian's Biography

As can be imagined, Julian Knotsofoolista hadn't always roamed the caverns of the Dalilennonian coastline tossing out one-liners or two-liners to anyone with ears to hear. In fact, he'd only been on the island, or at least back on the island, for about five years.

Julian had been raised an only child on Dalilennon, somewhat of a rarity in such a Catholic-rich nation without televisions: meaning married couples normally went to bed at the same time instead of one spouse staying up later than the other to watch the day's last clips of televised news or Jay Leno. J. K. had his basic church and school needs tended to and, as often as not, picked up a decent meal of vegetables and chicken stew whenever his mother felt inclined to cook.

Pardon, but we must take yet another retreat in time.

You see, childbirth, or rather the giving of such, had been a most traumatic experience for Julian's mother who'd bled mightily until, as a last resort, perplexed physicians had called upon the island's cantankerous midwife who'd hastily located the ruptured artery and held it closed until the supposedly skilled doctors in white could be instructed by Ms. Prissy Hampshire about what needed to be done to repair the damage and save the life of Julian Knotsofoolista's mother. To their credit, the normally staunch Dalilennonian doctors had scrambled for and helped man the tools requested by Ms. Prissy, and the lives of the very young mother and her newborn son had been saved.

The ordeal had been most draining for the unwed mother and she'd remained in bed for months on-end, dutifully giving suck to her son and morosely lamenting both what, to her, was a loss of womanhood (she having lost the capacity to give birth to any more children,) and her most pitiable plight as an unwed mother in a nation where unwed mothers practically were unheard of, and wholly unwanted.

Julian's father had been an adventurous sailor who, along with his shipmates, had spent two days and two nights on Dalilennon before catching out-puffing winds that took him world's away without knowledge or care of Julian's existence.

Being a bastard was enough of a handicap for any Dalilennonian child, but the added dimension of being a half-breed in a supposedly thoroughbred kingdom made life downright difficult.

While growing up, Julian experienced many morose days and had few friends.

A memorable 'up' moment came for Julian at age nine when, while chasing birds by the downtown fountain bench, he was approached by a kind man who stooped to share a secret. Without compromising king/constituent confidentiality, the man spoke nonsense nine-year-olds either fail to understand or completely forget when the next flock of birds lands nearby.

The man asked Julian what wish he most wanted to come true.

Without any semblance of hesitation, the Knotsofoolista boy asked to meet his father, of course, and the kindly man, whom we know to be good King Nocturnal, instantly surmised this to be a wish of unfulfillable proportions. Julian's back-up wish, aka his secondary wish, was to become the proud owner of something he'd first heard of that very day--a skateboard.

Not an easy assignment on Dalilennen, and when the good King's search for this novel item went into multiple years, the Knotsofoolista child, growing older and more cynical, lost faith in the promise, and in his good King.

Not having forgotten his inability to deliver on the promise of a skateboard, the good King came to Julian once more in the boy's early teenage years to see if the lad was willing to divert his aspirations to a third wish. This time, upon Julian's request, the lad was extended the opportunity to leave Dalilennon in exchange for a life at sea, as he believed his greatly romanticized father had lived.

Had he been older, J.K. likely would have anticipated the ingrained folly of the proposed voyage he was about to embark on. But, being an impressionable, unhappy lad of 14, any opportunity to leave Dalilennon for uncharted waters appeared golden.

Like his father before him, Julian left without saying goodbye to his already aging mother, and within months after his departure, her charge on earth completed, she died quietly and alone. Ironically enough, it was good King Nocturnal who discovered her body, having come to make good on a wish from years past by transferring ownership of a hard-wheeled skateboard. But, by that time, both Julian and his mother had moved on.

Had Julian Knotsofoolista been age 15 instead of 14 when he left for sea, J.K. might have suspected something was amiss when he first learned that he, an inexperienced cabin boy, and the ship's captain formed a bare-bones seafaring crew of two. But he only was 14 at the time, and it took Julian a few days to come to that realization.

Julian learned shortly after departure that his captain, too, had been granted a good King Nocturnal wish and, unlike Julian Knotsofoolista's wish, it had been granted quickly in the form of a particular ship equipped to seek 'a land to be saved.'

It took the young cabin boy no time at all to determine that his new captain neither was a man of the sea or a man of sanity.

By the hour, Captain Courageous, as Julian was instructed to address him, stood by the ship's foresail ordering the sail be yanked to and fro for maximum speed, and not direction. Now and again, Captain Courageous would blurt out profane truisms that had as much context to his and Julian's seaborne status as the wayward vessel over which he now purported control did to charted nautical direction.

Being an impressionable youngster, Julian Knotsofoolista initially thought the phrase "Ayetoo Brute" was a learned nautical term describing the process involved in altering the ship's course.

But phrases that followed from the lips of the voyage's helmsman soon confirmed Julian's fears that, indeed, he was adrift with a madman.

For strange quotes such as: "To err is human, to forgive divine" and "Satisfaction, even after one has dined well, is not so interesting and eager a feeling as hunger;" … what did they have to do with the sunrise or pink, late-day clouds that were of far more significance in J.K.'s eyes?

Still, much as Julian doubted the seafaring skills of Captain Courageous, he doubted his own seafaring abilities even more, and saw no recourse but to quietly go about his work of cooking, cleaning, swabbing, and polishing the captain's eyeglasses until a better life-alternative for him arose.

On the fourth day after departure, however, the natural law of magnetism brought the two of them together in a volatile collision.

It was late afternoon, hot, and the wind had dimmed to a whisper. The country-saving captain had no "sail" to catch, so began ordering Julian fore and aft for everything from bottled water to the lifeboat. Like a packrat, Julian Knotsofoolista dutifully fetched every fetchable upon the boat until everything from food to pitch caulking was, as instructed, placed at the captain's feet.

And then, as if chest-high in ocean surf at the moment the tide reverses itself, Captain Courageous, like the schizophrenic he might have been, suddenly did an about-face and yelled, "Fool!! Why are all these precious perishables laying willy-nilly about the deck waiting for a storm to wash them away?" Then, the No. 1 sailor on the small seaborne vessel erupted into a tirade of magnanimous proportions, using foul sailor-type language inappropriate any place other than at sea, and was far from having adequately expressed himself, at least to his own satisfaction, when Julian Knotsofoolista timidly said …

" … but I thought …"

Now, on Julian's part, those three words were a big mistake. So much so that Captain Courageous--deeming such utterances were of mutinous proportions because they obviously questioned his authority as 'top dog' on the ship--ordered the "treasonous scallywag" adrift in a lifeboat, without food or water.

From fire to the frying pan, or from the frying pan to the fire, he knew not which, but J.K. soon was lowered into the misleadingly calm sea and gradually lost contact with Captain Courageous and the larger boat the captain was in.

Many stories have been told about persons adrift at sea, and probably most of them are true. The scorching sun; the tantalizingly undrinkable water; the steady, lapping ocean waves; the mental wanderings to and away from the pains and injustices of reality; the occasional bird looking like a goddess overhead; the troughs and peaks that get deeper and higher as the accursed wind makes its face known--the absolute solitude.

Each of these horrors and anything more a 14-year-old mind could conjure up did young Julian Knotsofoolista experience over the course of three days of suffering. On multiple occasions he grabbed his tongue to check if it was swelling, and assumed the end was near.

But fate would allow no such thing.

After dark following the third day, an abrupt clunk awoke J.K. and, his heart thumping uncontrollably inside his chest, Julian scurried to see what manner of thing his lifeboat had come in contact with. Was he aground and needing to swim ashore? Was drinking water soon to be found?

With sleep now gone from his eyes, and pupils dilated in excitement, Julian Knotsofoolista's optimism was replaced with immediate terror when he realized whose boat his lifeboat had encountered. For, looking down at him from the deck of the larger vessel was none other than Captain Courageous.

But, what a difference three days can make!

Julian's fears of again being cast away in the night proved to be unfounded this 'go' as the inconsistent captain was most willing to share his decks with a fellow sailor cast adrift "on the seas of misfortune." As if J.K.'s appearance and soul had changed one-hundred percent from the child whose fate had been up for grabs three days earlier, Julian Knotsofoolista now was viewed as a heroic fellow seaman, not a mutinous cabin boy.

Captain Courageous, much to his or maybe good King Nocturnal's credit, had brought along ample provisions for the journey, and the last ten days at sea, at least for young Julian Knotsofoolista, were quite pleasant. He learned much about sails and how to rig them into and out of the wind. And he became the ship's navigator, knowing the general direction desired and moving toward it by references to the sun, moon, and stars.

At long last, land was sighted, and the two sailors beached their craft and found themselves in a busy world of people that took no notice of two new arrivals. Their questions of those they encountered fell on deaf ears, although the people seemed friendly enough and willing to point the way.

Again, it was direction and no real purpose that propelled the much wiser 14-year-old across roads and through villages, always asking simple questions and always being pointed in a consistent general direction.

Captain Courageous, in a prepared official proclamation, announced to Julian Knotsofoolista his belief that this new land didn't seem to be in need of salvation and, if his fellow mariner didn't oppose the idea, he, Captain Courageous, was of a mind to return to the boat and push off for uncharted waters.

Julian, who didn't mind in the least, trudged onward and began to sense that the only reason he didn't feel like a total stranger here was because everyone was a foreigner in this very big land. He'd become so accustomed to the pointing of a finger as the answer to every question he asked that it came as a shock when one man in his fifties responded to his query in a quiet, soothing voice, "You speak Dalilennonianese."

And so it happened that this man, who had a son two years older than Julian, took the wayward youth into his home and raised him as his own. Julian was schooled in that country's private institutions and found to be a quick learner. He proved agile at sports, and in so doing won acclaim from his peers. Yet, something wasn't comfortable inside his soul, and Julian Knotsofoolista began yearning for the peaceful, uncrowded shores of Dalilennon, and for his mother.

Since the land of his dreams was so many kilometers distance and the cost of personal transport no small matter, Julian was stumped for a means of conveyance back home until his newly found brother, one Norman Expedience by name, suggested that a career in espionage might see Julian getting paid to return to his homeland. Norman recently had embarked on such a career himself, and was finding it to be most entertaining.

And so, to reduce the amount of verbiage required to extricate us from this subplot and return to life on the wandering SlipSparrow, let it be said that Julian K. got schooled in spying, was quietly transported back to his homeland, and had little work to do there other than fill out monthly, routine reports, and collect his pay in Darian checks he had no place to cash.

Hence, on paper, Julian Knotsofoolista was getting richer every month.

It wasn't that Norman E.'s nation, Darius, felt a compelling need to maintain surveillance on Dalilennon, but some subsection of some clause somewhere said they had to have a spy in every country. And, boy were they glad some five years after Julian Knotsofoolista was assigned to Dalilennon when a delegation from arch-rival Eglicata, led by that nation's most-noted henchman, Manual McGetitdone, paid an unexpected visit to that island nation. That visit stirred the imaginations of Darius's top espionage thinkers and members of the nation's chess team, a recent bronze medal winner in the Olympics, who between all of their brilliant minds didn't have a clue why Eglicata suddenly had an interest in isolated, peaceful Dalilennon.

Time Passes the SlipSparrow

By this time, the mood on the stolen ship SlipSparrow had changed from one of goal-oriented espionage to one of outright confusion.

It was obvious that Manual McGetitdone was the ultimate villain, since his hands and feet had been bound in the most expert of manners by the only trained, unbound spy aboard, Norman Expedience, hence isolating Manual physically from the group's mainstream.

But, oh, what a diverse group it was, with only Ms. Nancy Droosha, who'd offended no one as far as she knew, experiencing enough peace to sleep without worry of mutiny.

For Norman didn't trust Norbert and Malcolm was unsure of Norman who, too, was skeptical of Ms. Sylvia, who knew Norbert too well to trust. Roger K. Rightjet, of course, had reservations about Norbert and wasn't willing to admit to, or grant absolute trust in his former lover, Ms. Sylvia Smitharomance, who held an unspoken grudge against no less a beloved creature than Ms. Nancy for loving her former lover. Toss in the undeniable facts that Malcolm trusted neither Ms. Sylvia or Norbert, that Roger K. still didn't know where the hell Norman had come from, and that the ship had neither priest or referee aboard, and it's easy to see why a ship wishing to travel six different directions, or seven if Manual's rope-bound will were to count, had as much cohesiveness as man's international policy on oil: i.e. 'these are my needs, and this is how I will proceed, regardless of who gets in the way.'

Their only point of agreement, other than that all were experiencing pangs of hunger, was the need to keep Manual McGetitdone secured by ropes. By nature, Manual was a vengeful man, and who has a stronger desire to exact revenge than one whom friend and foe alike have united to conquer?

When it became obvious the isle of Dalilennon wasn't to be sighted on schedule, or even close to schedule, Mr. Straight addressed the young foreigner, who'd assumed command of the helm, about the unconnected, dangling wires beneath each of the nautical devices Norman Expedience so cleverly had rewired.

It need be noted at this point in the story that Norman Expedience was a well-trained spy. He could wrestle (sort of,) he obviously could think creatively, he could do wiring (sort of,) he could navigate (sort of,) and he could sort of put on the garb of a spy and act the part.

But, when confronted by a peer about a personal error in judgment he wished to conceal, Norman Expedience's espionage training, no matter how well-versed it was, failed to prevent him from flushing pink and hot in the face until beads of perspiration popped upon his forehead, and his hands turned jelly cold.

Like a youngster still to learn that one's best recourse when caught in such situations is honesty, Norman began telling a fanciful tale to Mr. Straight about having seen a seagull messing with the instruments that very morning. And he would have continued down such a slippery path of attempted deceit had not Malcolm Straight, who might have seen Maxwell Smart reruns in a dream somewhere, cut him short and promptly ordered Norman's arrest for tampering with official navigational equipment. A secondary charge was tacked on for lying to his ship fellows (shippersons??)

Then, Malcolm Straight saw to it that Norman Expedience was tied with ropes, for they had plenty of rope on the SlipSparrow, and isolated him from the rest of the functioning crew next to Manual McGetitdone.

Which would have been somewhat of a seafaring coup had it not been that the only two people more than marginally capable of manning the ship now were confined by flesh-biting ropes. And so, for the sake of expedience, Malcolm Straight now elected himself to man the tiller.

Unlike a comparable story, in that instance a sub-story, a few pages back where young Julian Knotsofoolista had only self and the elements to overcome, those aboard the SlipSparrow had the added dimension of each other; a dimension that can work to one's benefit, or to one's detriment.

Those aboard the SlipSparrow--drifting, tired, and hungry--handled the situation relatively well by dividing into pairs: McGetitdone and Expedience, because of the ties that bound; Nodahead and Ms. Smitharomance, because of ongoing biological desires; and Rightjet and Ms. Droosha, because they were compatible.

Then, there was the loner, Mr. Straight, who filled his hours directing the ship's course toward any cloud, star, or seabird that caught his fancy.

Fresh water was the only commodity of quantity upon the vessel, and it was the life-saving qualities of this most basic liquid that kept all alive through those perilous times of heat, sweat, and boredom.

Tempers flared to combustion only once, and that between an odd pair of heat-stricken combatants: Norbert Nodahead and Malcolm Straight.

Meeting by chance at a water barrel, Straight told the fast-slimming 'plump' man to take his turn at the wheel. Nodahead retorted they'd be better off drifting in the wind than under his control, then accused Straight of suggesting such a diversion for the purpose of "sneaking into bed with my woman."

A shoving match ensued, sort of like shirt-pulling tussles between hockey players wanting to stay on their skates long enough to make a show before being sent to the penalty box, but, like the actions of such hockey players, it really didn't amount to much. For starters, both were ill-equipped for fisticuffs and the like, plus the verbal taunts and curses directed their way by nearby Manual McGetitdone helped dissipate their respective angers.

Not only were Manuel's words vulgar, but he was especially explicit in what he had to say to Norbert Nodahead; point-blank chiding Norbert for elevating self-proclaimed lusts for "my woman" ahead of any thought to serve his country by freeing Manual McGetitdone.

Unlike Sylvia and Norbert, Roger K. Rightjet and Ms. Nancy Droosha spent much of their time together quietly talking about their respective pasts, about gardening, and about work as a Dalilennonian secretary or a gristmiller. Ms. Nancy's eyes were filled with trust and a belief in Roger K., and in their future together.

Rightjet withheld some information, especially anything to do with his previous love for Ms. Sylvia. He also said nothing about political pressures in his past that had caused him to scramble for safety and solace in a new homeland or three.

Love, for that's what Ms. Nancy thought she was feeling for the white knight she'd found, sometimes has the vision of a near-sighted man who scrunches his brow in hopes of gaining clarity rather than going through the ordeal of searching out his missing bifocals.

Initially, Nancy didn't know there was anything Roger K. Rightjet didn't wish to share and, had she known, would have said it didn't matter.

They kissed and caressed as adults are want to do, yet she gave much more than he could receive. Her faith, her trust, her love, and her soul were more than Roger K. had bargained for. Too much vulnerability in this stuff called love, he thought, and his mind flashed upon a time when he'd gone to ask his first love to leave their homeland with him.

The memory pierced Roger K.'s heart, and made him wince involuntarily.

Ms. Nancy's soul sensed something was not right, sensed a buried pain in Roger K. too deep for her kisses to salve. And so her consciousness tried harder. She didn't want to start over again.

But, in many such cases, the final edict, the long-range outcome is governed by a higher realm.

After what seemed an eternity of drifting without food or direction, Malcolm Straight bellowed that land was in sight, a cry only Norbert Nodahead long had dreaded to hear. A confirmed bachelor for obvious reasons, stature and greed among them, Norbert now was in 'lust,' and knew these blissful days with Ms. Sylvia Smitharomance never would be repeated. He was too naïve to woo the beauty under normal circumstances, and lacked appropriate social skills to even tempt her if anyone else was in competition.

The two men bound with ropes, McGetitdone and Expedience, were elated about news that land was in sight. Both entertained hopes of being untied and fed.

Malcolm Straight had no doubt that his clever guiding of the craft was responsible for their imminent landing, and was bursting with pride.

Ms. Droosha was torn by the news.

Interesting enough, Roger K. Rightjet and Ms. Sylvia Smitharomance were the only two shipmates who never concerned themselves about whether or not they'd step on land again. Each, figuratively, had spent thousands of years adrift in the world called life, and knew that land would be sighted if and when it needed to be sighted … that food would be available if it need be made available … that their individual paths would cross some day and join, or cross and move apart depending on what needed to be.

Individually and collectively, neither had true hopes, aspirations, or concrete goals on such matters, but instead dwelt within auras of resignation, punctuated by faint glimmers of trust, that something good could arise some time in their futures.

Not consciously were these thoughts known to either of them, yet Roger K.'s soul was wrestling to prevent Ms. Nancy's love from penetrating his heart, and Ms. Sylvia's soul was wrestling with inherent sensitivities of a physical nature that should, but often aren't shared in the context of love.

The SlipSparrow quietly was guided into a big-pooled inlet and beached upon a narrow sandy spit dwarfed by massive granite boulders. The inlet looked like a cove where pirates lurk, and every nook and cranny of the shoreline was scrutinized to the max by Malcolm Straight (still at the helm,) and Norbert Nodahead, who reluctantly was beginning to take an interest in this landing.

Very little greenery was visible from where they touched ashore, and the only signs of animal life were lazily swooping seagulls and some smaller birds that sang lustily from the branches of stringy, leafless trees.

Mr. Straight assumed the role of Boy Scout leader, military officer, or whatever, and assigned different spots on the horizon for teams to explore, their current locale being the base they would report back to. Each of Straight's soldiers was given instructions to reconnoiter at the ship at nineteen-hundred hours.

The melodramatics of nineteen-hundred hours caught up with the Boy Scout-military leader, however, when Ms. Droosha asked what time nineteen-hundred hours was, and the sneering captive, Manual

McGetitdone, still confined by ropes, laughed leeringly, and growled, "How many of your troops got watches, Straight?"

But, a sorta good captain always is preferable to an evil captain, and Straight's crew gave little credence to McGetitdone's interjections. And so, at Malcolm's request, each set out to try and learn where the deuce they'd landed.

When the five troopers did return to base at nineteen-hundred hours, whatever time that might be, they found one of their captives missing, and the other one, Norman Expedience, fuming mad.

"That son of a bitch! That dirty son of a bitch! See if I ever do anything for him again! I work my butt off and get one hand free and can't get the other one loose for a day, and the son of a bitch says, 'Come on. Untie my hands and I'll do the same for you; and so I do, and you wanna know what the son of a bitch says? Heh? He says, 'April fools,' and skips off the boat pretty as you please as if I hadn't done him the biggest favor of his frigging life! Man, am I burned!!"

Malcolm Straight was less than sympathetic with the semi-bound man and his anger, in fact chided N.E. in front of the others for trusting such a scoundrel.

Practically in tears, Norman Expedience who, too, was under the strain of the scarcest of diets and the hot sun, blurted out something to the effect of, "Just who can I trust?"

Roger K. Rightjet stepped in then, said, "Us," and released the former captive's second hand over the objections of Mr. Malcolm Straight.

"He's certainly not going to steer us astray from where we are, since we already are astray, and we'll need all the help we can get to both survive and learn where next to go," said Roger K.

Roger's short speech was well received by all, even the logical-thinking Mr. Straight in a begrudging sort of way, but Roger K. Rightjet's tact at not naming where they wished next to go didn't go unnoticed.

It wasn't unnoticed by Ms. Nancy and Mr. Straight who wished to sail back to Dalilennon; it wasn't unnoticed by the spy, Norman E., who ultimately wished to sail to a large country very far away; it wasn't unnoticed by Ms. Sylvia Smitharomance, who knew she'd recognize the right place when she found it; and it certainly didn't go unnoticed to flighty Norbert Nodahead who didn't really want to go anywhere except back to bed with the high-spirited filly, Ms. Smitharomance.

The scheduled reconnoiter powwow with self-proclaimed leader Malcolm Straight proved little in regards to determining their geographical location, but did open doors for hope.

Roger K. Rightjet, a man familiar with plants and gardens, had come across some nettles which he boiled into a healthful broth. Mr. Nodahead, nodding his head in pleasant anticipation, had discovered and yanked from the ground tubers of a variety known in his youth that proved to be rich in flavor and glucose when eaten raw. (Remember, they were pretty darn hungry.) The other find of significance was a Mars bar wrapper that seemed to indicate that the land they'd discovered either was inhabited, or at least visited occasionally.

It was agreed by consensus that the body of land they'd touched upon was of a respectable size.

Norman E.'s right wrist was somewhat swollen from the restraints that had held him in check next to Manual McGetitdone, but not painfully so. Hence he agreed, with certain limitations placed upon him by both Mr. Straight and Mr. Rightjet, to study his erroneous rewiring job and, without changing existing circuits or wiring schemes, try to determine what negative effects the loose, dangling wires below the ship's nautical devices had triggered concerning their current whereabouts—wherever that was.

Such would be a tough assignment for anyone, let alone an individual with a swollen right wrist.

The assignment was complicated because, their one pen on the vessel having run out of ink, Norman's original plan of moving northward point X to the east by the number of degrees separating point Y (McGetitdone's destination,) from point Z (his own destination,) only could be calculated within his mind, and not on paper.

Norman's complex thought processes told him:

1) IF those loose wires tended to move Z to the west by a certain number of degrees, then that certain number of degrees could be added to the original difference between Y and Z to determine where X should have been placed in the first place.

2) IF the loose wires served to move Y to the east, quite obviously one must subtract that number of degrees from those originally computed to locate point X.

Of course, if those dangling wires had two or more separate effects on his overall rewiring scheme, Norman E.'s problem, already taxing the limit of his abilities in its complexity, would be compounded exponentially. In such an instance, a shoulder shrug and timeout would be the best alternative one could hope for.

It was a task of such magnitude that only a linotype designer would relish, and the recently released spy from Darius worked himself into a frenzy of exhaustion only commonplace among world-class chess players; such as those who competed on an international scale for Herr McCoffee, and Darian bronze-winning Olympians.

And, when Manual McGetitdone led a band of Eglicatan soldiers aboard the SlipSparrow the next morning, for the ship's seaward wanderings indeed had brought the sailors and the stolen vessel to no less a landing than on Eglicata itself, Norman Expedience was discovered slumped across the pilot's wheel suffering from a troubled, unsatisfactory sleep.

McTea to the Caves

Priest Precious didn't make his swing into Dalilennonian politics willingly but, like all else the gutsy clergyman set out to accomplish, the transition came quickly with a spirit consistently mindful of the priorities of whom he'd chosen to be.

Ten minutes into the job, and the feisty priest was told of Poncho McTea's observed dealings with the runaway diplomats from Eglicata and everything else crack Officer Oliver Ogilvie had uncovered before McTea had disappeared from view.

The good priest wanted to halt everything and pray for guidance right then and there, but his new boss, good King Nocturnal, proclaimed the time for prayer was in the evenings and on weekends, not during the employ of his forward-thinking government. This seemed to be an unproductive use of time, even contradictory to common sense to the man of the frock but, beings he now was on the clock and dealing with none less than the good King of Dalilennon himself, the priest-turned-advisor to the good King voiced no objections.

Besides, Priest Precious understood the need to honor the wishes of those placed in authority over him.

Good King Nocturnal seemed content to bemoan the current state of affairs on the isle of fancy and do nothing about them, but his new temporary advisor felt otherwise.

Over the course of many years, Priest Precious had journeyed to church conventions in other lands aboard the SlipSparrow, and had heard murmurings about a certain Herr McCoffee from Eglicata who seemed intent on spreading his influence, and his rule, far and wide. Since Dalilennon was by no means a strategically located base for any military actions--past, present, or future--you can readily understand Priest Precious's quandary in regards to McCoffee's sudden interest in remote, peaceful Dalilennon.

What did Dalilennon have that McCoffee wanted?

To the knowledge of the remaining Dalilennonian brain trust, which, if you remember, now consisted merely of good King Nocturnal and Priest Precious; the only chap on the isle of fancy who possibly could answer Priest Precious's armada of questions was the missing Poncho McTea. Hence, a massive manhunt was begun to discover McTea's whereabouts.

Or rather, as massive a manhunt as the lethargic Dalilennonian police force could muster. And, to be fair, their efforts did cause discomfort to the fugitive who no longer could stay in his own home or play Crazy 8's (Poncho had long since tired of Spades,) in local pubs.

In fact, Poncho McTea was forced out of the villages where his picture was slammed about in every prominent location promising a wish from the good King " ... for information leading to the arrest and capture of ..."

In all truthfulness, Poncho wasn't really a devoted family man, in fact only had married and had a son to further his political aspirations, so that portion of being a fugitive wasn't a major concern to him. He loved his wife and Stem to a point, however, and saw their salvation, like his, in the family's relocation to Eglicata.

Yet, Poncho, who'd grown up with silk sheets and servants ready to drive him to 7-Elevens for cigarettes and beer at all hours of the night, hated sleeping on rocks and wearing dirty clothes. As days passed, longer than he'd anticipated, Poncho McTea began to realize that the Eglicatan invasion of Dalilennon might come sometime beyond the immediate future, and that he would benefit by finding a temporary abode of relative comfort and semi-permanence to reside in.

And so, one evening, Poncho McTea stumbled upon a campfire-lit cave, and crept inside, until, looking across flames, he saw the unforgettable face of Julian Knotsofoolista intently peering into the fire between them.

By premeditated design, Poncho McTea bolted upon Julian Knotsofoolista's privacy waving a handful of Dalilennonian currency in front of the crazy man's face, as if flagging money in such dramatic fashion was the only way he could be understood.

Knotsofoolista, calmly watching this unexpected intruder, showed no signs of interest in the money; in fact, he hardly moved.

Their eyes met for several moments, as well as the flickering light would allow, and folks from the outside world would have been shocked to see which pair of eyes was glazed with fear. Admittedly, Julian Knotsofoolista was in a familiar setting, hence more likely to retain composure under stress, yet J.K. exhibited a look of comfortable acceptance that unnerved his uninvited guest.

The sharp crackling of shrub-like limbs in the fire punctuated what otherwise was silence as two very different men from worlds not as far apart as Poncho McTea thought, contemplated communication.

McTea spoke first. "I need your help, and am willing to pay good money for it."

The fire took on a new sizzling noise as a small pocket of pitch contributed its contents for warmth and light and sound.

"Do you understand what I'm saying?"

Poncho McTea's voice went high in stating the final words of his query, symbolic of the strain this strange interplay was having on a man used to dealing with Kings and Herrs, not would-be priests living alone in caves.

Still, Julian Knotsofoolista hardly had moved since his peace had been interrupted by this double agent waving Dalilennonian currency. J.K.'s stoic figure was silhouetted in black by the warming fire that radiated enough heat to warm their faces, hands, and front-sides. The outlined form of Julian's coal-black frock was all that kept him from looking prehistoric, squatting silently there with flame-shadows dancing behind him on the slanting rock walls inside the cave.

"Look," said Poncho McTea, taking an additional step forward, "I'll give you all this money if you'll feed me and provide me with shelter for seven days. What do you think? This probably is more money than you make in a year, and all you have to do is bring a little more food home for a week."

Poncho's words were reassuring the Eglicatan native (aka himself,) of eventual success in his proposed deal (wasn't money always the ultimate victor?) and he kept inching closer until he stood directly across the fire from Julian K.

Julian Knotsofoolista had decided earlier that the fugitive from the Dalilennonian police department--J.K. being the type of agent who did his homework judiciously, what little of it there was--could stay with him in his cave. He was willing to gamble that the culprit would do no harm to him, at least the first few days of his stay, since he, Julian Knotsofoolista, was to be the double agent's source of food, water, and shelter.

All Julian needed now was the right euphemism to seal their agreement.

At long last, the cave's caretaker broke his lengthy silence by saying in as eerie a voice as he could muster, which after five year of practicing alone in caves was a blue-ribbon type eerie, "He who trusts in his own mind is a fool; but he who walks in wisdom will be delivered."

Julian Knotsofoolista next pointed to a corner of the cool cave where some bedding was visible at the outskirts of the fire's flicker, nodded as if to confirm the deal, and took Poncho McTea's money from his hand, thus binding their contract.

Poncho chuckled to himself that evening as he skoo-shed into his warm covering of blankets, a chuckle of bland humor at how easily it was to direct the masses with the proper application of lucre. His cousin had taught him well, and within a few brief days his role in this dastardly affair would be consummated and a life of Eglicatan palatial leisure again would be his.

As McTea succumbed to exhaustion in peace and comfort, two beady eyes watched him from across the cavern, waiting until the guest's breaths reached a regularity not known in waking life. Then, Julian Knotsofoolista rose, his own tennis-shoe patter and the crackles of the late-evening fire drowned by Poncho McTea's snoring, and searched the other man's belongings for weapons. As expected, there were none, and the would-be priest returned to his side of the cavern and curled into his beloved fetal position, resting on his left side, and dropped off into a restful sleep of his own.

Instant Prison

When Manual McGetitdone's men captured the sailors of the wayward SlipSparrow, such was accomplished with little ado. Admittedly, Norman Expedience woke up in time to blaspheme McGetitdone, but the others--tired, hungry, and lost--accepted their collective fates as captives of the state of Eglicata with a 'what the heck' attitude. Nothing was to be gained from resisting arrest, and nothing was to be lost by not resisting. Their fates, individually and collectively, now were in the hands of others.

Since Mr. McGetitdone hadn't been shy about reporting, expounding, and tattling on the deeds of his fellow countrymen (countrypersons?), both Ms. Sylvia and Mr. Norbert Nodahead were rushed to prison as well as the others, being informed that one day soon their stories would be aired before Herr McCoffee himself.

Ms. Nancy Droosha and Ms. Sylvia Smitharomance were placed in the same cell in the women's section of the national prison, while Roger K. and Norman E. were placed in one cell and Norbert Nodahead in a cell of his own in the men's house of correction. Malcolm Straight, because of his most noble position as advisor to the good King of Dalilennon, was taken to a ritzy hotel where, with hot showers and television at his disposal, he was exiled from his peers while held under house arrest like a rich, dog-fighting football player with a good lawyer.

Herr McCoffee was unhappy and disappointed to hear of Ms. Smitharomance's apparent disloyalty and the percentage loss of the disadvantageous crop, but otherwise quite pleased with the results of the Dalilennonian mission.

Plans for an immediate invasion of Dalilennon, with a planned stop at the McTea-planted disadvantageous patch if needed, were made, and two fleets of Eglicatan seafaring vessels immediately left port to be on hand when the fowlawarfare--with Herr McCoffee, McGetitdone, and two soldiers aboard--arrived at the tiny isle to deliver a most fatal blow.

Two days it would take the powerful Eglicatan navy to speed into position, and scant hours for the mission's main man, the rugged fowlawarfare, to cruise into town and do his destructive thing.

During those two days when the Eglicatan navy was churning to Dalilennon, some interesting discussions took place in both the women's and men's prisons.

For starters, there's the women's prison, where a woman in love had been placed in the same cell as another woman whose strongest-ever affections, even after nine years, remained with that very same man.

Women may be known for their cattiness, but once enclosed behind prison walls tendencies toward philosophical discussions and straightforwardness aren't uncommon. And so it was with these two women, especially Ms. Sylvia Smitharomance, who unarguably was implicated to the max in the affairs of their captive state.

"I had no idea what a beautiful man he was until he left," said Ms. Sylvia, with no prompting from her presumed accomplice in crime. "He'd always been there before, and I just thought he'd always be there for me, no matter what I did or said to discourage him. I was wrong."

"My problem is of a different nature," pitched in the Dalilennonian secretary. "I love him too much. He can't be held or contained like I want to hold him, and I don't know how else to feel."

Scant kilometers away, two men also were contained by prison walls and openly voicing thoughts to each other.

Norman Expedience, bless his heart, was depressed by the turn of events that had led to their imprisonment on Eglicata, and blamed himself for the entire fiasco. Norman's recounting of his personal shortcomings during the just-concluded sea voyage was voiced more for his ears and soul to hear than for the ears and spirit of Roger K. Rightjet.

Roger K. listened intently, trying to discern from among Expedience's blubbering when the best opportunity might arise for him to ask the question he most wanted to ask.

Finally, that opportunity arose.

"You must either come from Lignatova or Darius, and I guess the latter," interrupted Rightjet.

His cellmate responded despondently, as if the secret he'd been carrying around for many days was no secret at all.

"Yes," Norman said evenly, without emotion, maintaining a distant look in his eyes as if he and Julian Knotsofoolista, kilometers and kilometers away in a warm cavern of his own choosing, were made from the same mold. "We, in Darius, know Herr McCoffee has developed a novel means of conducting warfare that could further his goal of becoming the most powerful man, and Eglicata the most powerful nation in the entire world. We know there's something on Dalilennon he needs to make his dastardly weapon operational, maybe even enable it to fly, but we don't know what it is. My guess it's that damnable weed, but figuring out what it's good for is a real boggler. And now that he's got the plant and we're locked up, who's going to stop him?"

Roger K. Rightjet, although beginning to take this hero business seriously, admitted he didn't know, then sat upon his single-wide cot, hands cupped beneath his chin, deliberating, with discernment, how to answer Norman E.'s penetrating question.

Roger had no way of knowing that the answer they both sought soon would arrive courtesy of a forgotten plump man sitting three cell doors away.

That individual, of course, was Norbert Nodahead.

Stated mildly, Norbert was morose about his new life as a convict. The overt inconvenience of a man accustomed to wealth and power being stripped of all privileges and dignity would have been reason enough, but the issue for him went much deeper. Norbert had no doubt but that Herr McCoffee would have his life permanently snuffed out; aka terminated, in short order. In the eye of Eglicatan glory, at least as Herr McCoffee would see it, one Norbert Nodahead had served his purpose, and now was a liability to the state.

These are indicators, samples of the feelings of fear and gloom Norbert Nodahead carried within his heart on that second morning in prison when an unusual coincidence (as if anything on this planet is coincidental, right?) brought new light into Norbert's fast-dimming future, and rekindled hope within his spirit.

For, parading past him in the wide aisle between jail cells was none other than Fat Albert Kazonkski, a childhood acquaintance who'd taken no small amount of verbal abuse early in life from Norbert Nodahead and their peers. Which would be no cause for joy were it not fact that Fat Albert had loved every minute of that abuse. When others were jiving him about his monstrous size; his inability to muster enough courage to ask hefty Olga McRibbonoski to dance at junior high school dances; or about the exposed backside gap between his shirt and jeans when he forgot to wear a belt, those were times of happiness for Albert: because they meant he wasn't being ignored.

To Fat Albert's noncomplex mind, those verbal assaults had been messages of love.

And Norbert Nodahead, whether to his credit or detriment, always had been a primary proponent of showering classmate Albert Kazonkski with this strange form of love. Norbert always was first and foremost to ridicule the slow-thinking giant, thinking such preemptive strikes, when Albert, figuratively, was thrown to the wolves, would help deflect the cruel juvenile vulnerability he faced because of his own pudgy, almost misshapen body.

And, for the most part, it had worked.

And so, seeing that Fat Albert, now a prison guard, had grown into a mountain of muscle, Norbert addressed Albert that second morning in prison with kindness and as much fondness as he could muster on short notice.

Kazonkski didn't bite, instead stating in a reverberating bass voice that prisoners weren't to address guards: Code 41E, Section 11P.

Norbert Nodahead was neither hip on prison code nor in a position to care one way or the other, so bypassed Fat Albert's guttural warning and said something more to the effect of, "It's me, your old buddy, 'Nory Nodahead." (God, how he hated the nickname, 'Nory!) "Don't you remember?"

Norbert was quick to stand back when the Goliath in uniform rattled his cage and, in that same commanding voice, repeated the code and section that put N.N. in violation of said statute.

Fat Albert hadn't been such an intimidating force in his youth, and was some three cells down the block before Norbert Nodahead regrouped his anger enough to bellow in frustration, "Take a hike, Albert!!"

Now, if you remember, when Malcolm Straight took an earlier tumble off the garden wall by the disadvantageous patch on Dalilennon, it had been prompted by an automatic reaction to an oft-repeated stimulus. In that incident, being overcome by amazement, Straight had rubbed his forehead, leaned backward, and fallen at an inopportune time.

Although Fat Albert Kazonkski's stimulus and response to N. Nodahead's desperate outburst were wholly separate from those made earlier by Mr. Straight, the same overall theory of conditioned automation held true.

The mountainous Eglicatan prison guard, standing at the time in front of Roger K. and Norman Expedience's prison cell--the two of them under the assumption Norbert would be flogged or worse for his emotional outburst--turned back in the direction he'd come with a flicker of recognition in his eyes, and said, "Nory, is that you, Nory?"

What happened next probably is unworthy of the tale being told, save that it reiterates the extreme level of stress these brave men and women were suffering from, or would that be 'under?'

Anyway, Norman Expedience, a top-notch spy from Darius who 'knew the score' as to how bad things appeared for our wanna-be heroes in prison, including himself, was tickled by the affectionate name of Nory, and began to giggle. Only a little giggle at first, and certainly nothing to usurp Nory's reunion with Fat Albert, but it quickly got out of hand to a point where Roger K. Rightjet, in the prison cell with Norman, began fearing for Expedience's sanity.

The loud, gasping laughter of one among many regularly draws the attention of those in proximity, which it did this morning at the same time that Norman Expedience, uncontrollably gasping for air by now, loudly discharged some fumes from his rear, an event that caused Fat Albert, the man mountain with the keys; Roger K. Rightjet; and Norbert Nodahead to all join with the Darian spy, Norman Expedience, in the universal joys of mirth and laughter.

Such a strange scene never before had been witnessed within Eglicatan prison walls, and the four roared loudly, especially the huge prison guard.

The other male prisoners nearby, possibly not under pressures of such magnitude, though who knows, failed to acknowledge the humor of the situation. Some possibly could have snickered a little in conformity, but few actually heard the noisy discharge of anal air that triggered the abnormal outburst of gaiety in what normally was, at best, a melancholy setting.

An aside.

One may notice when dealing with children that the bounds of propriety have yet to be determined. Some children loudly laugh at every Bob Hope joke whether they hear and/or understand the words or not. Some loudly laugh at the dinner table forgetting that food is in their mouths. And some, horror of horrors, even embarrass their parents by bursting into gales of laughter during solemn, God-fearing church services.

As growth and maturity occur, most children learn about acceptable boundaries that, for the sake of propriety, shouldn't be o'erstepped. In most cases, lessons like these aren't learned in heart-to-heart mother & son talks or in heart-to-heart father & daughter talks. Instead, they generally come from interacting with one's peers, one's environment, and the many settings those contributing life forces might share in common.

But some people, even with big hearts and bodies such as those belonging to good Fat Albert Kazonkski, lack the mental abilities, if abilities they be, to determine such boundaries. Not a fault, mind you, just the way God made them.

And so it was on this particular morning in an Eglicatan prison that an even stranger scene arose than the first one because, long after Norman Expedience, Roger K. Rightjet, and Norbert Nodahead had ceased to laugh, a giant of a prison guard continued to peak in the height of hysteria. Finally, tears of joy dripping down his face, Fat Albert collapsed to the floor just outside the cell of would-be heroes Roger K. Rightjet and Norman Expedience to best express his pleasure; bouncing on his belly and blubbering in merriment as he did so.

Roger K. Rightjet, emerging hero who he was, needed no written invitation to procure the sloppily kept keys from bouncing Kazonkski's belt, and all the good men now need do was await Mr. Kazonkski's imminent recovery and exit from their cell block, then release themselves and dash to freedom.

And that precisely is what Rightjet and Expedience did, taking Norbert Nodahead along with them. And, with the unwitting complicity of a sleeping Eglicatanese guard (in the man's defense, he was overdue for a smoke break,) soon they were outside prison walls. In sneak formation, the three of them sleuthed through the morning air until, several kilometers from the Eglicatan prison, they reached a tiny seashore cottage that Nodahead maintained for emergency purposes; which, since this obviously was a time of emergency, now became their hideout.

Mr. Rightjet became most authoritative when they reached the shack, even aggressive, and quizzed their nodding seashore host for every detail of the Eglicatan mission to Dalilennon. He nodded gravely when the planned disadvantageous use of the disadvantageous plant was revealed. He questioned long and hard about the fowlawarfare, learning of its capabilities and its limitations. Roger K. was most interested to learn that the beast had a heart the size of a thirteen-ounce tin of abalone.

"At least that's bigger than eight-ounce tin," he mumbled audibly.

Norbert, distracted at the time by surveillance duties, asked Roger K. what he'd just said, but Rightjet was too immersed in important thoughts to respond.

Nodahead was miffed, but didn't press the issue.

It now was becoming crystal clear to R.K. Rightjet that his options didn't include a backdoor exit and another seven or eight years of quiet introspection. Once that mental milestone was reached and hurdled, the lawyer-turned-gristmiller began warming to the task of hero-ship like a thoroughbred racehorse whose rider holds him back and holds him back until the throttled, speedy horse is so hyped to run that, once given full rein, he literally blasts by all contenders along the final curve and cruises before the grandstands to win the big race.

In many ways, Roger K. was like that thoroughbred. He'd been groomed to be a winner, been consistently held back (mostly by himself,) throughout the course of the race, and just now was beginning to steam full-throttle ahead to meet the challenge he'd dodged artfully nine years earlier.

Normally subdued, or at least introspective, Roger K. Rightjet never had been more animated about life than he now became in a tiny Eglicatan seaside cottage. The news of his homeland, for Eglicata always would remain so in his spirit, preparing to forcefully waylay peaceful Dalilennon en route to world conquest made his heart pound with the conviction of saintly Clark Kent or an energized Atom Ant.

In fact, the very thought pissed him off.

Not foolish, Roger K. tempered his contemplated invincibility to do the right thing through the filtered lens of reasonable, strategically based caution.

Only a few feet away from Roger K. Rightjet in the one-room cottage--unless you also want to count the tiny loo, where one had to turn his or her feet sideways in Charlie Chaplin fashion while sitting on the throne in order to close the door--sat a despondent Norman Expedience.

In spite of the fact Norman remained on a foreign payroll as a spy, the magnitude of the task looming before him left him empty and sad. Even the resurgent Roger K. Rightjet couldn't rally his spirit that insisted on dealing with past failures, especially his aborted attempt to recalculate and redesign the SlipSparrow's navigational systems, and, of course, their subsequent landing and capture in Eglicata.

Norman E. literally was engrossed in a mire of self-pity and self-loathing, as if unaware they no longer were locked in prison and been given a new opportunity to correct past wrongs, to again do wonderful things for God and country.

Norman's gloominess was the antithesis of Roger K.'s exuberance.

It would have taken a mighty man to stop Roger K. Rightjet from leading the charge that very day and, being the only one capable among those in the cottage to assume such authority, Roger K. designed an intricate game plan for the three former captives, now fugitives, to follow.

Aware that Norman E.'s willingness (he unthinkingly would have walked into a fire if given such a suggestion,) far exceeded his capabilities at this time, the day's true hero instructed Norman to join forces with Norbert Nodahead and free the two women from prison.

At the same time, he, Roger K. Rightjet, would proceed to confront the fowlawarfare and the many dangers thereof.

In response to a series of detailed questions, explicit directions from the noddingest of diplomats, or at this stage of the story the noddingest of 'fugitive' diplomats, Roger K. was pointed to a small brothel on the poor side of town where he ordered gin on the rocks and a woman.

That's right. That's exactly right. He ordered gin and a woman!!!!

Not what you'd expect a true hero to do in his first official act, eh? But, it was part of his intricate, clever plan.

Since Roger K. Rightjet had read a book or six in his day, he knew that such women weren't in the least evil by nature, simply fillies eagerly looking for the light to put them on top of the game, no pun intended, so that their lives, too, could experience renewed meaning and hope.

Let it be said that Roger K. Rightjet, no matter how quiet his Dalilennonian life had been, never had lost the gift of persuasion that at one time had propelled him into the heights of Eglicatan legalese.

And on this occasion, he needed every ploy in the book.

For Ruby, or maybe her name was Pearl, had heard every line man can utter, many of them more than once a day, and wasn't likely to be drawn into just any capricious caper our hero might have in mind.

But gin and intimate discourse with a former crack lawyer normally works to the lawyer's advantage, hence within an hour or three Ruby or Pearl agreed to be part of the program.

She slipped on a coat, for covering more than warmth, and visited a local household store, a chemistry shop, and a grocery store before returning to the brothel with one item from each.

"It ain't easy buyin' sun lamps 'n sun lotion round here, ya know," said Ruby-Pearl while chewing some orange-colored gum. "What ya gonna do with all this crap?"

Then Roger K., for the second time in this exciting narrative, 'stripped for gym' as they say, where his ultra-white, previously covered skin contrasted sharply with his seasoned, weathered face and arms.

"I see," said the hussy with a laugh, and roughly tossed Roger K. upon her bed beneath the sun lamp for treatments of suntan and coconut oil. By late afternoon, Roger K.'s temporary tan was complete and, instead of looking like a former soft Eglicatan lawyer, our hero easily could pass for a menial Eglicatanese laborer.

He thanked Ms. Ruby-Pearl (or was it Rose?) profusely for her assistance, and promised to return one day to thank her properly.

"Won't hold me breath, bucko," she retorted loudly. "Meet weird guys like you every day. Some come back, some don't."

And so the Rogerest of Rightjets exited the brothel through the front door and wound his way through narrow, jagged streets for over an hour looking for a place he knew all too well: the Eglicatan Congressional Headquarters (ECH).

You see, Norbert Nodahead, bless his heart, was one of few to possess secret information that he'd willingly shared with Roger K. at the seaside cottage, aka their hideout. And that information focused on the fact that the ECH--mysteriously closed so long for "nonpublicized repairs" that legislators now met in groups of ten at different Starbucks to conduct business--currently had a large, live-in guest. For it was inside Eglicatan Congressional Headquarters where the foulest of the fowl, the beast we know as the fowlawarfare, was anchored and chained in place.

Lambs were trucked in late at night to serve the animal's voracious appetite. And two days earlier, to the immense relief of Herr McCoffee and his military advisors, let alone the fowlawarfare itself, bales of cut Dalilennonian disadvantageous had been served to abate the painful case of bloat that had befallen the bird beast.

Still, security was high, and gaining admittance to congressional headquarters was no mean feat.

The precision password dance-step routine to help open the main door was so delicate and rhythmically oriented that no one believed an untrained outsider capable of learning it, let alone learning the synchronized outburst of song in the Eglicatanese tongue that, in harmony with the dance, released the lock mechanism granting admittance into what had become the fowlawarfare's chambers.

In fact, security precautions around the leathery beast were of such a stringent nature that neither McCoffee nor any of his close advisors initially could gain admittance to the building. The Herr soon resolved that dilemma by implementing an equally permissible identification badge system.

When Nodahead first informed Rightjet of the delicate dance step required for admittance to the ECH, Roger K. recognized it instantly as one he'd attempted to teach Herr McCoffee the night before R. K. Rightjet fled Eglicata. The Herr, or at the time soon-to-be Herr, hadn't availed himself of Roger K.'s free dance lesson, but instead had encouraged others to occupy the young lawyer while he, Max McCoffee, slipped away to romance Rightjet's anticipated bride-to-be.

Nodahead's miscellaneous and varied talents had enabled him to master the vocal half of the coded entrance to congressional headquarters, and he'd taught it quickly to a receptive Roger K. Rightjet at the seashore cottage.

And so, with happy feet and booming voice, our hero triggered the door release and, with a sporty suntan, entered the congressional hall where the giant fowl, no matter how strong the chains that bound, commanded the attention of all.

Roger K.'s initial thought upon first sight of the gigantic bird was, 'How the deuce do they plan to get him out of here?' The bird was that big, strapped as he was to numerous restraining blocks of stone. He seemed peaceful enough as long as ample numbers of lambs regularly were poked down his gullet.

Passing as an ordinary, everyday dark-skinned native soldier, Roger Rightjet sidled among the midst of a group of workers and soon was as natural a component of the landscape as any other. Which wasn't a noteworthy achievement in itself, since every thought of every man within the large structure was one-hundred percent focused on the fowlawarfare and his every movement. The fowlawarfare certainly was big enough to topple congressional headquarters if he chose to do so.

With ears tuned to hear words spoken in his native tongue, Roger K. overheard rumors that the fowlawarfare would fly to Dalilennon the following day with the "brave" Herr McCoffee, Manual McGetitdone, and two soldiers aboard. The plan was for the fowlawarfare to reach Dalilennon at the same time as two fleets of Eglicatan naval vessels that, among them, carried a boatload of lambs. They next would step ashore in a secluded cave-dominated area of the island to stoke the fowlawarfare and rest; then, at daybreak, march upon and conquer the unsuspecting nation of Dalilennon.

Very little resistance, if any, was expected.

Once late evening rolled around and Roger K.'s previously eager ears had been dulled by hours of monotonous gossip and rumor-telling, the fowlawarfare took it upon himself to squat in place for a preflight snooze, and the soldiers in attendance to the big bird gladly did the same. Waiting beak and claw on such a fidgety monster was tough work, and administrative types and soldiers still on duty, minus Herr McCoffee and Manual McGetitdone who'd left earlier to play cards and catch some z-z's of their own, eased into relaxed mode among the congressional chamber's 'cushy' seats where many public servants, aka legislators, soundly had slept in the past.

Rightjet noted with interest that all the sleeping soldier/workers soon were snoring in unison with the fowlawarfare's deep, resonant snore-song that warbled of munched lambs and little else.

It was apparent to Roger K. Rightjet, having the keen mind and wit that he did, that the act of placing a saddle on the beast was no small task. For even now, many hours before the scheduled flight to Dalilennon, the fwa (short for fowlawarfare,) already was saddled and ready for the journey. Which provided no inconvenience to the bird, since saddles for carrying four people and some bundles of disadvantageous were about as restrictive to the beast as prison walls to St. Paul or Richard Lovelace.

Norbert had said the prime steering device for the fowlawarfare's flight would be a live lamb dangled on a mechanized metal clothesline that cranked back and forth, at the pilot's choosing, in front of the fwa's strong smeller of a snout.

The theory was that the giant bird would follow the little lamb to hell and back to satisfy his appetite; and since the warfaring crew soon to be aboard the beast wanted to go to Dalilennon instead of hell, certain restrictions would apply. To wit, the fowlawarfare only would be allowed to chomp the sacrificial lamb once they'd arrived on the isle of fancy, and not before. Once on Dalilennon, with no culinary formalities to slow the process, he'd be allowed to slip the tantalizing wooly animal into his belly, where a snippet of disadvantageous would add blissful delight to his albacore-tin of a heart. And that scenario would be repeated many times.

In most instances, practice missions precede such major breakthroughs in the art of warfare--to wit, exploding bombs with radioactive fallout within the atmosphere of one's own nation or, better yet, over an island territory--but the Eglicatan experts were so convinced this plan was foolproof that the initial test would come with the mighty Herr aboard, and tiny Dalilennon as its first target. Besides, once the mighty fwa was aloft, the roof would be off their intentions, let alone congressional headquarters, and attacking such a peaceful island nation shouldn't exceed exercise proportions anyway.

After much midnight thought when he pondered the situation up, down, and sideways, Roger K. designed and began implementation of a plan whereby he, Roger K. Rightjet, would replace one bundle of disadvantageous in the port-side saddlebag of saddle No. 3.

Let it be made perfectly clear, as a less-than-honest leader used to say, that at this moment in time Mr. Rightjet knowingly abandoned any and all guarantees for personal safety. Placing himself in harm's way as a living sacrifice, Roger K. Rightjet was downright uncomfortable by the time daylight began peeking through the skylight windows of the Eglicatan Congressional Headquarters.

Saddlebags, even those custom-made to carry digestive supplies for a big, big bird, aren't conducive to harmonious human rest.

Expedience Sloshes On

It was during that same morning's predawn hours that another well-conceived plan was being implemented a kilometer or five away. It was there that a prison full of political inmates, female by gender, were catching final Z-z's on hard, uncomfortable cots purposely placed there to remind each of them about various and sundry iniquities they'd committed against the state of Eglicata.

While the women prisoners slept, a pair of suspicious-looking male bodies brazenly marched through preliminary admittance gates and on to an electrically triggered interior barrier they lacked the ability to penetrate without compliance from the on-duty female guard dutifully manning her post from the inside.

"Halt! Who goes there?" she challenged loudly, clearly, and with the authority of a seasoned Roman sentinel.

Nodahead nervously glanced at Norman Expedience. In the next few moments, they'd know whether or not their gamble as to the sum of Herr McCoffee's secrecy in this villainous plot would be rewarded with cherries or, horror of horrors, with lemons.

Norbert responded to the guard.

"It's Herr McCoffee's chief advisor, Norbert Nodahead, and I've come to interview two of your new prisoners at the request of the Herr, who had to leave the country on an urgent mission."

"I've received no orders to verify such a visit," responded the unseen woman.

"Of course not," snapped Nodahead in contrived irritably. "I only was given them myself within the hour. I was with Herr McCoffee when an urgent message called him away."

Norman Expedience was becoming more and more impressed with Nodahead's versatility, and could see no flaws in the interchange he was witnessing between Norbert and the unseen female guard.

Seconds later, a well-armed, (and well-endowed,) olive-skinned beauty appeared to the far side of the electronic beam that remained in place after the large, metal door between them had creaked open.

"Toss your papers beneath the beam," she said.

One of many things that had impressed the Darian Spy--meaning Norman Expedience in this instance, since Julian Knotsofoolista was busy entertaining a guest in a fire-lighted cave many, many kilometers away--in recent days was Nodahead's well-prepared seaside cottage that hinted of the pudgy man's lack of faith in his role with the existing Eglicatan government. Along with provisions, including an unopened box of Wheaties, plane tickets, money, and a motorbike, Norbert's cottage was equipped with multiple sets of identification papers to replace those taken away at the time of their incarceration.

Nodahead coolly tossed the replacement papers plus a counterfeit visitation form under the beam, correctly responded to the women's prisons rarely used secret admittance password, and was given an OK nod to step forward from the suspicious guard.

"What about him?" she asked Norbert in regards to Norman Expedience, who barely could understand the language, save respond to her with any level of coherence.

Norbert looked long and hard down the walkway he and N. E. had entered from as if fearing that evil ears lurked in the dawning hours, then bent close to the disengaged beam and whispered in one ear of the attractive female guard who sported long, dark hair with a bowed yellow ribbon in it; possibly indicating she yearned for Eglicatan soldiers everywhere to return to the safety of their homeland so she could find a husband, or at least improved employment.

Whatever was said obviously met the guard's approval, and the pudgy, soft-skinned Eglicatan diplomat-turned-fugitive and a young, handsome spy soon were through the beam and, following triggered releases for two sets of sliding metal doors, among the cell blocks of the women's prison.

"What did you tell her?" whispered Expedience.

"Stroke of genius, my friend. I merely said you are my boyfriend and accompany me wherever I go. I told her you were quite sensitive, but harmless. You see," Norbert added with earnest conviction, "a handsome gay catches pretty-ones with fingers in their own zippers every time."

One inmate woke immediately as they passed, and rushed to the bars of her cell to converse with this most unusual of sights in an Eglicatan women's prison: two men. "Hey, guys," she whispered with urgency in her voice, "I think if you come over here you'll find something you'll enjoy."

Norbert nodded his head in acknowledgement of her overture, yet kept walking, as did Norman Expedience. They now were men on a mission whose alternative actions didn't include the possibility of straying, even for pleasure, away from their assigned task.

Short moments elapsed before this pair of men, as likely to be a pair of seagull salesmen as near heroes, discovered the prison cell they were seeking in the eerily lit, predawn prison.

Ms. Smitharomance heard footsteps approaching, and gently nudged Ms. Droosha into wakefulness once the identity of their visitors was known.

"Our saviors have arrived," Ms. Sylvia said to the pretty maiden who would have been days and days away preparing for another boring day at work had her sleeping fantasies of love not taken her aboard the SlipSparrow while that ship was being hijacked.

Since the immediate order of business was to get the two ladies out of their dreary cell and the prison, then into the coming dawn, Norbert Nodahead conferred at length in whispers with Ms. Sylvia Smitharomance, talking through straight metal bars. Having worked most closely with Ms. Sylvia for numerous years at the top of Eglicata's power structure, Norbert had nothing but respect for the lady's intuitive mind which, if it had any real faults, occasionally was guilty of outthinking the opposition by two steps instead of one.

As the two Eglicatan advisors strategized how to escape a national prison from the inside, (Norbert's recently rejuvenated hormones put on hold by the seriousness of their predicament;) and as their two-person brain trust whispered and flexed its collective lips and minds seeking a workable solution to a complex problem … it was then that a most unusual scene unfolded scant meters away between two different players in our story.

Be it the intensity of the moment or the respective states of each one's vulnerability, Ms. Nancy Droosha and Mr. Norman Expedience focused eyes on each other through prison bars and suddenly experienced a peace neither could explain or understand. Their eyes locked in sensitivity, and each conveyed the pains, fears, and personal growth they both had been experiencing and clinging to for longer than they could remember.

Being younger than Ms. Nancy and more impulsive, Norman Expedience felt his heart glow to finally find someone who understood his pain. At that point, he gladly would have given himself a hernia to part the bars standing between them if he were physically capable of doing so. Self-doubts now were cast aside, and N.E. became an instant champion to save Ms. Nancy from this dilemma, and from any future pain.

The difference in age and experience between them toned Ms. Droosha's expedience in holding eyes with the young man, yet she greatly was moved to know that here was a handsome youth of sensitivity ready to treat her as a queen were a future occasion to arise.

'And maybe it might,' she thought while taking a second look at his wide open, trusting brown eyes. 'Maybe it might. Nothing withdrawn in his eyes'

That brief bout of foreplay concluded when Norbert Nodahead finally nodded his head in agreement to the plan of attack laid out by Ms. Sylvia Smitharomance, something he was less than excited to do because his own future was at stake.

Norbert motioned Mr. Expedience to his side and explained the plot thusly.

"The whole plan hinges on one man, that Fat Albert Kazonkski who accidentally allowed us to escape yesterday. Being less than a mountain of mental sufficiency, my guess is he either didn't discover the loss of his keys until the end of his shift or, not wishing to lose his job, didn't even report our absence. If so, our empty prison cells, at the earliest, wouldn't be reported until this morning. Since the Eglicatan prison warden makes it known he doesn't like being disturbed at night, the not-so-head prison guards won't know for certain whether our two cells should or shouldn't be empty. Since they won't wake the warden for the roster check until this morning, my guess is our escape hasn't yet been recorded or come to the attention of Herr McCoffee."

By now, the pudgy fugitive diplomat was getting into the scheme's intricacies like a math instructor speaking of advanced calculus, and Norman Expedience, following the drift but not the content of Nodahead's words, asked in a dreamy voice through love-smitten eyes, "Have you ever rewired a sextant?"

The magnitude of Norman E.'s gaffe caused Norbert to stop in amazement.

Was this man for real?

A time of silence, and N.N. began thinking about abalone-tin calibrations and gaffes as big as a giant, flying bird-of-war.

Norbert smiled then, a chubby sort of smile that exposed a seldom-seen, gold tooth that glittered like the giant, bad guy's front tooth when that oversized actor with few words thinks he has the jump on James Bond. Norbert's eyes beamed as he prepared to say more to Norman Expedience than Norman Expedience was going to understand.

He then put things into perspective.

"Which means, Mr. Spy," said Nodahead unkindly for Ms. Nancy to hear, "that, until 8:14 a.m., or until Herr McCoffee makes special orders to the contrary, I am the supreme ruler of Eglicata."

"Why?" asked Mr. Spy with skepticism in his voice.

"There's no doubt that the Herr wouldn't want my imprisonment on any legal records," said Norbert. "He plans to do away with me quickly and quietly, with emphasis on the former. The Herr is a very wise man, and long ago gave Ms. Sylvia and myself authority between 10:51 p.m. and 8:14 a.m. to carry out many actions during his sleep. This was arranged so he wouldn't be awakened for routine business. Of course, for fear of never waking up at all, such powers never were extended to Manual McGetitdone.

"So, if I don't awaken Herr McCoffee and don't o'erstep the many powers I have, much can be done between now and 8:14 a.m. But we'll have to move quickly.

"First of all, Mr. Expedience, I'll see that you get off of prison grounds so you'll be able to find Roger K. Rightjet and tell him what I'm preparing to do. Also," said Norbert Nodahead, who was heading toward the bravest moment of his life, "if this plan fails, it will be up to you to see that these two ladies are set free. Come on. I'll fill you in on the details as we walk."

As Norman Expedience was ushered away from the women's prison, Norbert planted a smoocher on Norman's left cheek for dramatic effect.

It already was half past six, and the sun was well above the horizon.

Posters and signs led Norman toward national congressional headquarters (its acronym ECH being of great value to a non-native, non-Eglicatan speaker and reader such as N.E.,) where the most fowl of warfaring birds was scheduled to burst into his daylight debut in little more than an hour.

Expedience had learned the vocals for entrance into the congressional building, but the dance step had him baffled. Hence, after locating the large building, he frantically set forth to figure a means, any means, to enter the structure before its top exploded and the dastardly fowlawarfare was loosed upon the world.

All Norman E. knew of Roger K.'s plan was Roger K.'s intent either to stop the flight altogether or be aboard when the giant bird burst the roof and walls of congressional headquarters en route to Dalilennon.

Precious minutes ticked away as the trained spy from Darius circled the sizeable congressional building, intently seeking any chink in the wall's armor that could grant him admittance.

Regardless of his relatively tender age, Norman Expedience was an able spy, and stalked the premises with gritty determination. Then, at half past seven, a mere thirty minutes before the fowlawarfare's flight was to wing (as verified by local soldiers using bullhorns cautioning all to move to safety before congressional headquarters exploded at 8 a.m.,) Norman's keen senses observed a manhole cover, and instantly he perceived his opportunity to shine.

Whereas his new friends from Dalilennon might have o'erlooked the innocent-looking manhole cover, N.E. had been the recipient of no small amount of television education in his day and, though having never previously explored a manhole himself, knew such entrances to otherwise closed buildings always led to excitement, dramatic music, and, ultimately, to the villain.

The element of excitement was fulfilled in the first seconds when Norman Expedience removed the metal cover, slipped inside, replaced it behind him, and then, in one foul (fowl?) swoop, leaped to the sewer floor.

Let it be noted at this point that Norman Expedience, a man of reason, immediately would have returned to daylight had time allowed. He would have purchased hip waders, nose plugs, and, if possible, bribed someone else to take his place. But, lacking such time, the brave soldier did what needed to be done. He slogged onward and tried not to retch as he whooshed through a wide channel of semi-liquid fowlawarfare poop droppings.

As the human body has the God-given ability to adapt to nearly any form of adversity--be it pain, sorrow, or fatigue--so, too, can it adapt to nearly any form of stench. As a seasoned paper-mill worker cannot smell the odor that daily tests his family's loyalty and a garbage collector's nose goes dormant during working hours, so it was this morning as Norman Expedience slogged onward through the fowlawarfare's smelly, mostly clogged sewer line.

Norman's steps were propelled by love, desire, and loyalty, but mostly by the compelling need to get out of that shit.

Soon, a vision of light was spotted in front and above him, and Norman E. knew that, if his calculations were accurate, he was somewhere beneath the building's legislative floor.

How wrong he was!!

Instead of being "somewhere" beneath the legislative floor, N.E.'s sewer hike had taken him directly beneath the structure's main occupant, the lamb-eating fowlawarfare.

To describe all the excitement and flurry created when Norman Expedience popped out of that sewer line beneath the awakened, skittish bird may be beyond the inherent limitations of any author short of Shakespeare, Kant, or Graham Greene. Yet, humbly sticking to a difficult task as Norman Expedience so nobly did his, this author will attempt to do so.

But maybe a trifle of stage-setting is in order.

TO WIT: Norman Expedience didn't arrive at just any time, but at 8:01 a.m. when all but one of the heavy chains holding the fowlawarfare in place had been undone in preparation for the big bird's launch.

TO WIT: The two brave soldiers chosen to accompany the great Herr and his henchman on this exciting, maiden voyage were less than keen on taking the trip; each being family men with their loyalties to their wives and children, though never expressed publicly, stronger than those held for Herr McCoffee and the nation McCoffee professed to represent.

TO WIT: Roger K. Righjet had a cramp in his neck of such severity that he gladly would have quit the operation and waved the white flag of surrender if only he could extricate himself from tight-fitting saddlebag No. 3.

TO WIT: Norman's B.O. problem had reached the magnitude of crisis. Such an odor in ancient times would have caused the Knights of St. John to abandon their Maltese fortresses or Hannibal to bail off his elephant and walk home.

And so, when odoriferous Norman Expedience blithely popped from the sewer directly beneath the already mounted fowlawarfare, bedlam broke loose.

Nearly all soldiers and diplomats within the building, forgetting the sky was about to fall, sprinted for the many exits of congressional headquarters gallantly and vainly trying to perform that goofy singing dance step to open doors to fresh air and the outside world.

Not a mass panic, this, but very close. Everyone sensed that something smelling that foul must be deadly.

As those forty to forty-five trustworthy Eglicatans danced and sang attempting to trigger exits that wouldn't allow them to exit, the two brave soldiers aboard the giant, warfaring vessel, the ones who loved their families more than their leader and country, found occasion to abandon ship.

Roger K. may have been trying unsuccessfully for hours to gain his release from half of a saddlebag built to carry the disadvantageous weed, but one whiff of Norman Expedience gave him that extra impetus to burst free and momentarily right himself in saddle No. 3 behind the nation's head honcho, Herr McCoffee, and henchman Manual McGetitdone.

Now, the fowlawarfare hadn't been born without a nose of his own, and acted up so brazenly after Expedience's unexpected arrival that McCoffee and McGetitdone failed to notice the desertion of their two chosen soldiers. In fact, it only was after Rightjet, wearing the olive (coconut?) skin of a poor soldier, had gained his balance in saddle No. 3 that McGetitdone turned around and looked his direction.

Now, the proper use of the human nose (other than in the Mrs. King's earlier court,) is a lost art, since eyes and ears so frequently are given top billing; so even in this extreme emergency situation, Manual McGetitdone's nose failed to focus on the true source of the stench, simply its presence.

Hence, seeing the needed fourth man for the journey standing beneath the big bird, McGetitdone gruffly ordered the soldier in saddle No. 3, aka Roger K. Rightjet, to " … bring 'im aboard, and strap him to the saddle."

Roger K. saw that proposed soldier #4 was an ally, aka Norman Expedience, and his nose totally and irretrievably was repulsed by the idea of pulling N.E. aboard the big bird. Still, in this instance, mental overruled nasal and, as the fwa was tearing from his final mooring, the stinking Darian spy was grabbed and hoisted on to saddle #4.

Let us point out that the past twenty-four hours, or at least most of them, had been less than a source of comfort, peace, and joy for Norman Expedience, who'd bargained for excitement in the spy business, but not to this extent. He'd been in prison with no hope of escape, escaped, been in a women's prison as a gay man, fallen in love, run over a mile to slug through a stinking sewer line, and now was being drug aboard the most destructive war machine yet devised by man as it left on its inaugural mission.

'Bullshit,' thought Norman Expedience, who'd reached his limit of tolerance, and he began summarily to thump the olive-skinned Eglicatanese soldier seated in front of him in saddle No. 3.

How can a man in saddle No. 3 reason with an intemperate man in saddle No.4 without being heard in saddle No. 1 or saddle No. 2 when war is about to break out? Especially without speaking in the one language understandable to the man in saddle No. 4 that would give away their spy status to those straddling saddles No. 1 and No. 2.

The answer is that you can't.

And so, since Roger K. had put in a nerve-frazzling day himself and wasn't overly fond of being struck from the rear, especially with his sore neck, he began to fight back, careful not to swear in any language other than Eglicatanese.

Up through the roof they smashed as Rightjet and Expedience struggled on the back of the big bird. Securely strapped to saddles No. 3 and No. 4, Rightjet and Expedience continued exchanging punches until Roger K.'s neck, cocked to the right to fight the man directly seated behind him whilst his earlier saddlebag confinement had seen his neck cocked to the left, felt better; and the two punched themselves into exhaustion, only their seatbelts preventing major falls from the sky.

Battered, but surprisingly content, Norman Expedience hugged low against the wind and sensed he'd fought this foe before. Then he thought of Ms. Nancy Droosha, of her eyes looking into his, and all pain was gone.

He didn't hear when Manual McGetitdone, only a few feet in front of him, turned to Herr McCoffee and yelled above the wind that the isle of fancy was only a few hours away. McGetitdone then managed to sputter an evil chuckle that caused his facial scar to flare pink.

Turning In a Villain

When the timing seemed right, Julian Knotsofoolista strolled into police headquarters in downtown Dalilennon--or would that be the unnamed capital of downtown Dalilennon--and offered to the first three police officers he encountered, they patiently standing in line to sip from a drinking fountain, the opportunity to capture Poncho McTea.

Not surprisingly, Julian was sort-of treated like the little boy who cried wolf, though the similarities weren't all that strong.

For one thing, J. Knotsofoolista never previously had cried "wolf," and for another, as far as the story's told, the boy in the fable hadn't worn high-topped tenny runners, red or any other color, or worn a priest's frock.

Still, for whatever reason, it was obvious from the get-go that Dalilennon's sleepy harbingers of unending justice--though 'harbinger' is the wrong term to use since the officers had no clue what valuable information was being ignored--were more leery about being fooled by the outlandish Julian Knotsofoolista than bent on catching the island's No. 1 fugitive.

Like any young man named Satchel in the rural U.S. of A. whose parents are on welfare and generally held in low esteem, it would have been easier for Julian Knotsofoolista to have stumbled over a rock and been picked up for public drunkenness than be believed as the source of vital information.

But, Julian Knotsofoolista was no ordinary frowned-upon citizen, as verified by his unstamped passport, and he again returned to police headquarters later that same day. On the second visit, the clerk on duty treated him with more civility than the officers had during his initial visit, but the practical results of the second visit paralleled those of the first one.

"We'd like to work with you and listen to what you have to say, but everyone simply is too busy just now."

Julian Knotsofoolista wasn't a stranger to Dalilennon, or a fool. He accepted the clerk's excuses for what they were, mere excuses. He was well aware of policemen spending what, to them, was valuable civic time sitting in on card games and doing bench patrol when the local garment factory released its pretty maidens to enjoy the sunshine on scheduled nineteen-minute breaks from their labors. On such occasions, those officers, donned in official-looking blue uniforms, occasionally were awarded by smiles from the young ladies.

Such smiles, if you have a good imagination, are synonymous to accolades at American rodeos where well-paid, safe announcers state to onlookers in the grandstands that the only pay the cowboy just ejected from his mount will get "is the applause you give him."

Not much of a reward, but possibly better than nothing.

J.K.'s inability to turn in the arch criminal was disconcerting to him. He wished to be done with McTea and prepare for future events he knew would come.

Julian desired to share his McTea-type concerns with the new advisor to good King Nocturnal, Priest Precious, but all church events had been cancelled until the precious priest's civic duties were completed; and, at this point in our story, Priest Precious, quite busy, had become a tough man to catch up to.

But, Julian Knotsofoolista was persistent and operated from an internal time clock that said putting Poncho McTea behind bars was an event that was past due. Something major was about to happen.

And so, being a spy and all, Julian Knotsofoolista stalked Priest Precious, finally meeting him face-to-face along a dusty lane when Priest Precious was walking home after many tedious hours of work for the state of Dalilennon.

"If you wish to confess, Julian, I'd rather not do it now," said Priest Precious. "I'm tired, my wife is cooking navy beans, and good King Nocturnal has insisted that my priesthood be put aside until my three months of service to his kingdom is up.

"It's only right, as I'm sure you understand, that I serve my country as well as my God."

In the falling darkness, Julian Knotsofoolista's eyebrows raised a notch or three. Why should the two be incongruent at all, he thought?

Then, J.K. spoke out and explained what his business was in regards to Poncho McTea, and Priest Precious dropped all else, including his desire to eat navy beans, to listened intently.

The exchange of a few words, and the two of them 'made tracks' to the home of crack Officer Oliver Ogilvie, who was forced to abandon a rather scrumptious meal of piping hot rabbit and creamed potatoes his wife was in the process of setting upon the dinner table.

"Couldn't someone else go this once, Ollie?" asked the most understanding of police wives, who simply couldn't comprehend the sudden cloak-and-dagger persuasion becoming commonplace on Dalilennon.

But her words were to no avail.

Under cover of night, with Julian Knotsofoolista adeptly guiding their steps, crack Officer Oliver Ogilvie and Priest Precious padded without speech to Knotsofoolista's latest cave dwelling.

When they arrived, voices were heard echoing inside the cavern, and Ogilvie looked to Julian Knotsofoolista for an explanation. He got none. But, Knotsofoolista stealthily did motion the others to wait outside while he checked for answers.

The closer J.K. crept to the interior of his cave, the more clearly and distinctly he could hear the words being spoken.

"I expected him back before now, Cousin Herr, but he's certainly not one to worry over. I gave him Dalilennonian dollars, and he's treated me like a king: food, clothing, and water. Whatever I want, he fetches. I overestimated him at first. He's really pretty thick up top."

A laugh followed from Poncho McTea's salivating lips, then a muffled voice, apparently spoken by someone with his back turned to Julian K., droned on in an upward tilt as if leading into a question.

Then, silence.

McTea spoke once more, louder than before, the projection of his voice directed toward the cave's entrance where Julian Knotsofoolista squatted and listened.

"The one to worry about is this Ogilvie fellow. Seems to have the patience of a saint, you know. He's the only reason I'm hiding in this cave right now."

A rock exploded in the fire and feet were heard shuffling away from the explosion.

"Where's the bird now?" asked McTea.

Again, the quiet response from the other man, whom we know as Herr McCoffee, encouraged Julian K. to creep a little closer in hopes of hearing more. The words "inlet," "lambs," and "tomorrow morning" were all the would-be priest with red, high-topped tenny runners on his feet could discern. Maybe another step or two closer …

… and the cruel, icy fingers of Manual McGetitdone clamped down on Julian Knotsofoolista's right biceps, instantaneously conveying the solemn message that the homely, skinny, tennis-shoed "crazy man" had best not try to escape.

"Ho-e-e-e," snorted McGetitdone in satisfaction for the benefit of those further inside the cave. "I caught me a sorta-priest here who's trying to listen in on your fireside chat. Ho-e-e-e, but he's an ugly wimp." And McGetitdone squeezed down more forcefully on Julian's arm, leaving bruise marks on the skinny spy's pale, thin skin beneath his frock.

It quickly was decided that Knotsofoolista, no matter how minimally he seemed to be implicated in the matter, must be bound to prevent any Paul Revere-type runs through the countryside. Leaving the fire ablaze, McCoffee, McTea, McGetitdone, and a securely bound, but walking Julian Knotsofoolista exited the cave and slowly wound their ways down to the sea where, as they grew closer, the bestial groans of an obesity-bent fowlawarfare could be heard distinctly above the sea's rock-smashing clamor.

Four men, three sailors from one of the lamb-carrying ships plus that off-colored soldier from saddlebag No. 3 who flew in on the big bird, were patrolling the inlet and feeding sheep and disadvantageous to the rechained fowlawarfare.

Norman Expedience, although having had a pleasant dream about Ms. Nancy before the fwa touched down on Dalilennon, awoke in a bit of a pickle. The boats from Eglicata had arrived shortly before the fowlawarfare, and when Norman opened his eyes to start a new day he was ringed by about twenty-five Eglicatan sailors holding their noses and pointing at him as the source of their displeasure.

At which point, still groggy from love, Norman E. swore at them in a non-Eglicatanese dialect and promptly was arrested for being the spy that he was. Then, most naturally, to everyone's relief, he was dumped into the sea for cleansing and overall detoxification.

The lamb-poking soldiers informed McCoffee upon his return from the cave with cousin Poncho McTea, Manual McGetitdone, and a tied up Julian K., that only three-quarters of the needed disadvantageous supposedly flown in from Eglicata had been found in the saddlebags. Without the other quarter, the quarter our hero Roger K. Rightjet cleverly had removed to earn himself a sore neck, they said the top warfaring weapon in the world would be reduced merely to a huge, mortal stuffed bird unable to restore his digestive tract well enough to commute the long distance to Darius.

Herr McCoffee immediately became exceedingly angry and swore at length, exhibiting flairs of aristocratic passion. And he spared his wrath on no one. By the time his animosity focused on Manual McGetitdone, waxing hotter and hotter all the time, the good henchman stated that, without doubt, the required disadvantageous had been packed by no less an authority than he, Manual McGetitdone, the henchman's henchman, and long-time loyalist to Herr McCoffee's fiendish causes.

As the two powerful men readied to square off in defiance of each other, McCoffee chanced to look aside and noticed something unusual about one of the nearby, listening soldiers, whose beautiful coconut-tanned skin was beginning to melt from the sun and excitement of the moment.

Both McCoffee and McGetitdone stopped to stare at the soldier whose beautiful golden suntan was beginning to drip from his body like rain from a greasy windshield.

The silence was deafening, and Roger K. knew, although he had nothing to say, that it was his turn to speak.

"Maybe the disadvantageous fell out when we left Eglicata," said Roger K. Rightjet meekly. "Maybe I fell into a vat of olive dye and it's finally coming off." Then, hastily, unthinkingly, "Maybe it fell out when Norman and I fought."

Which certainly was the wrong thing to say since no one from Eglicata, as often as they may or may not have scratched their heads on the matter, had been able to ascertain until that very moment, with any degree of certainty, either Norman E.'s first name or his cause. Of course, the loud gasp Roger K. followed his statement with didn't help one bit, and, as quick as Manual McGetitdone could get it done, our sorta-hero turned hero once again was bound in ropes with little hope of escape.

Yet, as is so prevalent in society today, here was just one more instance of a would-be hero being demoted to the familiar status of a potential would-be, sorta hero ... a scenario, like the lot of the Chicago Cubs, that one day will be reversed if ample patience is applied to the situation. The Cubs reference, of course, is a Biblically based axiom from James 1:4 saying, in rough paraphrase, that good trumps evil if one's willing to pay the price and hang in there.

McGetitdone huddled with McCoffee, speaking to the national leader about the cut disadvantageous in the garden plot that still might retain fwa- digestive-tract-type potency.

But, if you recall, Julian Knotsofoolista wasn't alone when he discovered McCoffee, McTea, and McGetitdone in Julian's cave, and the entire Eglicatan convey, including the sailing fleet and their big bird, wasn't alone now.

From a safe distance, crack Officer Oliver Ogilvie, who was beginning to see the light, and the nonpracticing priest, Priest Precious, gazed toward the waterside scene unfolding before and below them. The latter's heart fluttered at the sight of Roger K. Rightjet being bound, and a man who thought more than once that he'd seen the second coming was ready to do battle.

Still, they watched and waited.

When McGetitdone and one of the naval officers broke from the semi-sleeping group by the sea shortly before daylight and headed toward the garden plot near the island's only mountain, Officer Ogilvie was faced with a difficult decision. Surely, a priest of only a few days back wasn't capable of stopping a man such as McGetitdone from doing anything he wanted to get done. Who could? And to ask the priest to combat the bird (for Oliver was unaware that the fwa temporarily had been grounded for lack of prescribed, optimum disadvantageous to salve his digestive tract from massive lamb consumption,) would be ludicrous.

But, time was of the essence, and crack Officer Oliver Ogilvie responded to the stressful situation like the true general he was. He instructed Priest Precious to observe the comings and goings of Manual & Co., stay unseen, and report any pertinent information to him, crack Officer Oliver Ogilvie.

At this stage of our thrilling story, let us point out that truisms in life rarely follow a plot imagined by even the finest of authors. The events soon to unfold on these very pages will, once again, reiterate the worn adage that truth is stranger than fiction.

Or, in this instance, would that be vice versa?

"Why You Old Witch!"

That day's, 'D' day's first rays of sunlight peeped through a cottage window and, ever so gently, nudged a face of beauty from sleep to blissful, blind comfort. She didn't consider herself to be a beauty but, since all heroes and heroines either are handsome or beautiful, and she soon would prove to be the day's heroine, she was beautiful.

The deep lines in her face and ghastly overbite never were lovelier than on this special morning when Ms. Prissy Hampshire was awakened by the morning sun.

As in recent days, the resurgence of her personal good health was tempered by the uncomfortable bloated state her favorite donkey and friend, Blokehead, was suffering from. Since the night the island's only true ship had been stolen, which for sure had generated no tiny amount of gossip throughout Dalilennon, the animal's customary state of overt feistiness had disappeared from view; first to bloated bliss, and later to belly popping pain.

Being a former midwife of many tricks, Ms. Prissy had striven gallantly to reckon a cure; even administered an enema to her donkey friend, an intervention she hated as badly as Blokehead, but even that measure got little response. Well, as a point of accuracy, it did get a response, but did nothing to alleviate the stout animal's discomfort.

By the hour, the ailing donkey would stand with his head looking in Ms. Prissy's window, his donkey chin resting on the window sill itself. His eyes remained glazed.

Even the best antics of Jean Paul and Mary availed nothing as the donkey's pain persisted, then got worse.

On this particular morning when Ms. Prissy opened her eyes with God's warm sun beaming on her face, her thoughts immediately turned melancholy and pensive, again worrying about the gnawing pain her best friend, Blokehead, was suffering from. Though never spoken audibly to anyone, especially Blokehead, her inner fear was that this loved animal might not survive the ordeal he was facing, and such a possibility crushed her spirit.

A lady of many habits and rituals, some of them good, Ms. Prissy nearly always ate a hearty breakfast. "Best meal of ther day," she'd tell Blokehead seven times each week.

On this day, her sun-rising breakfast consisted of big-yoked eggs and lamb chops, but hunger wasn't with her, and she offered the final chop- and-a-half to Blokehead who, of course, was overseeing the meal with his chin on the ledge of the window.

To Ms. Prissy Hampshire's amazement, Blokehead grabbed at the lamb chop- and-a-half hungrily, ate it, and within seconds was prancing about as in the days of yore, cured of the bloat that had tempered his enthusiasm for life and so worried the elderly ex-midwife.

"An enzyme in need is an enzyme indeed," muttered the former midwife with a smiling shoulder shrug as she hurried out to view the happiest of sights: a rejuvenated, bouncing donkey.

Ms. Prissy had desired to perform a gardening favor for a neighbor of hers for several days, but hadn't wanted to leave her four-legged friend in agony. Following Blokehead's recovery, rapid as it was and undoubtedly complete, the crag-faced lady put a packsaddle aboard her suddenly frisky domestic partner and off they went to grab a key tucked under a rock for safekeeping while the neighbor was away.

Within twenty minutes after leaving her home, maybe closer to eleven and a half minutes, Ms. Prissy was inserting the retrieved key into the lock of a high gate, and entering a relatively good-sized high-walled garden plot, the type of garden plot where one normally would plant grape bushes, cabbages, a couple olive trees, potatoes, carrots, and some orange trees.

In fact, as you've probably gathered by now, it was the very same garden from whose wall Manual McGetitdone had leaped from and smacked the former midwife a good one, bruising her cheek and alarming a slumbering nation. You see, Ms. Prissy had no way of knowing that her neighbors, Mr. and Mrs. Jones, before they left on holiday, had leased the garden plot to a non-Dalilennonianese Dalilennonian diplomat named Poncho.

A dutiful worker and neighbor, Ms. Hampshire began gathering into one big pile the scythed disadvantageous weed that, to her amazement, was bundled with wire and neatly stacked in six-high bales at the point of the harvest. She questioned in her mind why the plant had gotten so out of hand in the first place and why so much of it had been cut down and not burned.

In addition, much of that disadvantageous had been left on top of the fertile garden ground in the form of seed, certainly not a welcome sight to any Dalilennonian gardener or farmer. Working as methodically and persistently as her age and body condition would allow--remember Ms. Prissy had been belted a good one and required bed rest only a day or two before--the cantankerous, loving old hag went about the business of placing cut, bundled shocks of disadvantageous in a central location, and prepared to torch a bonfire.

(As an aside, some might question the mentality of donkeys, but on this occasion Blokehead exhibited absolutely no interest in tasting the weed.)

"Yer gotta burn this stuff 'er it'll spread," she informed Blokehead. "Fer the life o me, I can't understand how all this weed got so all out o hand."

When Manual McGetitdone and one Eglicatanese sailor, followed by Priest Precious, did arrive at the gate outside the garden plot, a nasty-looking dark swizzle of black, black smoke was dancing skyward toward the cloudless heavens above the garden.

From a short distance away, Priest Precious watched what was unfolding before him and, anticipating what was about to happen, experienced an uncharacteristic surge of rage that seethed to the surface of his being. Not wanting to see Ms. Prissy hurt any further and, apparently, not willing to leave events to divine providence, the priest-turned-diplomat who'd once boxed poorly as a priest let out a bellow and charged the two-person Eglicatan envoy.

Not many folk in all of Dalilennon would have benefited even minimally from any attack on Manual McGetitdone, and letting out a harsh bellow thirty seconds prior to one's estimated arrival time, thus giving Manual ample advance warning, was sheer nonsense. By the time Priest Precious did arrive, weaponless and out of breath, he could have been hurt badly. In fact, he was justly cold-cocked by one McGetitdone punch, falling to earth with no more signs of life than a cold, cooked waffle.

Manual McGetitdone's face, with its flesh-tone scar only showing the slightest of color because the threat had been so minimal, looked puzzled as to why anyone during a state of war would act so foolishly.

Noble pronouncements of attack were out: winning was in.

The Eglicatan sailor with Manual pointed to the unlocked gate to the garden, and the pair of thugs, though maybe the sailor acting under the authoritative guidance of such a national leader as Manual McGetitdone shouldn't be stereotyped as a 'thug,' hurried inside to locate the source of the smoke.

What McGetitdone saw flashed his scar angry red, and again cranked his inner juices of hostility. Not only was the last of the scythed disadvantageous going up in smoke, but so was the entire conquer-the-world-on-the-fowlawarfare scheme (code name "c+wo+fwa scheme".) Only the rare enzyme in the almost fourteen-day-old disadvantageous plant could keep the big bird aloft long enough to fly to Darius, let alone prevent him from eating himself to death, and all that remained of what had been cut for that purpose was gingerly wafting upward like an Old Testament sacrifice.

More of the plant was around, to be sure, but Nature regularly plants seven, twelve, and thirteen-day-old disadvantageous plants next to and around the coveted nearly fourteen-day-old crop, making any attempts of harvesting only the latter nearly impossible.

Even the expertise of loyal Mr. McDove, were he not back in Eglicata, would have provided little help at this moment. Too little time to identify what remained standing of the nearly fourteen-day-old crop, even if exact science and scientists were available to do so.

And, to make matters worse, the best-made, fiendish plans from an entire nation, or more succinctly the elite upper strata of that entire nation, were being cast into flames by the same ugly hag (in Manual's mind, mind you, not ours,) and that same frigging donkey.

"Why you old witch," he bellowed at the top of his lungs in Eglicatanese, and took off running, scar a sizzling', to punish the meddling midwife for what Dalilennonian historians forever would describe as " … a God-fearing act of the gravest degree."

Let it be pointed out at this juncture that Manual McGetitdone, good henchman whom he was, did have some human failings. In this instance, it was one such flaw, his inability in the heat of battle to remember that his chosen adversary, Ms. Prissy Hampshire, had an ally standing by ready to counteract all the manual strength and get-it-doneiveness the enraged Eglicatan leader could muster.

For he'd forgotten Blokehead, the protective donkey who'd forced he, McTea, and Ms. Sylvia Smitharomance atop the wall the night he'd mercilessly and cruelly smacked the old hag on the mouth, or at least along the side of her face.

He'd forgotten, but Blokehead hadn't.

Like live meat in a trap purposefully placed to catch a killer lion, so was the not-so-agile old gal, Ms. Prissy Hampshire, who patiently waited while furious Manual McGetitdone stormed toward her with tunnel vision focused on her wrinkled, skinny throat.

At one moment in time, Ms. Prissy did experience some misgivings regarding her lion-killing savior, and glanced to the side to make certain Blokehead didn't miss his cue. But, that lapse in faith was temporary, and unnecessary, for she soon saw, with the timeliness of Zorro, Batman, and The Long Ranger combined, the hero donkey race in and give Manual McGetitdone a shot to his side that altered the bestial man's course ninety degrees to the left, and send him stumbling and tumbling into the base of an olive tree where he suffered a blow to the head that would have killed any civil man. In Manual's case, however, the blow created instant stardom, between the ears as well as behind the eyes, and he immediately gave way to a deep sleep characterized with dreams of extreme headaches and church steeples.

The warrior, or sailor, who'd arrived with Manual, made happy feet for the fowlawarfare's 'den,' a word that sounds better than inlet, where he knew, if nothing else, a rowboat of escape was waiting.

Blokehead trotted behind the sailor in sorta-hot pursuit, enjoying the gleeful cackles of Ms. Prissy behind him and the thrill of being a donkey hero.

The cackling ex-midwife stoked the disadvantageous fire one last time, then sauntered over to taunt her slumbering adversary with the scar; all the time pointing, howling with laughter, and chanting gleeful nonsense.

Imagine Manual McGetitdone's horror when, with head aching big-time, he opened his eyes and saw a cackling, pointing, jeering Ms. Prissy Hampshire standing over him with a fully stoked, crackling bonfire burning behind her.

A quick medical lesson.

Shock CAN occasion its recipient to go comatose in dumbstruck horror of what has been seen and/or experienced. At the other extreme, shock CAN readjust one's mental faculties and send that individual running in blind haste in a futile attempt to outrace one's own memories.

Manual McGetitdone's reaction, in this instance launched by the sight of this Macbethian ex-midwife laughing and taunting him in front of a bonfire for his personal misdeeds, took on the latter form of shock reaction and, falling twice and banging into an orange tree while looking over his shoulder to assure he really was leaving the horror behind him, McGetitdone raced posthaste through the gate and onward, his facial scar now a pallid white.

The sailor who'd accompanied McGetitdone to the garden was running, too, but in a planned direction. A chain smoker for God knows how many years, the frightened Eglicatan warrior, aka sailor, breathlessly was spent when he reached the hidden seashore cove and collapsed in the sand with more weight on his chest than a fool's wrath. He heaved and trembled until Nature restored his oxygen level.

Blokehead was close behind, bleating brays of glee.

Crack Officer Oliver Ogilvie (whose trusting wife had noticed and never commented on the scratch Ms. Prissy had planted on his back,) patiently had been waiting for the ideal opportunity to untie the knots binding Roger K. Rightjet and Norman Expedience. The arrival of the breathless naval warrior and the obnoxious braying of the frigging donkey on the slope above the inlet provided the necessary diversion, and Officer Ogilvie took the initiative to free his two allies.

Julian Knotsofoolista, watching from a nearby vantage where he was staked down across an open expanse of sand, responded with a foolish shoulder shrug as if to say, "Rats. Guess I'll have to stay here until all the fighting's over."

By this time, the stuffed fowlawarfare was in need of some digestive juices and moaned uncomfortably like a man who's eaten two additional pieces of peach cobbler Christmas day after being " ... too full to eat another bite." Between the fowlawarfare's gastric moans and Blokehead's loud, annoying brays of joy, the seashore inlet was no place for women, children, or pet parakeets.

The chain-smoking, panting warrior, after regaining his breath, informed Herr McCoffee that what remained of the nearly fourteen-day-old disadvantageous plant was going up in flames, and asked his national leader what to do next.

McCoffee instantly surmised the message's impact. Their mission to achieve world peace his way had to be scrapped, and now it was time to go home.

When asked by the panting sailor what was to be done about McCoffee's loyal, strong-armed advisor now mindlessly wandering around the island, the Herr responded that they now were at war, and Manual McGetitdone had known his chances.

Herr McCoffee then brought forth his communication wireless and contacted the ships offshore, instructing those aboard to pick him up for a return voyage to Eglicata.

A loud burst of laughter thundered through the receiver on McCoffee's wireless, and the Herr, in disbelief, shook the communication device like a doctor cooling a rectal thermometer. He repeated his instructions.

Again, the Herr's message was greeted with peals of laughter.

"What's the meaning of this disrespect?" barked Herr McCoffee in his final moment as leader of Eglicata.

The articulate response he received through the wireless left the abusive leader limp and pallid.

The end had come. Or more succinctly, his end had come.

According to radio communications to the ship now relayed to Herr McCoffee, an Eglicatan revolt (coup?) had taken place overnight in the Herr's absence from what had been his homeland. The revolt (coup?) had launched when every female in the national prison had been released after pledging support to a new government ruled by Norbert Nodahead and Ms. Sylvia Smitharomance. As a bonus for each female inmate's pledge, and a bonus for any desiring male constituents of the geographically large nation, blind dates were being arranged for all who wanted one. No promised favors, mind you, but ...

The sailors laughing at McCoffee were fearful that a similar deal soon would be orchestrated involving male inmates and female residents across the large land, hence were eager to set sail for home and strike their respective claims before pickings grew slim.

"Whatever happened to human decency?!" grumped the former Herr as his wireless permanently clicked into silence.

Blokehead was aglow with joy and merriment from his perch above the inlet, throwing his fuzzy donkey head in a-bray-sive laughter while squatting upon his back haunches.

Not one to keep anger contained within him, especially when it was prompted in part by an obnoxious donkey who'd help trump his best, most fiendish plan, the former Herr flashed Blokehead the international "bird" finger sign (the middle finger,) and at that very instant the groaning fowlawarfare in the cove below toppled to his side in a stuffed stupor.

As Roger K. Rightjet, Norman Expedience, crack Officer Oliver Ogilvie, Blokehead, Poncho McTea, and the former Herr McCoffee marched inland toward the midday sun, and three Eglicatan sailors/soldiers furiously rowed their boat toward their ships, Julian Knotsofoolista--still bound and gagged on the white sand beach--vainly struggled to get someone's, anyone's attention.

"Galatians 6:18"

It was two weeks later (or was it three?) when the SlipSparrow commandingly cruised into the Dalilennonian harbor amid lusty cheers from three persons on hand to witness the boat's arrival.

Cheering for the return of the nation's mightiest seafaring vessel, the three collectively had eyes for first looks at new international heroine, Ms. Nancy Droosha. Her role in the successful Eglicatan revolt, according to rampant rumor, ranged anywhere from a gun-totin' mama to that of a hard-dealing diplomat.

Malcolm Straight was aboard, too. He may have lacked the charisma, let alone the looks of the foxy heroine secretary, but Malcolm did know how to wave his hand in a circular motion like a princess in a Fourth of July parade; which, of course, he did on this occasion.

As Ms. Nancy stepped from the boat, in line to meet her were befrocked Priest Julian Knotsofoolista, sorta hero Roger K. Rightjet, and the young, sweet-smelling Darian spy, Norman Expedience.

She greeted Priest Julian first with a handshake and a light hug, commenting that his high-topped sneakers were missing and his frock new and clean.

In a somber voice she'd never heard from this man, Priest J.K. imparted these words. "Let all that you do be done in love, Ms. Nancy. Outdo one another in showing honor."

The message was clear, yet the lady of beauty, still holding his warm, comfortable hand, felt the need to ask.

"Yes," he responded with a smile so warm his face almost was handsome, (with emphasis on the word 'almost'.) "Never again will I be forced to swing from steeples to deliver my message. I've replaced

Priest Precious, and now have a hungry, attentive flock that needs all I can give them."

Ms. Nancy's attentions now shifted to Roger K. Rightjet, and neither spoke or moved for several moments.

What he'd known all along still was difficult to deal with once her kind, sad eyes communicated that she knew as well.

"Thank you," she said, holding back tears during a brief, final hug. Roger let her hand slip from his then, and boldly looked away for a new sign from the changeless, pulsing sea that had been giving and taking, ebbing and flowing since the time of Julian's Christ, and long before.

Rightjet sensed an answer still was somewhere on his horizon.

The hugs and kisses Ms. Nancy had reserved for Norman Expedience weren't brief or final. It was obvious to all, even those watching from a distance like the beautiful, olive-skinned Xandra from G. C. Corp., that many years of sharing, joy, and peace lay ahead in their futures together.

Feeling more numb than either sad or happy, Roger K. relayed to the new arrivals the Mrs. King's invitation for dinner that very evening, then walked away alone to reflect in his garden; tinges of melancholy gnawing at and rubbing the parameters of his soul.

By nightfall, good King Nocturnal's palatial banquet hall had become a scene of hectic organization. Never before had so many prominent locals been invited to dine at the good King's table, and never before had the Mrs. King shown such a zest for sharing the true merits of royalty.

The festivities received an early boost of good news when it was reported that, earlier that day, the tenacious Ms. Prissy Hampshire had administered the world's largest enema and, in doing so, had saved the life of a grateful fowlwarfare. The giant bird, no longer bound by chains, now would be renamed and become a fowlatourist. And, as Dalilennon became more and more known for the tranquil, beautiful, peaceful island it is, the fowlatourist, at advisor Darrell Precious's suggestion, would become a revenue source to permanently offset any future need for a dreaded sales tax.

Double-dealing diplomat Poncho McTea had been assigned guide duty atop the flying beast but, at the request of his loving wife and son, Stem, who was carrying a straight B average in school, had that stiff sentence commuted to one of popcorn-pusher at the fowlatourist's point of departure.

Ms. Patty Pickly and Ms. Frannie Finger had heeded the Mrs. King's turnabout in regards to nose picking and, pleased to be part of such a stately occasion, arrived early that evening to begin their habitually prattling conversations.

Malcolm Straight arrived next and, because of well-thought timing in regards to his entrance, was greeted as the mini-hero he'd hoped for. His "Oh, it was nothing's" were accorded as modesty by the banal former nose pickers who snooted for every detail Malcolm was willing to share.

Mr. Straight once again was pleased to be in a position to advise His Excellency, the good King. Yes, he was pleased with the prospects of working with Darrell Precious, the former Priest Precious, and, no, he had no idea when Mr. Precious's latest black eye would heal.

Next to arrive were possibly the true King and Queen of the ball, namely Priest Julian Knotsofoolista and the craggy Ms. Prissy Hampshire. She'd fought mightily to avoid coming at all, only relenting at the wishes of her good friend, former Priest Precious.

Ms. Prissy skillfully kept her politically and religiously untrained mind from considering which position, priest or advisor, gave Priest Precious more power; in fact was content to view former Priest Precious turned diplomat Darrell Precious as she always had, as a friend.

Blokehead accompanied the esteemed Knotsofoolista-Hampshire couple to the palatial gate, but was denied entrance beyond that point by good King Nocturnal's occasionally attentive guards.

Roger K. Rightjet arrived next. He looked handsome in a tailored suit and tie, and offered kind greetings to all he met; which, of course, was everyone in attendance, even stiff Hans the butler.

Crack Officer Oliver Ogilvie next strolled in to the good King's banquet hall, his dutiful, loving wife on his arm. He looked like a man of comfort and leisure because he'd resigned his police post to spend more time with his wife and study the arts of gardening and nephrology. Once seated, the former crack officer pointed out the craggy ex-midwife seated nearby and whispered to his wife, "You know that scratch on my back you never asked about and I never told you about? She's the one."

And former crack Officer Oliver Ogilvie's wife laughed aloud as if she'd just heard the funniest of stories.

The handsomest of couples, Norman Expedience and Ms. Nancy Droosha, came in next and quickly announced--amid heartfelt o-o-o-h-s and a-a-a-a-s--that Norman's sorta-adopted brother, aka Priest Julian Knotsofoolista, would marry them within a week and, following a leisurely Dalilennonian honeymoon, the couple would set sail for Darius where Norman would give up spying, enjoyable as it always had been, to spend time at home and raise a family with Ms. Nancy.

During the heart of the dinner, when Julian K., new in his position, was facing the dilemma of whether or not to eat his chicken with fingers or with knife and fork, two sets of eyes could be seen peering upon the bountiful gathering from a perch in a nearby pear tree. Of course, they were the eyes of little Jean Paul and Mary who'd come to see, more than anything else, the sight of Ms. Prissy Hampshire gussied for the occasion.

Mr. Precious pompously took the podium and gave a brief speech, predicting a prosperous future for Dalilennon for centuries to come.

General talk during the sumptuous meal ranged to and fro about most subjects imaginable, yet always seemed to return to the bizarre events of late that had given Dalilennon a new sense of international awareness and, almost by accident, had triggered new leadership in a faraway nation named Eglicata.

Good King Nocturnal was asked what he intended to do with the island's newest resident of infamy, Max McCoffee, and he responded in a most humane manner.

"To err is human, to forgive divine," stated the good King with a distant look in his eyes as if he, for possibly the first time, were viewing sights in the room that no one else could see. He added that if his advisors were in agreement, that former Herr McCoffee would be granted complete freedom to come and go on the isle of fancy as long as he became a burden to neither the people of Dalilennon, nor to their government.

As the isle's good wine began to flow freely, King Nocturnal again stood, glass aloft, and made a toast.

"Ladies and gentlemen," he stated gallantly. "This toast is to a spunky lady who has given everything short of her life for the people of Dalilennon and asked nothing in return. I don't believe for one second that she's done this because we are the people of Dalilennon, but instead because we are the people she can reach and touch with her sometimes misunderstood gifts of unconditional love. I offer this toast to the lady whose full midwifery pension now will be granted, Ms. Prissy Hampshire."

Amid the cheers and good-natured rails for a speech from the red-faced Ms. Prissy, her coloring not universally visible because of her warts and wrinkles, one chair quietly slid back away from the dining table, and its former occupant exited the festive gathering unnoticed.

The air was cool, ocean-like and healthy to Roger K.'s lungs as he strode down the narrow road to his garden-backed home one last time. Without hesitation or second thoughts, the lawyer-gristmiller-gardener packed a small duffle and trekked to the waterfront to wait for daylight and the next boat leaving Dalilennon.

Personal thoughts spinning in his heart and soul, Roger K. Rightjet was oblivious to a scene being played at a distance above his head; a familiar scene with a new player. For, hanging from the church steeple with one hand and swinging two bright lanterns in the other was a frock-robed man wearing red high-top tennis shoes. At the top of his lungs the man was chanting, " … He Himself gives to all men life and breath and everything. And two if by sea."

At long last, Manual McGetitdone was getting it done.

Roger paused on the dock and smiled sadly for seven or eight years well spent. His eyes narrowed in testy melancholy, but only for a moment. He thought of his friends in the banquet hall he'd just left, and felt warm inside for their joy.

"Life is funny," he stated audibly for his own benefit as he walked back into the unknown. "Maybe next time, I'll do it right."

At water's edge, Roger K. absently fished an obscure Welch plug from his pants pocket, shrugged his shoulders dumbly, and tossed the piece skyward, it landing on the deck of a recently confiscated, nonfunctional motorboat.

Then, he tramped on, seeking his own ship.

Watching from a higher vantage, Manual McGetitdone hollered "Galatians 6:18" to the retreating soul, extinguished his lanterns, and descended in the night.

THE END

AFTERWARD

An Isle of Fancy is not the first novel written, then taken to publication under the author's name of Rocky Wilson. In fact, it's Rocky's second published novel, following a Christian thriller entitled Sharene Death: A Prerequisite for Life that was released in January 2009.

With copies of Sharene in hand, Rocky went about the business of trying to place that novel into bookstores, generate sales, and get his work in the hands of people who would read it. Such proved to be a difficult task, no matter the quality of his writing, and Rocky soon learned his best recourse of action was to generate sales himself, one-by-one.

To date, the hundreds who've purchased and read Sharene overwhelmingly say they enjoyed reading that novel and have placed themselves on a list to order An Isle of Fancy when it's published and ready for distribution. Still, the process is slower than any author would want.

Both Sharene and now An Isle of Fancy are self-published print-on-demand novels, which in no way indicates they are inferior to novels published by big printing houses, simply without huge promotional budgets to ensure their placement in large bookstores and bookstore chains.

What you can do, if you believe in the literary quality of An Isle of Fancy or even Sharene, is help promote Rocky Wilson's novels by, to some degree, circumventing the power structure wielded by large publishing houses.

To do so, please feel free to talk to others about An Isle of Fancy, described by the publisher as "the most unusual book ever."

You could help as well by giving a copy of this book, or Sharene, to family members, friends, or even strangers as a gift. Paying it forward is another concept you could employ by giving a copy of An Isle of Fancy to people in the car behind you at Taco Bell, McDonald's, or even Arby's. By doing so, in the instance of An Isle of Fancy, you'd be sharing belly shaking laughter and allegorical insights to add unanticipated joy and edification into the lives of others. Sharene, on the other hand, is a page-turning thriller where its readers are exposed to the antithetical forces of good and evil.

If you have a Web site or blog, feel free to write on them your insights about either of Rocky Wilson's novels. If you so choose, encourage others to read An Isle of Fancy and/or Sharene, but please don't give away their respective plots. Also, encourage them to link to www.effectualhistory.com.

Rocky has a third novel, already written, that he plans to publish in the near future. Entitled Tread Softly, that epic work of historical fiction covers a 40-year period of time, but is focused on the events at Kent State University, May 4, 1970, when U.S. National Guardsmen gunned down four unarmed students during the turbulent Vietnam era.

Although Rocky is committed to follow through and publish Tread Softly, the successful marketing of An Isle of Fancy and Sharene would make that effort much easier and free him to write additional books in the future.

Rocky Wilson, whose best talent is generating the written word, hopes to write and publish more books, but asks for your aid in allowing him to do so..

Ways you could assist Rocky's future literary efforts include:

1) if you own a shop or business, consider placing a display of one or both of these books on your counter for resell purposes ... orders of five or more books to be sold for resell are available at discounted prices

2) buy one or more copies of An Isle of Fancy and/or Sharene and distribute them as gifts to battered women's shelters, prisons, rehabilitation homes, and the like

3) write book reviews for either of Rocky Wilson's novels and send them to local newspapers, favorite magazines, and/or commonly frequented Web sites

4) ask your favorite radio station to have Rocky Wilson on as a guest

5) ask authors, speakers, and politicians who impact many lives to review a copy(s) of either or both books, then make comments on their Web sites, newsletters, or distributed e-mails